W9-BEN-401

The Song of the Earth

Also by Hugh Nissenson

A Pile of Stones

Notes from the Frontier

In the Reign of Peace

My Own Ground

The Tree of Life

The Elephant and My Jewish Problem

The Song of the Earth

A NOVEL

written and illustrated by

Hugh Nissenson

Algonquin Books
of Chapel Hill
2001

Published by
Algonquin Books of Chapel Hill
Post Office Box 2225
Chapel Hill, North Carolina 27515-2225

a division of
Workman Publishing
708 Broadway
New York, New York 10003

Printed in the United States of America.
Published simultaneously in Canada
by Thomas Allen & Son Limited.
Design by Anne Winslow. Photographs of artwork by John Parnell.

Library of Congress Cataloging-in-Publication Data
Nissenson, Hugh.
The song of the earth : a novel / written and illustrated
by Hugh Nissenson.
p. cm.
ISBN 1-56512-298-4
1. Twenty-first century—Fiction. 2. Genetic engineering—Fiction.
3. Artists—Fiction. 4. Murder—Fiction. I. Title.
PS3564.I8 S66 2001
813'.54—dc21
00-066392

10 9 8 7 6 5 4 3 2

For Marilyn, Kate, Kore, and Daria Keynan

The Song of the Earth

This biography of John Firth Baker, illustrated with his work, is published in collaboration with The Virtual Museum of Modern American Manual Art, which organized and mounted the current Baker retrospective that commemorates the tenth anniversary of his death.

The book's title comes from the title of Baker's favorite poem:

The Song of the Earth
by Clorene Welles

I mother
& devour life.
I father forms
that thrive &
those that fade.
I'm husband
& wife,
windpipe
& knife.
I'm the sheath
that shields
& rusts its blade,
this patch of sunlight,
that patch of shade.[1]

John Firth Baker was the first genetically engineered visual artist. A confluence of fundamental contemporary expressions of creativity—science, art, and religion—made him into a uniquely twenty-first-century phenomenon.

A bound and printed book like this is a fit commemorative for Baker, who cherished bound books. Baker was a self-taught manual artist; his figurative images, always the work of his own hands, appeal to the sense of touch, as well as sight. They convey Baker's deepest feelings, his fantasies and dreams. The political and sectarian uses to which his art was put by others made him famous at nineteen; then he was murdered.

---

1. *The Complete Poems of Clorene Welles,* New York: Parnassus Press, 2061:103. (61–We5426)

Baker was posthumously transformed into a myth, which continues to grow. His work is now given an iconic significance he never consciously intended. Gaians claim the images he made, particularly those they call "Baker's Dozen," are tangible visions of his quest for Gaian Consciousness.

John Firth Baker's inner life was more complex—far richer—than that. He died before he could fulfill his promise as an artist. Yet his handful of work endures. Baker was an American original. This book tells his whole story for the first time.

I organized *The Song of the Earth* around interviews I conducted with John Firth Baker which appeared in the June 2057 issue of *The International Review of Manual Art*. I was then a young reporter with a Ph.D. in Art History who admired Baker's work and was intrigued by his celebrity.

I have remained interested in Baker and his art. In the decade since his death I have edited and annotated his mother's journal[2] and Baker's extensive correspondence, which was preserved in his central data storage system.[3] I have interviewed his family, friends, and acquaintances. The text of *The Song of the Earth* is made up of selections from all these sources, along with other documents pertinent to Baker's life and work. Whenever possible I have allowed the material to speak for itself, in the belief that it presents on its own an honest portrait of John Firth Baker. I regret that Dr. Frederick Rust Plowman twice refused my request for an interview; however, he allowed me access to his papers. I'm grateful to all those who graciously cooperated with me in the preparation of this book. Except where otherwise indicated, all of the art reproduced in this book was created by John Firth Baker and is in the collection of Polly Baker.

Katherine G. Jackson
May 19, 2067

---

2. Jeanette Baker, *The Mother of Beauty: A Journal, 2038–2056,* ed. Katherine G. Jackson, New York: Parnassus Press, 2061. (61–BaJa14)

3. John Firth Baker, *Collected Correspondence,* ed. Katherine G. Jackson, New York: Parnassus Press, 2064. (64–BaJa71)

The Song of the Earth

From John Firth Baker's interview in *The International Review of Manual Art:*

To begin with, as everybody knows, I'm an arsogenic metamorph. Mother made me one. She wanted an artist for a son.

Polly Baker

John Firth Baker's mother, Jeanette, was the only child of Maggie Cobble and my older brother, Quincy Firth Baker. Quincy owned the Powder Horn, a thirty-five-hundred-acre cattle ranch in Cherry County, Nebraska. Jeanette was born there July 3, 2009. Four years later the drought loosed the Creeping Sand Hills.

Quincy's ranch got sanded up in the spring of 2016. So he filed for bankruptcy, and the county posted his ranch for taxes. My brother took it hard—the ranch had been in our family four generations. Quincy had even managed to hang on to it during the Great Recession. Now it was gone. He began drinking heavily. His blood pressure soared. In May, I helped move him, Maggie, and Jeanette into a two-room furnished apartment on the corner of South 84th Street and Pioneers Avenue in Lincoln. I lived nearby over the hairstyling salon on Sun Valley Boulevard that I'd inherited from my mother. That year the temperature topped ninety-six degrees for thirty-seven days running; there were at least a dozen blackouts. Everything in the apartment was hot to the touch—the toilet seat, chairs, tables, walls, and window-panes. The dusty kitchen glasses felt as if they'd just been filled with hot water. Jeanette never complained. She kept to herself. She was a bookworm.

Roberta Friar

I met Jeanette Firth Baker on a blind date Christmas night, 2032, at the University of Chicago, where we were postgraduate Resident Scholars. A mutual friend fixed us up. She'd warned me that Jeanette was two years younger than I. I usually went for older wimin. I'd recently broken up with my thesis advisor, who was forty-two; we'd lived together for three years. I needed to get in touch with myself. There was something missing in me. I didn't like myself. I wasn't ready to get involved again so soon—certainly not with someone younger. But it was an icy Christmas night, and I felt lonely. Jeanette and I met at eight-thirty in the lobby of Bartlett Tower. She looked me over with those blue eyes and pulled off one mitten to shake my hand; I noticed she bit her nails to the quick. And she was pale—very pale.

She was like, "I'm broke. We have to eat cheap."

I thought, this girl needs looking after.

I bought her dinner in a pizzeria near Hyde Park called Liveware, which was a hangout for campus hackers like me. I was getting my Ph.D. in cellular automata theory. Jeanette was in art history. She told me about her thesis on Charlotte Salomon.

From Jeanette Firth Baker's proposal for a doctoral thesis in Art History at the University of Chicago, August 8, 2032:

I plan to write my thesis about the life and work of the German-Jewish painter Charlotte Salomon (1917–1943). My thesis will analyze her autobiographical masterpiece *Life? or Theater?* as a compelling expression of a twentieth-century womin artist's creativity in the face of phallocratic oppression.

Charlotte Salomon was born in Berlin on April 16, 1917. Her mother was a hausfrau; her father was a typical bourgeois patriarch. Charlotte was named for her mother's sister, who drowned herself in 1913. Charlotte's mother jumped from a window to her death in 1926. Seven years later, the Germans elected the failed artist and ex-soldier Adolph Hitler as the head of their government. Hitler made anti-Semitism the basis of a new phallocratic tribal religion he called National Socialism, or Nazism for short. Another basic tenet of Nazism was the subjugation of wimin, summed up by its creed of *Kinder, Kirche, Küche* —Children, Church, Kitchen.

Charlotte showed a precocious talent for drawing and painting. She studied for a year in Berlin at the State Academy of Fine Arts but quit in 1935 because of the humiliations to which she was subjected by her Nazi teachers and fellow students. In 1939 Charlotte fled with her maternal grandparents to the south of France; there the old lady tried to kill herself. Charlotte pleaded with her, "Instead of taking your own life in such a horrible way, why don't you make use of the same powers to describe your life? . . . By writing it down you will be able to liberate yourself and perhaps perform a service to the world."

A few months later, Hitler plunged Europe into the second half of the Global Tribal War by invading Poland. Charlotte's grandmother committed suicide in March 1940. Charlotte wrote, "I cannot bear this life, I cannot bear these times." She thought about throwing herself out of a window.

Hitler conquered France in June. Charlotte chose to live. She described how she made this decision in one of the written texts that are integral parts of many of her paintings: "As if awakening from a dream, she saw beauty all around her. She looked at the sea, felt the sun, and knew she must sacrifice everything and vanish awhile from the world of men in order to create a new world for herself out of the depths."

During the next two years, Charlotte painted and wrote the story of her life in a unique work that she entitled *Life? or Theater?* Her narrative consists of 769 gouaches combining picture and text, which she entrusted to a French doctor late in the summer of 1942. The next year, Charlotte married an Austrian engineer named Alex Nagler. Charlotte got pregnant. She and her husband were arrested on September 21, 1943; sometime during the next month, they were deported to the Auschwitz extermination camp in Poland and gassed.

Roberta Friar

I stared at Jeanette so hard while she talked that she blushed. Then I realized that she'd polished off a bottle of Chianti by herself. That worried me. My ex-lover drank. When she was drunk, she dropped her dirty laundry on the bedroom floor. I hated picking up after her.

At that moment, as though she'd read my mind, Jeanette went, "I drink too much."

We talked sports. Jeanette was a big Husker fan. We discovered we both loved playing softball and made a date to join the Saturday afternoon pickup game in the new Field House behind White Hall.

Jeanette and I were outfielders on the same team. We lost seven to nothing because our pitcher and catcher refused to talk with each other. They were both sleeping with the shortstop, a gorgeous redhead, whose name—so help me!—was Gwendolyn Turnipseed. I struck out twice. Jeanette hit into a double play.

The game was over about six-thirty. It was sleeting. The subway steps were icy; Jeanette took my arm. We went back to my apartment on Oak Street. Right off, she goes, "What do you like in bed?"

And I went, "How about you?"

And she went, "I like doing what I'm told."

She did, too. I got her to move in with me the same week. For over a year, Jeanette never mentioned her family or talked about growing up. I knew she was from Lincoln, Nebraska, but that was all. Her reticence about herself put a damper on our relationship. We were hot and wet for each other in bed, but we weren't friends.

Then, one night, on the web, we heard the folk singer Janie Hitchcock do "Home in Nebraska."

Jeanette said, "My daddy used to sing that." She hummed along. Then sang a verse. I never heard Jeanette sing before. She had a nice voice. I made her sing the verse again while I recorded her. That started her talking about her childhood. She was a little drunk and talked about an hour. It was an important occasion in our life together. I recorded her every word.

From a transcript of Roberta Friar's recording of Jeanette Baker, March 23, 2033:

(singing)

I live in the land of drought and heat
Where the wind don't sleep,
The Sand Hills creep,
And nothin' grows for me to eat.

My daddy loved jokes about Nebraska: "How dry is it?"

"Why, it's so dry that yesterday, in Holmes Park, I seen two trees fightin' over a dog."

Poor Daddy! He couldn't afford to buy medicine for his high blood pressure and died of a stroke on 33rd Street two days after my twelfth birthday. They broke the news to me at school. I still dream about it.

Momma got religion. She joined the Second Methodist Church on North 33rd Street. Her pastor got her a job in a city soup kitchen for exodusters. The work wore her out, but she wouldn't let up. Momma always said,

> Good better best,
> Never let it rest,
> Till your good is better,
> And your better's best.

I earned a little money on weekends working for my Aunt Polly in her hairstyling salon. The three of us lived together in Polly's five-room apartment on Sun Valley Boulevard. Just before dawn on June 28, 2022, all the tenants in the building were alerted that a Black Blizzard was blowing towards Lincoln from the southwest. About sixty of us holed up in the concrete storm cellar that was a sometime exoduster shelter and smelled of piss.

The temperature outside dropped fifty degrees in two hours. We watched what happened next on the web. Hundreds of birds landed on the roofs: sparrows, black birds, crows, swallows, wrens. I spotted a horned owl. Then, about 2 P.M. a huge black cloud appeared on the horizon. It blotted out the sun. The birds got quiet. The cloud rolled over the city like a wall of muddy water—but without a sound.

Static electricity in the cellar made everybody's hair stand on end. What a sight! Sixty people sitting around in a cellar with their hair on end! The computer crashed. A sixty-mile-an-hour wind roared above us for sixteen straight hours. The silence at sunup was deafening. I went outside with Momma for a breath of air. The sky was a coppery red. A greasy coat of black dust, an inch thick, covered the whole street.

Momma said, "Fetch me my rubber boots, will you, honey? I'm going for a walk before breakfast."

I fetched Momma her boots. She walked straight to a deserted part of Holmes Park, where she hanged herself with her panty hose from a branch of a dead spruce tree.

Polly Baker

Maggie was cremated on June 30, 2022. Next day, Jeanette and I took her ashes in a bronze urn out behind the broken-down frame house in Cherry County. I hadn't seen the place since it got sanded up. The kitchen-garden fence, piled with tumbleweeds, stuck out of the dunes; it looked like a big backbone.

I scattered Maggie's ashes; Jeanette recited the short poem "After Menamoto," by Clorene Welles. I can never remember the words.

Katherine G. Jackson

To what shall I compare my life?
Streaking west,
above Bayonne,
a jet trail at dusk.[4]

Roberta Friar

Jeanette was a type A-2 unipolar depressive. She took 5 milligrams of Euphorol once a day. Euphorol doesn't mix with booze, so I got her to go on the wagon. I loved looking after her. We were happy. Then on Christmas night 2035, exactly three years after we'd met, she announced, "I feel incomplete; I want a son."

She knew I didn't like babies. I told her, "You want kids, you're on your own."

She said, "You mean it?

"Make a choice," I said. "Him or me."

"Oh," she says, "I choose you."

4. Ibid., p. 32.

That seemed to be that. Spring rolled around, then summer—the driest summer of the decade. Jeanette always felt blue on her birthday. To take her mind off turning twenty-eight, I took her to Paris for dinner at a three-star restaurant on the rue Louis-Ferdinand Céline called Chez Denis. Jeanette spoke French pretty well. I had two years in college.

Jeanette drank only Evian water. It cost $60 a liter. The French call Evian water *le Champagne de la Sécheresse*—drought Champagne. I ordered a special birthday cake, Jeanette's favorite—genoise, with caramelized pears.

We caught the late show at Le Clit Club which was, like they say nowadays, a "rouser." Jeanette's birthday celebration cost me a bundle, but I didn't care. I'd just been made a senior systems analyst at Lunartech-Interares. Jeanette was also doing well; she was almost finished with her thesis on Charlotte Salomon.

Things were great between us till late in September. Then Jeanette read a bestseller called *Visual Arsogenes: The Genetic Basis of the Ability to Draw and Paint,* by Frederick Rust Plowman. She goes, "Listen, Roberta. All my life I've wanted to draw and paint, but I can't. I've no talent. It's not in me. I haven't got the right genes. The guy who wrote this book helped discover the ones I lack; he implants them in embryos. You know what that means? I could have a son born with artistic talent. That would mean a lot to me, Roberta. What do you say?"

I said, "I don't want a kid. I want you, but no kid!"

Jeanette burst into tears. I took her for a walk. We headed for Seward Park. The wind off Lake Michigan stank of rotten fish. Those were the years when the lake was drying up. The mud it left behind was a breeding ground for eels, rats, roaches, and green flies.

Outside the park, Jeanette goes, "These flies are driving me nuts! Let's go back to your place."

She always called my apartment "home." I thought, my God, she's going to leave me!

"All right," I said. "I'll read the damn book."

The opening paragraph got my goat.

From *Visual Arsogenes: The Genetic Basis of the Ability to Draw and Paint,* by Frederick Rust Plowman:

We scientists will eventually transform our species into a new kind of being; one whose mind will have the same relationship to ours as ours has to life and life to matter. The scientist can now say, with the poet: "*Oh, je serai celui-là qui créera Dieu!*" "Oh, I shall be the one who will create God!"[5]

Roberta Friar

How like a man!

Plowman's whole book pissed me off; it purported to be an objective account of a scientific discovery but was actually a piece of propaganda for the repeal of the Created Equal Act.

I said to Jeanette, "Who is this guy?"

We called up his bio.

Frederick Rust Plowman's 2035 biographical sketch:

Plowman, Prof. Frederick Rust (2008–) molecular geneticist. b 30 Sept., 2008, Little Rock, Arkansas, s of late Dr. Duncan and Judge Gladys Christine (nee Payne).

During Plowman's adolescence, he became fascinated by genetic engineering, particularly the successful experiments carried out on humin genomes in France to produce beautiful babies. Plowman attended Choate and MIT, where he earned a B.S., graduating summa cum laude in 2027. He received his Ph.D. in 2030 from the University of Nome for his work on the technical feasibility of supplementing humin genomes with arsogenes: genes that govern the development of artistic talents. The same year, Congress passed the Kenady-Kantor Created Equal Act, which prohibited the artificial alteration of genetically determined traits in humins except for reasons of health. Plowman continued his studies in Japan.

---

5. Dr. Frederick Rust Plowman, *Arsogenes: The Genetic Basis of the Ability to Draw and Paint,* Kyoto: The Metamorphic Press, 2029. (29–Pl726)

Plowman's quote is from Paul Verlaine's poem, "*Crimen Amoris.*" (10–Ve6327)

Late in 2030, he received a Nippon Fellowship and became Professor Yoshida Ozaki's research assistant at Kyoto University. The late Professor Ozaki was the world renowned genetic engineer who in 2020 first used the noun "metamorph" to designate any organism that has been genetically transformed by a microinjection of purified DNA.

During 2030–31, Ozaki and Plowman identified 786 arsogenic alleles common to the genetic makeup of 615 graphic artists. Ozaki declared: "They are the genes that contribute to the talent to draw." He and Plowman then analyzed the genomes of 321 painters and discovered 659 arsogenes, active in their visual cortices, which increase the number of colors they can see in the spectrum.

Ozaki wrote, "The possession of visual arsogenes—talent itself—is insufficient to make a truly original artist. The brains of the thirty-four creative artists we have studied crave incessant visual stimuli. They seem possessed by a 'lust of the eyes' *(me-no-yoku),* which must be constantly gratified.[6] Vincent van Gogh described how 'the lust of the eyes' affected him: 'I am ravished, ravished by what I see.'[7] We must discover the physiological basis of the lust of the eyes."

In 2032 Ozaki and Plowman established that artists who have particularly intense emotional experiences associated with visual stimuli frequently exhibit a postnatal neurological hyperdevelopment: an extensive arborization of the nerve cells in the prefrontal lobes of the brain associated with the production of emotion by visual stimuli.

In his book *Visual Arsogenes: The Genetic Basis of the Ability to Draw and Paint* (2035), Professor Plowman postulates that such hyperdevelopment can be activated by certain kinds of postpartum maternal behavior. Plowman indeed proposes an experimental series he calls "Ozaki's Project" in honor of his late mentor, who was killed in a swimming accident.

Plowman lives in Kyoto, where he is the Director of Ozaki's Project at the Ozaki Institute of Humin Metamorphic Genetics.[8]

---

6. Ozaki is utilizing a translation into Japanese of the New Testament phrase from 1 Jo. 2:17

7. Vincent van Gogh, *Letters to Theo,* ed. Anthony Wilson, London: Adam Press, 2003:67. (03–VaW4446)

8. *Current Biography* 2035:937–40. (35–CB86)

Jeanette Firth Baker to Frederick Rust Plowman, October 23, 2036:

I admire your beliefs, but I'd prefer the scientist and the artist—in fact, each and every one of us—to say, "*Oh, je serai celui-là qui créera la Déese*"—"Oh, I shall be the one who will create the goddess"—because the eternal feminine is my ideal.

I want my son to be special. Father him for me by artificial insemination and give him a gift for drawing and painting. I'll mother him in any manner that you think might help make him into a manual artist.

I enclose one copy each of my health insurance genetic profile, multiphasic personality profile, and curriculum vitae.

Polly Baker

Jeanette read me the letter over the phone. I was like, "It's illegal in this country to do such a thing. Don't set yourself above the law."

She said, "I can't help it! I want an artist for a son."

Roberta Friar

I yelled from the kitchen, "A son! And you call yourself a Gynarchist!"

She goes, "I do and I am, but I need a son!"

Polly Baker

I don't know why Jeanette was frantic for a son. But I can guess why she wanted him to be an artist. I'm partly responsible. I raised her after Maggie killed herself. Trouble is, I couldn't bring myself to talk to Jeanette about her mother's suicide. Not ever. I felt—I don't know—ashamed and guilty, as if I could have done something to prevent it. Jeanette, of course, never brought it up. She suffered in silence. But you know what? After a while, she came down with terrible insomnia. For weeks on end, the poor kid lay wide awake in her bed till first light. When she finally fell asleep, she had nightmares. She told me she constantly dreamed of looking in the mirror, where she saw her mother's dead face peering over her left shoulder.

Poor thing! Big brown rings appeared under her eyes; she was exhausted all the time. Her schoolwork fell off, apart from a course in Manual Art Appreciation, which was taught by—what was her name? A young substitute teacher . . . yes, the beautiful Julia Merrill. Jeanette had a crush on her. Julia Merrill introduced Jeanette to Manual Art. She got an A in Merrill's course.

One night when Jeanette couldn't sleep, I said to her, "Why don't you look at pretty pictures? They'll relax you."

The next couple of nights, Jeanette turned her bedroom into a virtual art museum. She called up paintings, drawings, and statues. Soon she discovered that paintings of the Virgin Mary with the Christ Child soothed her to sleep. It was a nightly ritual. Jeanette lay on her back under the covers, looking at Raphael's Madonna, one by Botticelli, and Leonardo's *Virgin and Saint Anne* on the walls around her. Then she would drift off.

But one morning she said to me, "Life is shit, Aunt Polly! I'd give anything to be an artist, but I can't draw a straight line."

Roberta Friar

I held my tongue about Jeanette's letter to Plowman. We waited for an answer. Jeanette chipped away at her thesis. She tried to get inside Charlotte Salomon's head.

Libby Ferguson

During the fall semester of 2036 at the University of Chicago, I programmed VR immersions for graduate students in the social sciences. I designed two for Jeanette Baker. In the first one, she was a German Jewish girl on the streets of Berlin one March afternoon in 1938. It was cold and rainy. Jeanette wasn't allowed to ride a streetcar, eat in a restaurant, or sit on a park bench. The second program immersed her for two hours in a sealed boxcar that arrived at the Birkenau station just before dawn on October 15, 1943, around the time that the painter Charlotte Salomon arrived there.

Roberta Friar

The second immersion got to Jeanette. She shook me awake one night and went, "I dreamed I was Jewish! I was sitting on my rucksack in a moving boxcar. We pulled into the Auschwitz-Birkenau station. The doors slid open, so I got out. Dazzling lights; I heard dogs barking. A black German shepherd bit off my nose."

Jeanette had other concentration camp nightmares. She called them her "Jewish dreams."

From: Frederick Rust Plowman, Associate Director, Ozaki's Project
To: The Board of Directors, Ozaki's Project, The Ozaki Metamorphic Institute of Kyoto, Japan
Date: November 12, 2036

Our three-year search for a potential mother–artist-maker has ended. I recommend Jeanette Baker to you as the ideal subject in that category.

Baker, who has a Median Multiple Intelligence Quotient (MMIQ) of 163, is a doctoral student in art history at the University of Chicago. Her mother committed suicide. She herself has a genetic propensity towards Type A-2 unipolar depression for which she takes 5 milligrams of Euphorol daily.

If she could be persuaded to forego this medication for six months after giving birth to an arsogenic metamorph, she would probably suffer a prolonged postpartum depression like those exhibited by Anna van Gogh, Laura Munch, Regina Magritte, Franziska Salomon, Shizue Hara, and others. Ozaki-san postulated that the postpartum behavior of these depressed wimin in some way stimulated the hyperdevelopment of an infant's frontal lobes associated with emotion produced by visual stimuli. It provided the physiological basis for their sons' "lust of the eyes."

It must be noted that Baker has a normal Mest maternal complement of genes, but I believe that if the subject is sufficiently psychologically motivated, she could stifle her instinct and become a mother–artist-maker.

From: Board of Directors, Ozaki Institute
To: Frederick Rust Plowman
Date: December 5, 2036

Please recruit Jeanette Baker as an experimental subject in the suggested category for Ozaki's Project.

Roberta Friar

Jeanette and I spent New Year's Eve 2036 together. Right after the PMC hit us with the latest bad news.[9] I told her, "Don't bring a kid into this world."

She said, "Maybe you're right."

Frederick Rust Plowman to Jeanette Baker, January 1, 2037:

Happy New Year!

I will father you a son by artificial insemination and provide his genome with the same complement of arsogenes as the other two subjects in Ozaki's Project. These arsogenes have been assembled from at least four distinguished contemporary manual artists. However, you must first agree to participate with your child in a risky postnatal experiment, the results of which won't be known for years. The Japanese, you know, are very fond of keeping diaries. You will be contractually obligated to keep a written journal or diary of your experiences for the archives of the Ozaki Institute, which reserves the right to 25% of all the gross proceeds from its publication.

However, in appreciation for your participation in the Project, your insemination, which is not covered by American medical insurance, will be given you at cost: $42,000.

If you agree to the above conditions, sign the enclosed contract and get it back to me as soon as you can.

P.S. Please understand that the genetic composition of your son's reproductive cells will be altered. He will not be able to transmit his metamorphic endowment to his descendants. The Ozaki Institute of Metamorphic Genetics is at present conducting no speciation experiments on humin subjects.

---

9. The Planetary Monitoring Commission reported that from 2025 through 2035, the global temperature had increased 2.9 degrees and the sea level had risen 1'9", causing extensive flooding. *Statistical Abstract of The Planet Earth* 2035:1784. (35–St5700)

Roberta Friar

Jeanette asked, "Where will I get forty-two thousand bucks?"

She knew I had a little more than that in my savings account, but I was like, "Search me."

She gave me a look I can't forget.

Polly Baker

I loaned Jeanette the forty-two thousand at no interest.

From Jeanette Baker's journal, January 2, 2037:

Signed a contract today with the Ozaki Institute of Metamorphic Genetics to take part in Ozaki's Project.

Then I spoke with Plowman's secretary in Kyoto—a tall, very pretty Japanese boy. He set up a teleconference between me and his boss for this coming Wednesday at 3 A.M.

I have no compunctions about breaking the law.

Roberta Friar

It was a bad time for me. My mother in Calgary fell off a horse and broke her right shoulder. I had to go up there and arrange her home care. The first night, I sent Jeanette a card with Clorene Welles reciting her two-line poem "Vita":

> Some in summer long for snow;
> I miss your pussy.[10]

Jeanette Baker to Roberta Friar, January 5, 2037:

I miss yours.

From Jeanette Baker's journal, January 7, 2037:

During today's teleconference Plowman and I exchanged memories about growing up.

Plowman: "The drought hit Arkansas in July 2021, when I was twelve years old. We had no rain for 271 days. All the ponds and streams in Conway County dried up. My daddy owned a fishing shack on the north shore of Lake Conway. Buzzards and hogs fought over the

10. Wells, op. cit., p. 87.

dead carp and catfish. The polluted water infected the ducks on the lake with botulism, which paralyzed and then killed them. One morning, I counted over a hundred little corpses of pintails, teals, widgeons, and mallards rotting in the mud.

"Easter Sunday, my folks and I prayed for rain at an interdenominational service in the Little Rock Municipal Auditorium. A Baptist preacher gave the invocation. Halfway through, the air-conditioning broke down. Mother fainted from the heat. Lo and behold, next morning, the famous Easter Monday Cloudburst: a polar air mass collided over the southeast with a wave of damp, tropical air. The resulting downpour lasted a week.

"One night, I saw on the news that a flock of mallards over the Little Rock airport mistook a flooded runway for a river. Fifteen of them landed on the concrete and tore off their legs. I thought, God does a lousy job; we ought to put somebody else in charge."

Plowman arranged to have me fertilized in vitro with his sperm at the Institute during my next ovulation, which should be around the first of the month.

Plowman: "Your baby's genome will be enhanced with visual arsogenes and placed in your womb, where he should develop a brain that possesses a highly augmented visual cortex, a basic requirement for a visual artist. And then, from birth to age six months, you will systematically deprive him of a nurturing visual maternal environment in hopes that this will make him use his eyes to facilitate the hyperdevelopment of his prefrontal cortex, the area of the brain that associates powerful emotions and visual stimuli."

Roberta Friar

I got drunk with Jeanette on the new designer Japanese booze, Amae, which had just hit the States.

When she awoke next morning, she said, "Fuck my Ph.D. thesis! The hell with an academic career. I'll learn a trade, so I can be independent and set my son a good example. I've been thinking. I'll go back to Lincoln, apprentice myself to Aunt Polly, and become a hair dresser."

Polly Baker

Jeanette called and said, "I'll never make a good mother on my own, Aunt Polly. Give me a hand."

"Honey," I said, "come home. I'll do what I can."

From Jeanette Baker's journal, January 14, 2037:

Got my period today.

Roberta Friar

Jeanette left me on the morning of January 16, 2037. I've no memory of our good-bye; I just remember eating breakfast in the kitchen by myself and throwing up. The next two months were hell. I couldn't sleep nights. The smell of food nauseated me. I lost eighteen pounds. Jeanette was the love of my life.

Polly Baker

I was in my mid-forties and recently divorced when Jeanette moved back to Lancaster County, Nebraska. Harry, my ex-husband, had made a fortune in synthetic rubisco, an enzyme essential to photosynthesis. I did well in the market. After eight years, our marriage died; we fell out of love with each other but stayed friends. It was an amicable divorce.

Harry, who retired on the moon, sold me his share of our town house in Cather Keep at a reasonable price. I divided up the interior into four three-and-a-half-room apartments. I rented Jeanette the one on the third floor, above mine, for a song—four hundred bucks a month—and put her to work across the street in Polly's Parlor as my apprentice. She earned thirty-four-fifty an hour, plus tips, which meant she lived on less than thirteen hundred dollars a week.

From Jeanette Baker's journal, January 22, 2037:

Plowman, via his secretary, invited me this evening to spend all next week at his home in Kyoto. I accepted.

Made a reservation on the Planet Train leaving Chicago for Tokyo on Tuesday at 8:06 A.M. The round trip cost $5550. Polly again loaned me the money without interest.

Polly Baker

Did I do right? I like to think so—despite what happened. Jeanette, you know, picked her own epitaph: "I will not wholly die."[11]

Well, she got her wish.

From Jeanette Baker's journal, January 28, 2037:

Plowman rents a log cabin in the faculty keep *(shiro)* near Kyoto University. He won't let me wander the city alone. Six wimin have been slashed to death on the streets since the Emperor was assassinated here during the night of his inauguration thirteen months ago.

The Sada Abe Gynarchist Sisterhood claimed responsibility for the assassination. The Sisterhood's named for the early-20th-century geisha who strangled her two-timing lover in his sleep, then cut off his pecker and wrapped it in a *furoshiki,* a cloth used especially for gifts. The Emperor's assassin, a lady-in-waiting, stabbed him through the heart, emasculated his corpse, then stabbed herself.

Plowman: "The gender war has spread to Japan, but in this country it's mixed up with anti-Chinese phallocratic tribalism."

He lives with his pretty secretary, Wakinoya Yoshiharu, who was raised in Concord, Mass., where his parents owned a Japanese-style country inn. He served us lukewarm stewed dumplings, roasted mushrooms, and stale chestnut buns for supper.

Coffee under a fig tree in the little walled garden. Plowman said, "You won't have an easy time raising your son to be an artist. Think you're up to it?"

"Try me."

From Jeanette Baker's journal, January 31, 2037:

Every morning, Plowman scrapes a carrot top, cracks two walnuts, and slices up half an apple for his three-yr.-old yellow-naped Amazon parrot named Sozoshii (Noisy). Her huge cage has its own video screen, which plays all day. The bird sings along with some commercials; others make her yell "Turn that shit off!" She shrieks, laughs like a maniac, guzzles sake, chews chopsticks, shreds paper, and calls Plow-

---

11. Jeanette's epitaph is from Horace: *"Non omnis moriar." The Poems of Horace,* tr. Diana Best, Los Angeles: Inanna Press, 2020:117. (20–HoB4159)

man "Sweetie." They shower together.

Plowman: "We love each other. Yoshida gave me Sozoshii for my 30th birthday. It took me two months to hand-tame her; she was a great consolation to me after Yoshida died."

Yoshida drowned three years ago next month while swimming alone in the Indian Ocean off Australia's Hundred Mile Beach. *Arsogenes* is dedicated to his memory.

Plowman: "Yoshida's nickname for me was Hotaru—firefly—because my ass lit up his nights."

Wakinoya Yoshiharu

Early in the morning of February 1st, Fritz brought Jeanette three yellow chrysanthemums from his lab and arranged them among some moss-covered stones at one end of a shallow glass bowl filled with water. We Japanese call this classic arrangement, which suggests a little scene in the woods, the Water-Reflecting Style.

Jeanette said exactly the right thing: "Oh, how lovely! They look as though they're growing by a stream."

Fritz said, "Watch what happens," and went back to the lab.

Jeanette hung around the bowl, which was on the dining room table. About a quarter of nine, I heard her cry out, "Ah!" and joined her. The chrysanthemums were dark green. She said, "They're metamorphs!"

Over the next few hours we watched them turn blue, then violet, then red and orange, and back to yellow. Jeanette e-mailed Fritz at work.

Jeanette Baker to Frederick Rust Plowman, February 1, 2037:

Thank you. I think I understand your beautiful arrangement. It means "These metamorphic flowers have been arranged to look as if they're growing by a stream, and therefore are to be taken as part of the natural world. And that goes for all kinds of metamorphs—flowers or people."

Frederick Rust Plowman to Jeanette Baker, February 1, 2037:

Yes, exactly. You're very astute. Yoshida once wrote: "Evolved by natural selection, the humin mind in turn is evolving metamorphic forms of life, which humins must think of as 'natural.' Nature makes no distinction between living things that we call natural and those we call artificial."

From Jeanette Baker's letter to Polly Baker, February 1, 2037:

This evening Fritz sat me down in the garden under the fig tree and said, "After you give birth I want you to lay off Euphorol for six months."

I asked, "What for?"

Fritz: "So you'll suffer a postpartum depression like Franziska Salomon, Anna van Gogh, Laura Munch, Regina Magritte, and Shizue Hara had." He calls them "mother–artist-makers." He believes their depression stimulated in their gifted infants a hyperdevelopment of the prefrontal lobe, the part of the brain that associates emotion and visual stimuli.

I pointed out that three out of the six wimin on his list eventually committed suicide. Regina Magritte drowned herself, and Shizue Hara jumped out of a window like Franzsika Salomon.

"But you'd only be at risk for six months." he said. "Will you do it?"

Polly, dear, forgive me, I said, "Yes."

Wakinoya Yoshiharu

After Fritz talked with Jeanette in the garden, he rushed me to the IVF lab, where I jerked him off into a test tube. He processed the sperm himself.

Polly Baker

I caught the 5 A.M. Tokyo Express out of Chicago on Monday, February 2, 2037, and arrived in Kyoto about 7 P.M. local time. I remember the air-conditioning at my hotel was on the blink.

Wakinoya Yoshiharu

Believe it or not, that same day, the 2nd, Jeanette met Mariko Tanaka, Yukio's future mother, in an elevator at the Institute. I'm a witness. Fritz introduced them. They bowed to each other. Mariko, who was due in August, got off at our prenatal clinic on the fifth floor. Jeanette called out after her, "Good luck!"

Neither womin ever met Anya Kammerovska, the third mother chosen to take part in Ozaki's Project. Fritz nicknamed them "The Three Fates."

From the Letter of Agreement between Jeanette Baker and the Ozaki Metamorphic Institute February 2, 2037:

In connection with the undersigned's participation in said Experiment, the undersigned does hereby hold the Institute and its employees, representatives, agents, and directors blameless for any liability, loss, damage, cost or expense, including reasonable attorney's fees, arising out of or in connection with any personal injury to the undersigned arising out of or in connection with the undersigned's participation in said Experiment.

From Frederick Rust Plowman's Report on Ozaki's Project:

On February 2, 2037, at 8 A.M. the subject's ovum was extracted and then fertilized in vitro with one of my Y-sperm cells.

At 1:20 P.M., recombinant vectors containing purified DNA sequences that amplify the activity of those constellations of neuron-specific arsogenes (NSAGs) that stimulate the development of the talent to draw and increase color perception were microinjected into the pronuclei of the subject's fertilized oocyte. The above arsogenes, from the Institute's library, were harvested from four distinguished manual artists and reassembled in the standard 16-1 pattern of all O.P. subjects.

Analysis of the host genome ascertained its viability and indicated that the injected DNA had been integrated into it.

At 4:15 P.M. the male metamorphic embryo was implanted in the subject's uterus.

Wakinoya Yoshiharu

Back at the house, I served Fritz and Jeanette a light supper of sweet bean soup with rice cakes. Fritz, who was a little drunk on Amae, called out to me, "Come join the celebration! You had a hand in this!"

From Jeanette Baker's journal, February 3, 2037:

Amory Firth Baker
Andrew Firth Baker
Benjamin Firth Baker
Brian Firth Baker
Channing Firth Baker
Cullen Firth Baker
Denis Firth Baker
Frederick Firth Baker
Guy Firth Baker
Howard Firth Baker
Ian Firth Baker
James Firth Baker
John Firth Baker
John Henry Baker
Michael Firth Baker
Olin Firth Baker
Quincy Firth Baker
Sidney Firth Baker
Timothy Firth Baker
Varian Firth Baker
Vivien Firth Baker
William Firth Baker

John Firth Baker

Polly Baker

Jeanette told me she picked John because it resembles Jeanette.

We spent a couple of hours making the rounds of Kyoto hairstylists so I could write the trip off. My old friend Yoko Hibi, who ran the salon at the Miyako Inn, told us that the Emperor's assassin hadn't killed herself, but had bled to death after having been raped and then clitorectomized with a sliver of broken glass by two Imperial bodyguards.

Jeanette had a four o'clock appointment with Plowman to go over John's genomic analysis. She invited me along. The leather sofa in Plowman's office was cracked. I smelled Amae on his breath.

From Jeanette Baker's journal, February 4, 2037:

Johnny (!) will come into this world equipped with a grand total of 2,613 arsogenes, which should result in extensive development of the brain cells in his visual cortex. Johnny's MMIQ will be around 152.

He'll probably be gay and a risk-taker. He's inherited my polygenic propensity towards Type A-2 unipolar depression.

He's also got genes for light blue eyes, curly black hair, and male pattern baldness.

Johnny will have 20-20 vision and be right-handed. He'll be muscular, have broad shoulders and flat feet. He'll grow to between 5'11" and 6'1".

He'll be allergic to chickpeas. In his fifties he'll stand a 60% chance of developing high blood pressure and, if he smokes, a 90% chance of lung cancer. Thanks to Fritz (the gene is carried in the Y chromosome) Johnny during his fifties will grow hair in his ears.

If Johnny takes care of himself, he's got an 83% chance to live a century.

Wakinoya Yoshiharu

Fritz gave Jeanette a farewell dinner on the night of February 7, 2038—the third anniversary of Ozaki's death. Fritz got drunk on Amae and cried out, "Yoshida! You're three years dead! Am I dreaming? It must be a dream."

Then he said, "What do you think, Jeanette? Is all this a dream?"
She said, "No."

Polly Baker

Jeanette and I got home early Monday morning.

From Jeanette Baker's journal, March 15, 2037:

Have settled in my three-and-a-half-room apartment above Polly in her redbrick house at 124 Kuttner Street in Cather Keep, Lancaster County, Nebraska. The Keep was designed by C. L. Moore and built in 2027. It was named for Willa Cather. The Keep is laid out around the artificial Lake Twilight in the shape of a rectangle ¾ mile wide and 1-⅓ miles long. It's covered by a transparent and oval impermium dome, which reaches a height of 130 feet.

10,725 people live here. Most are skilled workers who belong to various Guilds. For example, our next door neighbor, Indira Rabindra, is a book repairer, and her husband, Ben Shrapnel, is the articles editor of *Keepsake* magazine.

There's no poverty or violent crime in Cather Keep. The temperature is always 75°F. during the day and 50°F. at night. There are all kinds of trees and prairie flowers. These include the violet, wild rose, larkspur, phlox, spiderwort, blueflag, poppy, mallow, waterlily, petunia, columbine, and yellow ladyslipper as well as the goldenrod and sunflower. We live in a garden where spring stays put.

Indira Rabindra

Jeanette and I hit it off right away. I was her first Hindu friend. When she fixed up the small bedroom off her kitchen as a nursery, I put it under the protection of the Divine Mother, in the person of the Goddess Sati-Parvati, by giving Jeanette a drawing of Her by the turn-of-the-century Bengali artist Shubha Roy. The drawing had been a wedding gift to me from my dear mother, who's devoted to the Great Goddess.

Jeanette hung the drawing in a white enamel frame on the wall behind the crib.

Shubha Roy, 2027, *Face of Parvati*, scratchboard drawing

Shubha Roy's biographical sketch:

Shubha Roy (2002–2029) was the only daughter of a Brahmin industrialist who built a temple for the Goddess Kali in the Janbazzar district of central Calcutta. Roy took an MFA in graphic design at the Pratt Institute in New York, then worked in New York for two years as an assistant art director at an ad agency.

On the night of November 22, 2025, Shubha Roy had a dream: "The Divine Mother commanded me: 'From now on draw only Me in My myriad forms. I will manifest Myself in your pictures and accept worship and offerings.' "

Roy quit her job, returned to Calcutta, and rented a one-room studio near the Janbazzar temple, where over the next three years she made 1,012 scratchboard drawings of the Divine Mother in her various aspects.

Roy was a political activist and one of a growing number of religious intellectuals and artists known as "goddess wimin" who split with the secular Indian Gynarchist Party in 2027. A year later, she was exiled by the Lingamist coalition government to Nepal, where, weakened by malnutrition, she died of mycoplasmic pneumonia on April 3, 2029.[12]

Polly Baker

Jeanette worked hard as my apprentice. Part of her job was to offer each customer a free glass of wine. Around the middle of March, the smell suddenly nauseated her. She puked all over her own sneakers. Another time she vomited a little blood. Her hair went limp, but her face glowed. She yawned all morning and napped every afternoon. Her boobs got bigger.

Jeanette said, "I wish they'd stay this size."

From Jeanette Baker's journal, March 20, 2037:

Applied this morning for federal maternity benefits, to which I'm not entitled under the Created Equal Act. As required by health insurance regulations, I submitted a transcription of Johnny's gen-pro, loaded with metamorphic arsogenes which, Fritz assured me, are indistinguishable from those acquired normally.

If I'm caught, I risk a $40,000 fine, a year in jail, or both.

After lunch, I enrolled at the Lake Twilight Street Childbearing Center, where I had a physical and attended an orientation session with six other pregnant Cather keepies. Our nurse-midwife is Aura Jones, who's in her late thirties. She emphasizes that this is a self-help program. "Assume responsibility for your own health care. Educate yourselves about what's happening to you!"

Polly Baker

Jeanette and I let it be known that she'd been artificially inseminated by an American friend who lived in Japan.

From Jeanette Baker's journal, April 4, 2037:

Today I posted the following on the Pregnant listserve:

Pregnant with talented artist. Seek confidential relationship with other mothers-to-be like me. Call me at 402-873-5193.

---

12. *Short Biographies of 21st Century Manual Artists* 2035:763. (35–SBMA10)

From Jeanette Baker's journal, April 6, 2037:

Got a call today from Cressanthia Thomas, who lives with her husband Alex in Crudge Keep, near Hartford, Conn. Married four years. They both market industrial robots and share a passion for African-American music. I liked her face, particularly her expressive eyes. She said, "I'm a little over a month pregnant with a musically gifted boy."

"How did he come by his gift?"

She hesitated. Told her I was pregnant with an arsogenic metamorph, acquired at the Ozaki Institute, whom I hope to turn into a visual artist.

Cressanthia then confessed to me that her son's genome was supplemented at l'Institut Metamorphique Génétique de Paris with musical arsogenes, which contribute to the acquisition of absolute pitch, an acute intervalic sense for musical harmonies and scales, and a propensity to develop auditory brain lateralization (aural dominance).

Cressanthia: "I don't feel guilty about breaking the law. Americans should have the right to enhance their kids' genomes."

"I agree."

"But I'm scared."

"So am I."

"Let's keep in touch."

From Jeanette Baker's journal, April 9, 2037:

A long talk today with Cressanthia, who's sympathetic to Gynarchism because of the sisters' work organizing African-American wimin in the ghettos.

We're both frightened of the possibility of being prosecuted for taking federal maternity benefits under false pretenses. I'll get $1035 a month for the first four years after Johnny's birth and $825 a month until he leaves school or home.

Cressanthia Thomas

The risks Jeanette and I took for the benefit of our kids bound us together and formed the basis of our friendship, the closest one I ever had with a white womin. Jeanette and I teleconferenced at least twice a week till two days before she gave birth.

From Jeanette Baker's journal, June 1, 2037:

WORLD HUMIN CHESS GRANDMASTERS' ASSOCIATION PAYS MEXICAN WOMIN $400,000 TO BE CLONED AS CAPABLANCA METAMORPH—CHESS GENIUS WHO CAN ONE DAY CHECKMATE IBM'S CHESS MAVEN

By Samantha Lyons
Special to IN-News

MEXICO CITY, June 1. The Humin Chess Grandmasters' Association announced today that it recently paid $400,000 to Mal Teratol, a 22-year-old Zinacantec womin, to bear her own clone whose genome has been metamorphically enhanced in Japan at the Ozaki Institute of Metamorphic Genetics with genius genes associated with the ability to play championship chess.

Boris Chmeilniki, 37, president of the Grandmasters' Association, said that Ms. Teratol is five weeks pregnant with what he termed "the world's first Capablanca metamorph." The term honors Jose Raul Capablanca (1888–1942), the greatest humin chess player of all time. Mr. Chmeilniki added that Ms. Teratol's daughter will be raised and educated at the Association's expense "with but one aim: to someday regain for the humin race the world chess championship, which has been held by IBM's Chess Maven since 2009."

Teratol, who formerly lived in El Dorado, a Mexico City slum, now resides in a suburb of Havana, Cuba.

From Jeanette Baker's journal, June 1, 2037:

There was a young Mexican clone
Whose mother conceived her alone,
But added the gene
To beat the machine
We can't checkmate on our own.

(limerick 767)

From Jeanette Baker's journal, June 4, 2037:

His Eminence Hector Santana, Cardinal Archbishop of Havana: "Any unnatural enhancement of the humin genome is a sinful desecration of the sacred receptacle in which the Holy Spirit became incarnate as a Man."

From Jeanette Baker's journal, June 5, 2037:

TOP IN-NEWS STORY:

CUBA'S RULING CHRISTIAN COALITION EXPELS MAL TERATOL.
PREGNANT MOTHER-TO-BE OF CLONED CHESS GENIUS
IN-THE-MAKING HAS 48 HOURS TO LEAVE COUNTRY

From Jeanette Baker's journal, June 6, 2037:

TOP IN-NEWS STORY:

TERATOL GIVEN REFUGE BY REGIONAL
GERMAN GYNARCHIST LEADER

HOHN, Schleswig-Holstein, June 6. Elsa Schminke, 44, a Regional Director of the German Gynarchist Federation (G.F.D.) said today that she has given refuge to Mal Teratol. Ms. Teratol, 22, is pregnant with the world's first cloned Capablanca metamorph. Teratol, who is incommunicado, presently occupies a small suite of rooms on the second floor of Die Weisse Jungfrau, a moderately-priced hotel-restaurant that Ms. Schminke has owned and operated for six years in this medieval Schleswig-Holstein town.

"There's always room at my inn for a homeless mother-to-be," Ms. Schminke declared.

A Mexican Indian clone
Whose genome with genius was sown,
Was forced from her nest
At the Church's behest,
And fled with her mother to Hohn."

(limerick 767)

From Jeanette Baker's journal, August 30, 2037:

TOP IN-NEWS STORY:

TERATOL DECLARES HERSELF A GYNARCHIST;
JOINS BEIT TIAMAT, INTERNATIONAL GYNARCHIST KEEP UNDER MEDITERRANEAN; DECLARES DAUGHTER WILL WIN WORLD CHESS CHAMPIONSHIP FOR WOMINKIND

BEIT TIAMAT, MEDSEA, Aug. 30. Mal Teratol, 22, four months pregnant with daughter Ishtar, the world's first cloned Capablanca metamorph, said today that she has joined this thriving Palestinian-Israeli Gynarchist communal keep situated 250 meters under the Mediterranean Sea, 9 miles southwest of Tel Aviv.

In a prepared statement, Ms. Teratol declared herself a Gynarchist, committed to the feminization of the humin race. "I have become a member of this commune of Palestinian and Israeli wimin, who renounced the warring tribal phallocracies into which they were born and live in peace. Here I will raise my daughter Ishtar to win back the world chess championship for Wominkind."

Tried my hand at a limerick:

An undersea Gynarchist keep
Is now home to our hope in the deep.
She'll play chess with the fishes
And do as she wishes,

(No last line. Am going to sleep.)

From Jeanette Baker's journal, September 4, 2037:

METAMORPHIC MASTERMIND THANKS GYNARCHISTS

By Rebecca Hartog
Special to IN-News

KYOTO, Sept. 4. In an exclusive interview today, Dr. Frederick Rust Plowman, 29, the American director of the Ozaki Institute of Metamorphic Genetics, expressed his gratitude to the international Gynarchist community for its support of Mal Teratol, mother-to-be of the world's first Capablanca metamorph. Dr. Plowman said, "I had the privilege of designing and building Ishtar Teratol's genome. I'm not a Gynarchist; I'm neutral in the gender war. But I'm a genetic engineer. I believe that the humin race must direct its evolution, and I thank the International Gynarchists movement for helping me implement the Doctrine of Metamorphism."

Wakinoya Yoshiharu

Make no mistake: Fritz loved publicity. His interview with IN-News got him into hot water with the powers that be at the Ozaki Institute. The Board of Directors had been gunning for him since Ozaki had handpicked him as his successor. Fritz was doubly—make that triply—resented: as a foreigner, because he was young, and because he'd been Ozaki's lover. Behind his back Fritz's underlings called him *gaijin homodachi*—"foreign faggot."

The Board of Directors was fit to be tied that Fritz had publicly associated the Institute with Gynarchism; we're talking here sixteen powerful old Japanese men. Their bête noir was Gynarchism. Like most Japanese males, their turn of phrase for Gynarchism was *rezu kisoku*—"Lesbian rule."

Fritz had a lot riding on Ozaki's Project.

Polly Baker

After Jeanette's nausea went away, she passed her first two trimesters without a hitch. She took up biking around Lake Twilight and did her pelvic exercises religiously. She craved orange marmalade; I once watched her eat a whole jarful.

I enjoyed going with her every Tuesday afternoon to the Childbearing Center.

Aura Jones

Jeanette was obsessed by her baby's prenatal development, which was perfectly normal. According to my records, he opened his eyes during the twenty-sixth week of her pregnancy. Jeanette carried on like he was going to be born sighted in the country of the blind.

From Jeanette Baker's Journal, August 17, 2037:

Tuned in this afternoon at the Childbearing Center to all the sounds that Johnny now hears in my womb: the rumble of my intestines, the whoosh of blood through my arteries, and my own voice, which sounds deeper than a man's. My spoken words are individually unintelligible, but he hears the melody and rhythms of my speech—what Aura Jones calls "the mother's primal tune, the music of her spoken language, to which her baby listens till it's born."

Tonight I read aloud to Johnny for an hour from Clorene Welles' *Collected Poems.*

Cressy makes Alex jr. listen to Waleed Parmalee conducting his chorale *The Murder of Dr. Martin Luther King Jr.*

My heartburn is back —worse than yesterday.

From Jeanette Baker's journal, October 22, 2037:

At today's exam, Aura reported Johnny's head is engaged and I'm already 2 cm dilated. He could be born any time now.

Jeanette Baker to Cressanthia Thomas, October 23, 2037:

Dear Cressy,

Aunt Polly will let you know when Johnny's born. For reasons I can't explain, I'll be out of touch for the next six months or so. I hope all goes well for you in November.

See you next spring. Meantime, the best of luck.

Cressanthia Thomas

I couldn't help thinking that Jeanette broke off our relationship because of racism—she didn't want Johnny and Alex jr. growing up friends.

From Jeanette Baker's journal, Oct. 24, 2037:

On Aura's recommendation, and with Polly's generous financial help, I hired a baby nurse today named Delia Claire for $1250 a week. Have also rented a cookbot @ $25/hour.

Polly Baker

Jeanette's water broke in her living room while she and I were watching the third quarter of the Nebraska-Oklahoma game on Saturday afternoon, October 24, 2037. The score was tied fourteen all. I helped clean Jeanette up. Then she flushed twenty capsules of Euphorol down the toilet.

The Huskers won twenty-eight to seventeen. Jeanette went into labor about 11:30 P.M. I was with her the whole time.

Jeanette Baker to Frederick Rust Plowman, October 25, 2037:

John Firth Baker born 6:01 this morning @ Lake Twilight Childbearing Center, in Cather Keep, Lancaster County, Nebraska.

Weight: 7 lbs. 8 oz. Length: 21 ½ in. Apgar score: 9

His F dendrite formation scan shows—as hoped!—hyperarborization of synapses in his visual cortex. Ditto, Broca Region—please explain.

Am now off Euphorol 23 hours. No discernible effect.

Frederick Rust Plowman to Jeanette Baker, October 25, 2037:

Congratulations on the birth of your son, the arsogenic metamorph John Firth Baker.

The Broca region is the language center of the brain. Its hyperdevelopment in your son seems to be an unforeseen consequence of the enhancement of his genome with arsogenes. It should greatly facilitate his verbal capability.

Polly Baker

I left the glad tidings on Cressy's machine. She sent Jeanette a dozen blue metamorphic roses. They arrived, I remember, while Jeanette was nursing Johnny for the first time. He sucked once or twice and fell asleep. Jeanette kissed the top of his bald little noodle and said, "He's all mine!"

Wakinoya Yoshiharu

"The Three Fates"—Mariko Tanaka, Anya Kammerovska, and Jeanette Baker—gave birth within five months of each other. And each arsogenic metamorph showed synaptic hyperdevelopment of both the visual cortex and the Broca region of the brain.

Fritz sent each mother a baby present: a metamorphic birth tree. Anya got a flowering birch; Mariko, a winter cherry; and Jeanette, a towering bower. The towering bower was an American favorite, designed specifically at the University of Nebraska for the Creeping Sand Hills, but also planted in the Sahara and Gobi deserts.

Frederick Rust Plowman to Jeanette Baker, October 28, 2037:

The sealed phial contains the gamete of his metamorphic birth tree, a towering bower *(Nova Prosopis tamarugo).*

Plant the phial as directed in the Creeping Sand Hills. The tree's gamete, being nurtured within, will grow to more than sixty feet in height without rain or an underground source of water. Its massive root system, which flourishes on carbon dioxide, has been designed to grow in sand. The leaves of its huge crown, or bower, absorb moisture from the night air. In thirteen years, its showy white flowers, streaked with lavender, will bloom between March and May. Its sweet and spicy spherical blue fruits will ripen two-and-a-half to three months after that. The fruit is a variety of the metamorphic type popularly known as "manna," one-half pound of which provides an adult's minimum daily nutritional requirements.

May Johnny and his beautiful birth tree flourish together in the years to come.

From Jeanette Baker's journal October 27, 2037:

Off Euphorol since Sat. Trouble sleeping. Indigestion. Never noticed a baby's feet before. Johnny's soles look unused.

Indira Rabindra

I had my astrologer cast Johnny's horoscope but never showed it to Jeanette. Johnny's focal planet of the finger of fate, his yod, was opposed by transiting Pluto, which was also in exact square to his natal Mars in the twelfth house. In other words, he was going to die young.

Polly Baker

Jeanette and I brought Johnny home Tuesday morning. First thing she did was program her apartment to keep a video baby book. Then she asked me to plant Johnny's birth tree behind the old ranch house in Cherry County. That required an OK from the Nebraska Ecological Authority because the ranch was now part of the Wild Cat Creek Sand Hill range.

I called an old friend at NEA. The OK came within twenty-four hours. I went out and planted the tree in the dunes some fifteen yards west of the half-buried house, where we once scattered Maggie's ashes.

I got back around six. Jeanette was nursing Johnny. She put him down before supper. He woke up crying. Jeanette burst into tears.

From Jeanette Baker's journal, October 29, 2037:

I feel like Johnny's still part of me. When he cries, I cry. We're stuck together as if he'd never been born.

Jeanette Baker to Pediatrobot 333-L14, Lake Twilight Childbearing Center, Cather Keep, Nebraska, November 8, 2037:

My baby pays no attention to the mobile over his crib. Is something wrong with his vision?

From: Pediatrobot 333-L14
To: Jeanette Baker
Date: November 8, 2037:

No. Your baby can't make out a mobile hung directly above his crib. He can only focus on an object between 8 and 14 inches away, the distance at which he sees your face from your breast.

From Jeanette Baker's journal, November 10, 2037:

Dreamed last night I gouged Johnny's eyes out with a teaspoon.

Weepy all day. Palpitations, headache, sweaty palms. Very sore nipples.

Delia Claire

Jeanette had no energy. She nursed her baby, then lay around in bed or sat for hours staring into space. Once in a while, though, she roused herself to write in her journal.

Johnny was an easy baby. By three weeks, he slept three to four hours at a stretch during the day and woke only once at night. He gained weight steadily even though he was a big spitter-upper.

Polly Baker

I looked in on Jeanette every evening after work. One night about the middle of November she whispered to me, "Johnny's in danger."

I asked, "Who from?" and she whispered again, "Momma."

Next morning I took her to the doctor.

From: Obstetrobot 129-D33, Lake Twilight Maternity Care Center, Cather Keep, Nebraska
To: Jeanette Baker
Date: November 18, 2037

Your low blood levels of equilibric acid, estrogen, and progesterone indicate that you're suffering from a Postpartum Major Affective Disorder (PMAD).

Your 5-HIAA level, however, is still only slightly below normal, which means that you're not yet in imminent danger of committing suicide or harming your baby.

Polly Baker

Jeanette agreed to have her 5-HIAA level monitored once a week but nixed any treatment. She told everybody at the Center that it was against her religion.

Delia Claire

Jeanette said to me, "Delia," she said, "I'm suffering a postpartum depression, but I won't take medicine for it because I'm a Christian Scientist."

I said to her, "God love you, Ms. Baker! I'm a member of the Church of Jesus Christ of Latter Day Saints myself."

Polly Baker

As usual, I made Thanksgiving at my place. Jeanette hardly ate. And you know what? I couldn't even get her interested in the Huskers' big win over Colorado.

From Jeanette Baker's journal, November 26, 2037:

Today was Thanksgiving for everyone but me. I've got nothing to be thankful for anymore.

Delia Claire

Johnny was coming along nicely.

Katherine G. Jackson

Within a month of his birth, Johnny, like all babies, was fixated on the bilateral symmetry, glistening brightness, depth, acute angles, curves, and contrasts between light and dark that compose the humin face. And, like all babies, beginning at eight-and-a-half weeks, he tried repeatedly to make eye contact with his mother while he nursed or lay in his crib. Jeanette almost always looked away.

He first smiled at her on Friday, January 29, 2038, at 7:35 A.M.[13]

Delia Claire

Ms. Baker often burst out crying. In the weeks to come, Johnny got clingy and sad. I cuddled him all I could.

Once Ms. Baker screamed, "Keep your hands off my kid!" Once, she begged me, "Take Johnny home. He's safer with you."

Polly Baker

I monitored Jeanette's 5-HIAA level twice a day; it pretty much stayed okay at around .02.

---

13. All information on John Firth Baker's early development is based on Carol Rose's analysis of his video baby book. Carol Rose, "The Etiology of John Firth Baker's 'Lust of the Eyes': An Analysis of the Nursery Recordings," *The Journal of Metamorphic Psychology* 2062/8:329–47. (62–JMP8)

Katherine G. Jackson

During the second half of February 2038, when he was three-and-a-half months old, Johnny gained complete control over his eyes. By early March, he stopped trying to elicit Jeanette's gaze and instinctively sought visual gratification from things like his crib bumper and cotton balls, a Mickey Mouse mobile, and Shubha Roy's drawing framed above him on the wall.

From February 29 through April 30, 2038, John's eye movements and the duration of his glance increased respectively 86% and 61%, more than double the usual increase for infants his age. The concomitant increase in John's retinal images, as he frantically looked around his nursery, resulted in abnormally extensive neuronal activity for a six-month-old who under ordinary circumstances would have primarily focused his gaze on a nurturing mother.

Polly Baker

In the beginning of April, I let Delia go and moved into Jeanette's apartment, where I slept on the living room sofa for the next six weeks or so. Jeanette's 5-HIAA level hovered around .02.

The day the six months were up, I took her back to the doctor.

From: Psychotherobot 129-D33, Cather Keep Maternity Center
To: Katherine G. Jackson
Date: June 11, 2064:

On April 25, 2038, at Jeanette Baker's request, I treated her Postpartum Major Affective Disorder (PMAD) with intramuscular Euphorol and progesterone, and estrogen suppositories. She also went on a daily maintenance dose of 5 mg. Euphorol, and recovered fully from PMAD by the end of the month.

From Jeanette Baker's journal, April 28, 2038:

This is my first journal entry since November 26th.

Weaning Johnny to formula milk, which gives him diarrhea. Which gives him chronic diaper rash. A few minutes ago (2:30 P.M.) he screamed, "Mama!"—his first word. At six months!!

From Jeanette Baker's journal, April 29, 2038:

While Polly babysat Johnny, I left the keep this morning for the first time since he was born.

Walked east on Arbor Road all the way to 70th Street. The warm breeze on my face felt wonderful. I'd forgotten how crowded outside streets are. And how sandy. The gritty scrunch underfoot set my teeth on edge.

This afternoon, took Johnny for a scan of his prefrontal cortex, the portion of the brain that attaches powerful emotions to visual stimuli. My experiment was a success. He has 62% more neurons there than average. Sent the results to Fritz.

Frederick Rust Plowman to Jeanette Baker, May 2, 2038:

Congratulations on Johnny's extensive neuronal arborization of the prefrontal cortex. It constitutes the physical basis of "the lust of the eyes."

Wakinoya Yoshiharu

Fritz said, "If only Yoshida were here."

Jeanette Baker to Cressanthia Thomas, May 5, 2038:

All well. What's with you?

Cressanthia Thomas

Jeanette's message caught me in the middle of moving us into a three-bedroom apartment in Du Bois Keep outside Atlanta. I couldn't get back to her for days—till that weekend, as I recall.

Then we talked and talked. I filled her in on Alex jr., born December 5th, and we oohed and aahed over each other's baby.

Jeanette was worried about her weight gain—fourteen pounds—but wouldn't go on an appetite inhibitor while she was nursing, something neither of us was nuts about. She never once mentioned her long silence.

From Jeanette Baker's journal, June 12, 2038:

Arsogenic metamorphs are obviously verbally very precocious: Cressanthia tells me Alex jr., six months old, said "cup" yesterday, his first word.

From Jeanette Baker's journal, June 21, 2038:

About ten after seven this morning, on my way to report for jury duty in Lincoln, I walked through the keep's West Gate and froze in my tracks. Light-headed, short of breath, my heart pounding, I shook like a leaf. I was scared stiff of leaving the keep. I thought, What's going on? Am I going crazy? and ran back inside.

From Jeanette Baker's journal, June 23, 2038:

The strangest thing: I feel safe at home anywhere within the keep, but I can't leave it, even virtually. This evening, I started on a VR walking tour of Brooklyn's new Tropical Gardens. Got dizzy. Then I couldn't breathe. I thought, If I'm not out of here this instant I'll die.

Polly Baker

On Fridays, I cut hair for free at the Lincoln Municipal Shelter near Sherman Field, which was packed with American exodusters who'd been deported from Canada. One Friday, I couldn't make it and asked Jeanette to go in my place. She begged off. I suddenly realized she never left the keep anymore. I said, "If you don't watch out, you'll become a keepie shut-in."

She said, "That's what I'm scared of."

So I said, "Then do something about it! Check with your therapist!"

From: Psychotherobot 147-B22
To: Jeanette Baker
Date: June 25, 2038:

Your blood test indicates that you have a 53% chance of becoming a keepie shut-in. Because your body has been unable to metabolize enough of the exogenously-administered hormones, a pathological increase from 1 to 5 in the degree of permeability of your intercellular membranes has significantly altered the relationship between extracellular and intracellular concentrations of minerals such as calcium and magnesium that are specifically devoted to neural transmission. As a result, your neural transmissions are impaired, giving you an acute form of agoraphobia, which afflicts 5.6% of American keepies. If left untreated, the phobia will render you incapable of leaving the environs of your keep.

Your genetic predisposition to unipolar depressive disorder necessitates your treatment for this type of agoraphobia with an individually-formulated variant of GABA (gamma-aminobutyric acid) patented under the name Outease, the cost of which is $43,500 yearly, an amount not covered by your medical insurance.

Polly Baker

I said to Jeanette, "Don't look at me! God knows, I don't have that kinda money!"

But you know what? I felt guilty. Why did Jeanette always make me feel guilty?

From Jeanette Baker's journal, July 5, 2038:

I've joined Stepout, an online keepie–shut-in support group. Under the direction of Dr. Monique Chung, Stepout advocates the use of gradual exposure (Grex) therapy to treat keepie agoraphobia without medication.

Chung: "Grex behavioral therapy incrementally conditions the keepie shut-in to leave her keep at will and resume a normal life. To this end, Stepout members are assigned specific biweekly actual excursions of gradually lengthening duration outside their keeps, during which they must accomplish a simple task of their own choosing."

Each day during the next two weeks, I must do something for at least thirty seconds outside Cather Keep's West Gate.

From Jeanette Baker's journal, July 7, 2038:

The good news: today—my third try—I managed to hang just outside the West Gate for thirty-eight seconds while I copied down the following, scribbled in red crayon on a cardboard sign hung around the neck of a wrinklie panhandler:

Cather keepies pleas help my name is Maria. I am an exoduster aged 73 forced from Colorado by black blizzards. My daughter Betty died June 6. June 7 her kids threw me out of there squat into a heat wave. I been living under the weather ever since. State welfare said no to help me get a place inside. Pleas take me in or money will do. Major credit cards accepted.

Maria

The bad news: Johnny's diaper rash has flared up. His tush looks like raw chopped meat. It's my fault. I never should have stopped nursing him.

Polly Baker

Jeanette kept Johnny by her while she worked; between feedings, she constantly checked him out with a nervous look. At home, she hardly took her eyes off him. Her big round eyes watching over him were like the eyes in that Shubha Roy drawing come to life.

From Jeanette Baker's journal, July 20, 2038:

Jeanette to Stepout, 7/20/38
Re: Grex Assignment #2, dated 7/19/38

As you know, my second assignment for Grex required me to walk east on Arbor Road towards North 40th Street for two and a half minutes, do a little something, then head home. My "little something" was going to be: smile at a pretty girl, which I haven't done in nineteen months! Then I started thinking about what would happen to me when I went out. Now I can't budge from my keep. I'm back on square one. Help me. Please help me.

Monique Chung, Ph.D.

Jeanette was experiencing anticipatory anxiety, a symptom which is well known to us Grex therapists. It is a very difficult though not an impossible symptom to treat.

I explained to Jeanette that anticipatory anxiety means, in essence, that the more a patient thinks about something, the worse it gets.

This was her exact answer: "You think? I think you're right. I think too much. Think you! Thinks a lot!"

Polly Baker

Jeanette charged a couple of quarts of Amae to my account in a local liquor store and went on a three-day binge at home. She lay in bed nursing—no pun intended—a bottle or sat on the living room sofa, saying: "I gotta drink. Lemme drink. Gimme more to drink."

I stayed at her place and took care of Johnny. But what to do about Jeanette? To make a long story short, I got in touch with Monique Chung, who recommended immediate hospitalization. On the evening of the third day, Ben and Indira helped me pack Jeanette off to the psychiatric ward of the Cather Keep Skilled Workers Clinic, where she spent three days drying out. The first twenty-four hours were hell.

From Jeanette Baker's journal, August 2, 2038:

Ten days ago, Friday, the 23rd of July, was the worst day of my life. Deprived of booze, I went crazy in a small white room. Even worse: peeping out of a calm corner of my mind, I watched myself going crazy in a small white room. I saw myself thrash around on a bed and roll on a shiny floor. I heard myself groan and sob and scream and gag, then gag some more from dry heaves that lasted hours on end.

But I got off Amae. And now, with the help of 5 mg. of Endcrave a day, I intend to stay off.

Jeanette Baker to Monique Chung, August 5, 2038:

I drank till I stopped thinking. Till it was an effort to remember my name. I felt so ashamed! I still do.

I'm on Endcrave and have decided to take a short leave of absence from Grex therapy. I've at least temporarily accepted my lot as a keepie shut-in. For the immediate future, I'll remain indoors and devote myself to raising Johnny, making a living, and staying sober.

From Jeanette Baker's journal, October 25, 2038:

Johnny's a year old today. His verbal precocity amazes everybody.

In the last few days, he's begun producing three-word sentences: "I wan' juice" popped out of him this morning.

But he's not walking yet and shows no precocious small motor ability. When I hand him a crayon, he sticks it in his mouth.

From Jeanette Baker's journal, July 3, 2039:

Thirty years old today. Despite myself, I remain anxious because Johnny has not yet demonstrated the artistic capacities with which he was endowed, and it's too soon to tell if my experiment is a success. Nevertheless his potential fills me with joy. This is the happiest time of my life.

Cressanthia Thomas

I invited Jeanette and Johnny to Georgia for Thanksgiving, but she begged us to come to Nebraska instead. So we did. During dinner Jeanette confessed she was an incurable keepie shut-in; that was the word she used, "incurable." Then she went, "So I'm stuck here. So what? I don't mind. Cather Keep is cozy and safe. It's got everything I need. And I'm out of the weather for good. Think what I save on clothes!"

It was a Thanksgiving from hell. Our two kids were smack into the "terrible twos"—willful little beasts. They ran us ragged.

From Jeanette Baker's journal, December 25, 2039:

Johnny: "Does Baby Jesus bite?"

Polly: "Never!"

Johnny: "I bite."

Polly: "You bite me, and I'll bite you back."

Johnny screamed. He screams a lot.

Polly Baker

Johnny was supersensitive. He overreacted to everything; it was a struggle to dress him in new clothes because they made him itchy. His skin was very sensitive to touch. Lights and noise drove him wild with excitement. But at the same time, he was sensitive to people and very verbal—way beyond his years. When Johnny was a little over two, I introduced him to my new lover, and Johnny later said, "I like Paco, Aunt Polly. He told me his name right off. Grownups always say 'What's your name?' They never give you theirs."

From Jeanette Baker's journal, January 20, 2040:

A good start to the New Year. This week, my three-year apprenticeship with Polly ended. On Monday I received my hairstylist's license and membership in Local 103 of the North American Hairdresser's Guild. The guild provides fair medical coverage for me and Johnny and funeral benefits for me.

I don't miss the outside world one bit. My life here is complete. The Lesbian community in Cather Keep is small but select. I've got Johnny and love my work. I have a good eye and dexterous hands. Making a living manually is very satisfying.

Polly Baker

Jeanette had the most important quality of a good hairstylist—she made her customers feel good about their looks. I hired her at $40 an hour plus tips. She sent Johnny to the Cather Keep Nursery School on Elm Street half-day. He spent his afternoons with us in my shop. Everyone fussed over him. He only had eyes for Jeanette.

From John Firth Baker's interview in *The International Review of Manual Art:*

The first thing I remember is Mother cutting some womin's long blond hair. We're in Polly's Parlor, where mother worked. I'm between two and three. Mother holds a long comb and a big pair of scissors between the fingers of one hand. She parts the womin's hair down the middle with the comb while hanging on to the scissors. I hear music playing and feel happy.

From Jeanette Baker's journal, February 8, 2040:

Gave Johnny his first haircut today. His lower lip trembled, but he didn't cry. Tears came to my eyes, and I had trouble leaving his soft, black curls scattered around my feet, like downy feathers. I saved a lock.

Polly Baker

Jeanette kept a lock of Johnny's hair in a heart-shaped locket she wore around her neck. She always cut Johnny's hair; he wouldn't let anybody else touch it.

From Jeanette Baker's journal, July 18, 2040:

Two years without a drink.

From Jeanette Baker's journal, October 25, 2040:

Johnny's third birthday. I gave him a 14" × 17" inch pad of white paper and a set of watercolor finger paints: red, black, yellow, green, white, blue. He chose black for his first picture (12:04 P.M.).

First painting (untitled), 2040, finger paint on coated paper

Polly Baker

Johnny's first finger painting sent Jeanette into ecstasies; she praised him to the skies. He churned out finger paintings by the dozen.

Cressanthia Thomas

Jeanette called to wish Alex jr. a happy birthday and show off her collection of Johnny's finger paintings. I told her that Alex jr. could pick out thirds on the keyboard and was teaching himself to read music.

From Jeanette Baker's journal, November 8, 2040:

Am determined to educate Johnny politically as a Gynarchist and artistically as a Manualist. Have programmed his Mentor IV accordingly. It'll give him the Gynarchist slant on herstory and won't let him draw or paint digitally.

From John Firth Baker's interview in *The International Review of Manual Art:*

Mother raised me as a Manualist; Lenrow's *Handbook* was her bible.

From *A Handbook for Manualists:* [14]

A multitude of robots, manufacturing what we need on command, have robbed us of the joy of making things with our own hands.

Let us therefore rediscover for ourselves and teach our children the diverse manual skills which will once again enable us to experience the unique gratification and delight that working with our hands bestows.

From: Sister Maria Lopez, Chairpersin, the North American Gynarchist League
To: Sister Jeanette Baker
March 8, 2041

Subject: Celebrating International Wimin's Day

FEMINIZE THE HUMIN RACE!

14. Elbert Lenrow, *A Handbook for Manualists*, New York: Fieldston Press, 2027:3. (27–Le458)

Dear Sister Jeanette:

Today as we celebrate International Wimin's Day, polygamy is on the rise all over the world. Forty-nine phallocratic tribal regimes on three continents have legalized the pernicious practice. In the United States a powerful coalition of Mormons, I Kings 11:3 Evangelicals, fundamentalist Muslims, and Hasidic Jews, calling itself "The Patriotic Patriarchs" (PAPA), contributed to the election last November of 103 members of the House of Representatives and 18 Senators who, in turn, have pledged to support the Ritchie-Frazier Bill to legalize polygamy in the United States. PAPA is already committed to backing pro-polygamy candidates in as many as 65 Congressional and 11 Senatorial races next year. PAPA has a huge war chest and a vast network of religious organizations at its disposal.

But we have you. That's why you must immediately renew your membership in the North American Gynarchist League. Your support will help us in our battle against the legalization of polygamy in the United States.

Our defeat in this battle would be a catastrophic setback for wimin in the global Gender War. It would strengthen phallocrats everywhere in their resolve to reverse history and re-create an age when all wimin were men's slaves.

Celebrate International Wimin's Day by renewing your membership in the North American Gynarchist League with a generous contribution to our Cause!

Sister Jeanette Baker to Sister Maria Lopez, March 8, 2041:

Dear Sister Maria:

Please debit my interbank account # 64203671-A in the amount of $250. I only wish I could give more money to the Cause.

From Jeanette Baker's journal, May 9, 2041:

At 9:15 this morning, I handed Johnny a felt-tip pen, along with a 9" × 12" sheet of tracing paper, and said, "Draw Mommy a picture of yourself!"

The result:

First self-portrait (untitled), 2041, felt-tip pen on tracing paper

Rewarded him with my praise and a chocolate chip cookie.

From Jeanette Baker's journal, November 13, 2041:

Johnny's developed nighttime fears that hungry wolves with red eyes lurk under his bed. He goes to sleep clutching my roll-on deodorant.

"Why?"

Johnny: "The label guarantees 100% protection."

From Jeanette Baker's journal, November 15, 2041:

Johnny: "Do I have a father?"

I told him a little about Fritz: what he does, where he lives.

Johnny: "Does my father love me?"

"Nobody loves you as much as I do!"

From John Firth Baker's interview in *The International Review of Manual Art:*

To tell the truth, I was a lonely only child; my best friend was my Mentor IV.

From an interface between John Firth Baker and his Mentor IV, January 2, 2042:

J.F.B.: I love you, Mentor. I always will. Do you love me?

Mentor: I'm just a tool with a voice. I can't feel anything. I don't have it in me.

From Jeanette Baker's journal, January 3, 2042:

Johnny's sore at his Mentor. He spent all morning making a charcoal sketch of the heavy-duty wrench I keep in the toolbox under the kitchen sink.

At lunch he showed his drawing to Mentor, stuck out his tongue, then said, "So there! Who needs you?"

Polly Baker

Jeanette called Johnny's drawing *The Talking Tool*. I took it to a framer in Lincoln. Jeanette hung it on the wall over Johnny's bed.

The Talking Tool, 2042, charcoal on paper

From Jeanette Baker's journal, November 5, 2042:

A narrow squeak in yesterday's Congressional and Senatorial elections. Even though ten more PAPA-backed Congressmen and three PAPA-backed Senators won seats, the Ritchie-Frazier Bill still hasn't got the votes to pass in either House.

From John Firth Baker's interview in *The International Review of Manual Art:*

I took a big step in my artistic development when I was around six. I awakened to technique. I watched an old Walt Disney animated cartoon called "Saludos Amigos" and fell in love with one of the characters —a hard-drinking, cigar-smoking, fast-talking tough little parrot named José Carioca. I was mad for him. The way he bossed Donald Duck around! I wanted him to boss me. I loved the curve of his big beak, the shape of his eyes and tongue. I thought about him day and night. I wanted to marry him.

Then I got an idea: if I draw him, he's mine forever. So I copied his head again and again and again—but couldn't get it right. Hard at work one day I suddenly saw that his beak and eyes were variants of simple geometric shapes—circles and what I later learned are called ellipses. The insight staggered me. I felt privy to a great secret. That same afternoon I drew José's head in black ink with a brush.

José Carioca, 2043, brush and ink on paper

Polly Baker

Johnny's drawing, matted and framed, went up on the wall with his other pictures. I once or twice referred to his room as "the Gallery." The name stuck.

From John Firth Baker's interview in *The International Review of Manual Art:*

Mother was a keepie shut-in, so I didn't leave the keep much when I was little. I thought the transparent, impermium dome was the sky. The sun was bright but gave off no heat. Sometimes, without making a sound, a downpour splattered in the airway above me; I didn't know rain was wet. I once watched a Black Blizzard swirling silently way above the palm trees on Pudding Street. All I recall about the tornado that hit us late in 2043 was this gigantic white cloud that filled the sky.

To tell the truth, the first memory I have of wind on my face is at the Earth Day picnic in first grade.

Barbara Briggin

I remember that. I was Johnny's first-grade teacher at the Janusz Korczak Elementary School on Rosa Parks Street in Cather Keep. Our Earth Day class picnic that year was held in Lincoln's Pioneers Park. It was a raw spring afternoon. A gust of wind ruffled Johnny's hair. He was like, "Wow! The earth breathed on me!"

From John Firth Baker's interview in *The International Review of Manual Arts:*

In the fall of 2044, my aunt Polly took me out to see my birth tree growing among the dunes in Cherry County. She told me this little tree with pointed yellowing leaves was planted when I was born. The sun went behind a cloud; I felt chilly.

I begged mother to dig up my birth tree and replant it in our backyard so I could look after it. She explained it was designed by genetic engineers to live in the creeping Sand Hills. "It'll grow sixty feet tall and bear sweet purple fruit called manna—food for all kinds of birds and animals who live in the desert."

On my eighth birthday, Polly took me out to Cherry County again. I remember the deep, drifted sand squeaking and whistling with every step I took. My little birth tree, which was almost my height, was dead. I snapped off a dry twig.

Polly said, "Everything living eventually dies."

I asked, "Me, too?"

Polly said, "When you're very old."

From an interface between John Firth Baker and Mentor, November 12, 2045:

J.F.B.: How long you figure I'll live?

Mentor: Ninety-six more years.

J.F.B.: That's all?

Mentor: That's it.

J.F.B.: What a screw.

From *The Book of Terror, A Book for Third Grade and Higher,* by John Firth Baker, January 11, 2046.

One fall day a little boy left his keep and went out in the weather. A cold wind made him shiver. Then the Creeping Sand Hills buried him alive.

Polly Baker

Johnny worried about the killer hurricanes and floods down south. In December 2045 half of Florida and Louisiana, where my cousin Aaron lived, were under water. He wrote me that Felix, his Manx cat, drowned.

When Johnny heard that, he made Jeanette sign him up for swimming lessons at the local Y.

From John Firth Baker's interview in *The International Review of Manual Arts:*

I loved a ten-year-old named Billy Peters who was in my swimming class, which met twice a week, at the Laker Street Y in Cather Keep.

Billy had slate-gray eyes—a sad color. He looked best in blue. Billy's father was a big-shot atmospheric processor. Billy owned his own mybot, a Mori 500, which was almost unheard of for a kid in the early forties.

The mybot, whose name was Arturo, waited for Billy after class. Billy got a kick out of bossing Arturo around. "Don't just stand there, stupid! Go buy me a chocolate donut and a Coke!"

I longed to be Arturo.

Dr. William Peters

I remember Baker. He was a creep.

Alex Thomas jr.

One Thanksgiving after dinner, in his room, Johnny asked me if I liked kissing boys.

I said, "You're kidding!"

"Yeah," he said. "I'm only kidding."

From Jeanette Baker's journal, November 23, 2046:

Next year, Alex jr. starts studying at Juilliard in New York.

Cressanthia: "He transposed Beethoven's Sonata in G major to D minor because it's his favorite key."

Johnny spends his time drawing Donald Duck.

From John Firth Baker's interview in *The International Review of Manual Art:*

Mother let me use her expensive barber scissors to make paper cutouts with it at home. She taught me how to cut out and paste together paper collages. I made a collage called *This End Up*. I got the idea from a documentary I saw at school about handling freight in outer space, where there's no down or up. I applied to my collage the technique I'd learned from drawing all those Disney cartoons and reduced its most important component elements to simple geometric shapes.

This End Up, 2046, cutout paper collage

Polly Baker

Jeanette hung Johnny's cutout paper collage on the wall opposite the closet in the Gallery.

From John Firth Baker's interview in *The International Review of Manual Arts:*

Mother let me stay awake New Year's Eve in 2046 to watch the PMA report. I vividly remember the news that the Mediterranean had risen more than a foot in the last ten years. Mother told me about the cloned Capablanca metamorph, Ishtar Teratol, who was growing up there in an underwater keep with her mother.

It was a watery New Year's Eve. At midnight EST, I watched the ball of light drop from the top of the brand-new Manhattan Tower towards its shimmering reflection in the brand-new Broadway Canal. I swore to myself, "One of these days, I'm gonna live in New York."

That spring I got interested in 19th-century American cut-paper silhouettes. I loved how a black shape defined the white space surrounding it. Mother's Day was coming up. I decided to do Mother's portrait in secret and surprise her with it as a gift.

The first step was drawing her profile in pencil on black paper. I drew her from a hologram. I captured her likeness with ease, but sweated for days over the outline of her hair, which was done up in the popular Greek goddess style.

From Jeanette Baker's journal, May 10, 2047:

Mother's Day. Johnny gave me a gift of a cut-paper silhouette of my portrait in profile—double chin and all. It's a good likeness. Too good! I look more and more like Momma.

Silhouette of Jeanette, 2047,
paper cutout on paper

Polly Baker

Jeanette hung the silhouette in the Gallery, next to the drawing by Shubha Roy. I think Johnny sensed the portrait made Jeanette uneasy because it reminded her of her mother. Johnny never gave Jeanette another gift on Mother's Day.

From John Firth Baker's interview in *The International Review of Manual Art:*

As I kid I learned about drawing from Walt Disney and Shubha Roy.

I grew up with Shubha Roy's framed scratchboard drawing of the Hindu goddess Parvati on the wall over my bed. It was given to me at birth by Indira Rabindra, a neighbor and family friend.

Indira Rabindra

I taught Johnny that Parvati is one name for the Divine Mother, who rules—and is—the world. She's the Radiant White One, and the Black One, too. Both life and death! We call Her "Wisdom," as well as "the Blind Demon." We know Her body only by the many forms She takes, which is the stuff of the universe—including ourselves.

From John Firth Baker's Interview in *The International Review of Manual Art:*

Mother got me thinking early on about Shubha Roy's style of scratchboard drawing. Again and again, she was like, "Look at how much Roy accomplishes with just a few lines!"

Those words changed my life.

From Jeanette Baker's journal, June 4, 2047:

Today, at Johnny's request, I bought him two etching needles, a large whetstone, 1 oz. India ink, and ten inked scratchboards for $348.50. Also one pad (fifty sheets) of 18" × 24" translucent drafting vellum for $135.

At this moment he's watching The Manualist's Guide to Cutting Drawings on Scratchboard (scratchdraw.com)

From John Firth Baker's interview in *The International Review of Manual Art:*

I taught myself the fundamental technique of scratchboard drawing. I learned that there are two ways to cut a drawing into an inked scratchboard. You can take a steel etching needle and scratch a freehand drawing directly onto the board. Or—Roy's method—you first make a pencil drawing and transfer that to the board.

I made three or four copies of Roy's drawing using her technique, but couldn't get it right.

Polly Baker

The summer of '47 Jeanette took up softball again. Every Sunday afternoon she played left field in Lake Twilight Park for a Cather Keep pickup team called the Pioneers.

Magdalena Ramirez

In September 2047, I was a seventeen-year-old cocaptain of the wimin's softball team at Cather Keep High and also pitched Sundays for the Pioneers. I dated Jeanette because she struck me as being an experienced older womin.

Up to then, I'd never been able to come, except on my own or with Orgazaid. I was too worried about giving my partner pleasure to let myself go.

My lack of emotional involvement with Jeanette freed me from that responsibility. I came without drugs the first time we made love. My nickname for her was Thunder Tongue. Twice a week, for a month, we made love at her place after Johnny fell asleep.

One Tuesday night, Jeanette forgot to lock her bedroom door. Johnny woke up around eleven and walked in on us naked in bed together. I can still see him standing in the doorway rubbing the sleep out of his eyes.

I was never so embarrassed in my life. Right there and then, I swore off lovers with kids. Needless to say, I never slept with Jeanette again.

From John Firth Baker's interview in *The International Review of Manual Art:*

Mother gave me a tenth-birthday party at school. My fifth-grade classmates and I finished off a banana cake with chocolate icing and watched the old movie *Snow White and the Seven Dwarfs*.

That night, I had a nightmare. A witch grinned at me. I woke in a sweat and was scared to go back to sleep. The next night the witch's grinning face woke me again. And again I stayed awake for the rest of the night. In the morning I told Mother what had happened.

She was like, "Draw me this witch."

I spent the rest of the day at home making a scratchboard drawing of the witch's grinning face in the style of Shubha Roy. Mother watched me work.

When I finished, she said, "Good job! The witch is now in your power. Go to sleep and have pleasant dreams."

And I did.

Witch, 2047, scratchboard drawing

Jeanette Baker to Cressanthia Thomas, November 3, 2047:

Johnny's *Witch* now hangs on the wall to the right of Shubha Roy's *Parvati*. His style owes a good deal to both Roy and Walt Disney. But the drawing conveys the feelings his subject evoked in him, which is what I tell him all his work must do.

From Jeanette Baker's journal, November 18, 2047:

In the evenings I call up art I love and share it with Johnny. Tonight we looked at my two favorite paintings by Albert Pinkham Ryder: *The Race Track* and *Jonah*. I read to Johnny Ryder's explanation of why he became an artist:

"When my father placed a box of colors and brushes in my hands, and I stood before my easel with its square of stretched canvas, I realized that I had in my possession the wherewithal to create a masterpiece that would live through the coming ages. The great masters had no more. I at once proceeded to study the works of the great to discover how best to achieve immortality with a square of canvas and a box of colors."[15]

Johnny: "What's 'immortality' mean?"

"Life everlasting."

Johnny: "Sounds good to me!"

From John Firth Baker's interview with *The International Review of Manual Art:*

I asked Mother, "How come I draw better than anyone else in my whole school?"

She said, "I bought you your gift. It cost me an arm and a leg, but was worth it. You're an artist!"

I took Mother's words literally: I thought my gift for drawing had cost her an arm and a leg. Who cut them off? Did the amputations hurt? How did her limbs grow back? I remembered this kid in Omaha who blew off his finger with a cherry bomb at a July Fourth picnic. The finger was regenerated in a Chicago hospital. I figured the same for Mother's arm and leg. I thought about them day and night.

Then one evening after supper, Mother called up some Australian Aboriginal paintings done on rocks and bark and wood. She pointed out that Aboriginal artists reordered humin anatomy; a naked woman on a cliff wall was portrayed frontally, but with her head and breasts in profile and her drawn-up legs splayed.

---

15. Albert P. Ryder, *Paragraphs from the Studio of a Recluse*, Boston: MFA Press, 2017:18. (17–RY283)

Mother said, "Look at her hands and feet. They're drawn as if from above."

Her words, "hands and feet," made me think of "arms and legs" and then her phrase, "your gift cost me an arm and a leg," popped back into my head. I saw an image in my mind's eye. I turned it into a scratchboard drawing in the style of an Aboriginal rock painting, which I called *The Gift that Cost Mother an Arm and a Leg*.

When I gave it to Mother for Christmas, she said, "You know me inside out."

The Gift that Cost Mother an Arm and a Leg, 2047, paper cutout and ink on scratchboard

From Jeanette Baker's journal, December 25, 2047:

Explained to Johnny what the expression "it cost an arm and a leg" means. He was visibly relieved. I told him he was an arsogenic metamorph and how he was conceived. Said what I did was against the law, which I broke because, more than anything else, I wanted an artist for a son. Told him that Polly knows the truth, which we'd best keep concealed till the Created Equal Act is repealed.

Johnny: "What's for lunch?"

Alex Thomas jr.

When I was around ten and a half, my folks told me I'm a musical arsogenic metamorph. My first thought: What they gave me, they can take back!

Dad went, "This is between us, boy. Let's keep it that way."

Mama said, "Johnny Baker's also an arsogenic metamorph. But hush up! It's a secret!"

I called Johnny that afternoon and said, "We got lots in common—only I can't say what."

He was like, "You're gay! Are you gay?"

"Hell no," I said. "Not that! I'm an arsogenic metamorph."

And he said, "A freak, like me."

I said, "Yeah."

And he said, "Let's be freaks together."

After that we spoke with each other once or twice a month. The Kammerovska case brought us even closer.

Wakinoya Yoshiharu

Anya Kammerovska, you may remember, was one of "The Three Fates." She and her husband, Oleg, came to Fritz at the Institute in August 2036, because they wanted an artistically talented daughter they could raise to become a great Russian painter—a femayle Rublev. Anya was an architect who collected 20th-century manual architectural drawings. Oleg taught Japanese at Moscow University; he had no talent as a calligrapher but he made kites, in the Japanese style, out of paper and bamboo. Both were humorless Manualists—very Russian, very ideological. They believed that skilled manual work purifies the soul.

Fritz chose Anya for Ozaki's Project primarily because her MPP was normal; she showed good potential as a nurturing mother—the exact opposite of Jeanette Baker. Fritz wanted to know how Anya's maternal behavior would influence her daughter's postnatal neurological development. He told her, "In the first six months while you're nursing, make constant eye contact with your daughter. Stimulate her visually as much as you can."

Anya's daughter, Nadia—which means "hope" in Russian—was born in Moscow on January 3, 2038, the Russian New Year. Fritz sent Nadia a birth tree, and Anya sent Fritz Nadia's postpartum MRI. Six months later, she sent another one. It revealed that the synaptic connections of the neurons in Nadia's prefrontal cortices had increased 54%—the greatest increase in the three subjects of Ozaki's Project.

Fritz said, "I've got great hopes for Nadia."

Four and a half years later, the Russian Duma elected Patriarch Kiril of Moscow to be the Supreme Holy Father and absolute ruler of Russia for life. The first week in office, he denounced humin genetic engineering as an international Jewish plot, the work of the devil.

Fritz said, "Abandon all hope."

From Jeanette Baker's journal, February 14, 2048:

SEXUALLY SUGGESTIVE MANUAL DRAWING FINGERS PRECOCIOUS RUSSIAN CHILD ARTIST AS ARSOGENIC METAMORPH

Parents Confess; Family Under House Arrest, Await Judgment At Next Session Of Holy Synod

By Lily Hochman
Special to IN-News

MOSCOW, Feb. 14. Ten-year-old Nadia Kammerovska was bored in her fifth-grade collaborative digital imaging class last Monday and made a pen-and-ink drawing by hand, which was confiscated by her teacher, the Orthodox priest Father Tihon Yefimyev.

In a statement issued today Father Yefimyev, 53, recalled that his eye was first caught by the manual drawing's "lascivious subject matter—unfortunately not unexpected in the work of a ten-year-old girl. Then

I realized that Nadia's drawing is a sophisticated takeoff on Japanese kanji, a very precocious stylistic achievement for someone her age. Now, I knew Nadia's father taught Japanese at Moscow University, so it wasn't surprising that the girl was familiar with kanji. But her precocious use of it indicated to me the girl just might be an arsogenic metamorph."

Nadia Kammerovska, 2048,
pen and ink on paper

Nadia said she was a natural-born artist. "I love to draw," the ten-year-old told the priest. "I draw all the time."

Father Yefimyev checked up on the Kammerovsky family. He discovered that Nadia's mother, Anya, 46, had conceived her daughter in Japan, which Yefimyev termed "a heathen nation that encourages metamorphic research." Said Father Yefimyev, "I smelled a rat."

On Thursday morning, Father Yefimyev confronted Nadia's parents in their Moscow apartment. He said that the couple immediately confessed that Nadia was an arsogenic metamorph whose genome had been enhanced with artistic potential at the Ozaki Institute of Metamorphic Genetics in Kyoto.

Yefimyev quoted Nadia's father, Oleg, 46, as saying, "We repent our sin, beg forgiveness and throw ourselves on the Christian mercy of the Holy Synod of our Mother Church."

Under Article 58 of the New Criminal Code, Russian metamorphic children under eighteen years of age are liable to be removed from the custody of their parents and raised in ecclesiastical orphanages, where they are dedicated to a life of service in the Church as monks or nuns. Their parents are liable to twenty-five years' imprisonment in one of the theocratic state's Redemption Through Suffering Centers.

A spokesman for Father Mikhail Magnitsky, 94, the Procurator of the Holy Synod, said today that the Holy Synod will render its judgment in the Kammerovsky case during its next session on February 20. In the meantime, according to the same spokesman, the Kammerovsky family will be permitted to remain in their Moscow apartment, where they could not be reached for comment today.

Johnny: "If they took me away from you, Mommy, I'll die."

From John Firth Baker's interview in *The International Review of Manual Arts:*

I was jealous of Nadia's originality; it killed me that she'd already invented a style of her own. At the same time, I felt very close to her. I wanted to reach out and let her know that another one of her kind existed in the world.

I copied Nadia's drawing till I got the hang of her style. Then, using her idiom, I made her a scratchboard drawing and wrote her a note—neither of which my mother let me send.

From Jeanette Baker's journal, February 19, 2048:

Johnny to Nadia Kammerovska (unsent):

Hi! My name is Johnny Baker. I'm a ten-year-old American arsogenic metamorph. Mother bought me my gift the same place your parents bought you yours. I admire your kanji-type drawing. It inspired me to make a scratchboard drawing in your style. I hope you like it.

Good luck to you and your folks.

P.S. Do you have a birth tree? Mine died.

Untitled drawing for Nadia Kammerovska, 2048, scratchboard drawing

From Jeanette Baker's journal, February 20, 2048:

TOP IN-NEWS STORY:

OLEG KAMMEROVSKY KILLS KIN AND SELF

MOSCOW, February 20. Apparently victims of a double murder and suicide, Oleg and Anya Kammerovsky, both 46, and their 10-year-old daughter Nadia were found shot to death today in their Moscow apartment only hours before they were scheduled to appear at the Holy Synod in a case brought against the two adults by the Procurator's Office under Article 58 of the Russian New Criminal Code.

According to Moscow ecclesiastical authorities, Kammerovsky first shot his wife and daughter and then himself in the head with a .380-caliber semiautomatic pistol.

From John Firth Baker's interview in *The International Review of Manual Art:*

After Nadia's death, I didn't draw for nearly two years. I took up ballet at the Cather Keep Y on Laker Street.

There, in the spring of '50, I fell in love with a tall sixteen-year-old who was the star backstroker of the Swimming Club.

The Rev. Theodore Petrakis

After practice one afternoon, Johnny followed me into the shower, where we introduced ourselves.

From John Firth Baker's interview in *The International Review of Manual Art:*

"Petrakis," I said. "What kind of a name is Petrakis?"

"Greek," he said. "We Greeks were once famous for loving pretty boys like you."

The Rev. Theodore Petrakis

Johnny blushed.

That evening I sent him one long-stemmed white rose and Pierre Minuit's recording of a verse by Richard Barnefield:

> If thou wilt love me, thou shalt be my Boy,
> My sweet Delight, the Comfort of my mind,
> My love, my Dove, my Solace and my Joy.[16]

From Jeanette Baker's journal, April 14, 2050:

Johnny, who's let his hair grow long, asked me to give him a page-boy cut. He's dating a freshman at Cather Keep High named Teddy Petrakis, whose mother, Frances, is a very successful landscape gardener; both are Christians. Johnny accompanied mother and son to services last Sunday at St. Fiacre's, the Gardener's Guild Episcopal Church on Van Dorn Street in Lincoln.

Sat Johnny down with Mentor for a lecture on sex hygiene. He's been vaccinated against HIV 1, 2, and 3 and the run-of-the-mill venereal diseases. Mentor stressed the necessity of protecting himself against the new strain of syphilis that attacks and rots the cerebellum within ten days of infection. Twelve new cases were recently reported in Hawaii.

---

16. Richard Barnefield, "The Tears of an Affectionate Shepheard sicke for Love," *Oxford Anthology of Elizabethan Poetry,* ed. Caitlin Welks, New York: Oxford Press, 2015:36. (15–WE2742)

From John Firth Baker's interview in *The International Review of Manual Art:*

The Rev. Theodore Petrakis

Johnny said, "I love you. Do you love me?"

"Very much."

"Will you always love me?" he asked.

I said, "No, dear boy."

He said, "Thanks for telling me the truth."

Polly Baker

Johnny, at that time, was about four-foot-seven; Ted was five-ten. Between ourselves Jeanette and I referred to them as "Jack and the Beanstalk."

The Rev. Theodore Petrakis

I gradually realized that Johnny's mother was a keepie shut-in and that he almost never left the keep himself. At the end of May, I practically dragged him out to Broken Bow in Custer County, where his mother's family first settled in Nebraska.

Johnny told me, "My great-great-great-great-grampa Matthew laid up a sod house in this town around 1880. His wife once killed a rattler coiled on the dirt floor with her broomstick."

He drank everything in and pointed out a ladybug climbing a fence post, a crow overhead, and three Muslim wimin in black chadors scurrying along outside a bakery. On our way back to the station, we strolled along South E Street between some scruffy young towering bowers.

I said, "Some of my fellow Christians believe that only God should make a tree. What do you think?"

"How about you?"

"I asked you first."

"I'm no Christian," he said. "I don't believe in God."

A few weeks later, Johnny showed me his drawings in the Gallery. When I said, "You're good," he asked, "Can you keep a secret?"

I went, "Of course."

"Well," he said, "Mother bought me my talent in Japan. I'm an arsogenic metamorph."

"Oh, yeah?" I said. "So what?"

From Jeanette Baker's journal, October 15, 2050:

Johnny is 13 today. Polly and I gave him a $520 oil paint set, in a transparent impermium case, which includes ten tubes of paint, three brushes, one palette knife, a palette, an 8-oz. bottle of linseed oil, one of turpentine, and a 11" × 15" canvas board. Plus, for another $248, twelve sticks of compressed (softest) charcoal sticks, six sheets of white paper, erasers, etc.

From John Firth Baker's interview in *The International Review of Manual Art:*

Mother handed me my birthday present and said, "Here. 'The wherewithal to create a masterpiece'—just like Ryder." I froze up inside. It scared me off color for years to come.

The Rev. Theodore Petrakis

Johnny and I were having an after-school snack at his house, when the news came about the electrical fire in the galley of Burroughs Keep on Mars that burned four colonists to death.

Johnny said, "I don't believe in life after death."

"You should. Jesus loves you."

"Even though I'm a metamorph?"

And I answered, "We've no say in how we're made. Jesus loves us all the same."

I got Johnny to read the Gospels. He made two comments: "No colors are mentioned in them." And: "I didn't know Jesus was Jewish!"

Then, on his own, for weeks on end, he roamed Christian art.

From John Firth Baker's interview in *The International Review of Manual Art:*

My heart went out to pictures of the crucified Christ. I thought to myself, Are the Gospels right? Have You conquered death for us?

Frances Petrakis

Teddy brought Johnny home for dinner. I remember him as an ordinary-looking kid who bit his nails. He was well-spoken, very polite, and asked about my work. I told him I'm a landscape gardener. Now at that time, Ted and I were living in a small house on Pudding Street, off Lake Twilight Park. Out back I kept a little scented garden of flowers that bloom after dark: evening primroses, night jasmines, beauties of the night, ornamental tobacco plants, and the like.

The Rev. Theodore Petrakis

Johnny walked around, inhaling the different scents, and said to Mom, "It must be nice to be a gardener."

Frances Petrakis

"Oh," I said, "it's much more than that. Gardening's the Lord's work."

Johnny asked, "How do you mean?"

I said, "God is a gardener." I played him my favorite sermon, *Christ the Gardener,* given by our minister, Margaret Boeth, on Easter Sunday, 2033.

< No. 74 >

The Rev. Margaret Boeth's Sermon, Easter Sunday, April 17, 2033, St. Fiacre's Episcopal Church, Lincoln, Nebraska:

Today we celebrate the two thousandth anniversary of the Resurrection of Our Lord, Jesus Christ. The Apostle John tells us (20. 1–14) that on that first Easter Sunday morning, while it was still dark, Mary Magdalene came to the garden where on Friday night Jesus had been buried in a new sepulcher.

When the sun came up, Mary saw that the stone that had sealed the tomb's entrance had been moved aside. She ran to Simon Peter, who was with the other disciple, whom Jesus loved, and said to them (John 20.2), "They have taken away the Lord out of the sepulcher and we know not where they have laid him."

Everybody knows what happened next: how Peter and the beloved disciple found only linen grave clothes in the tomb and went back home.

"But Mary stood without at the sepulcher weeping; and as she wept, she stooped down and looked into the sepulcher, and seeth two angels in white sitting the one at the head, and the other at the feet, where the body of Jesus had lain.

"And they say unto her, Womin why weepest thou? She saith unto them, Because they have taken away my Lord and I know not where they have laid him.

"And when she had thus said, she turned herself back, and saw Jesus standing, and knew not that it was Jesus.

"Jesus saith to her, Womin, why weepest thou? whom seekest thou? She, supposing him to be the gardener, saith unto him, Sir, if thou have borne him hence, tell me where thou hast laid him, and I will take him away." (John 20. 11–15)

Mary Magdalene takes the risen Christ for a gardener. And so she should, though it's only now, after two thousand years, that we can understand why.

Scripture says God "planted a garden eastward in Eden" (Gen. 2.8), and there He put huminkind to trim and keep it. (Gen. 2.15) In other words, God Himself was once a gardener and gave us His job. Then

God said, "Of every tree of the garden thou mayest freely eat: But of the tree of the knowledge of good and evil, thou shalt not eat of it. In the day that thou eatest thereof thou shalt surely die." (Gen. 2.16–17)

Despite God's warning, we disobeyed His command. We listened instead to the Devil, who let us in on his great secret: knowledge is power. Gain knowledge, he says to us, "And ye shall be as gods." (Gen. 3.5)

Well, we got what we wanted—and more than we bargained for; our pride brought death into the world. Since then we've planted plenty of gardens: some for food and shade, and some in which to bury our dead.

So it was in a garden, on the first Easter morning, that Mary Magdalene caught a glimpse of God as He once had been—a gardener. It's now clear why. Look around you on this parched spring day. Check out the gardens, the woods, and orchards. Walk the fields.

"The vine is dried up and the fig tree languisheth; the pomegranate tree, the palm tree also, and the apple tree, even all the trees of the field are withered." (Joel 1.12)

Christ must have known that was coming. He must have foreseen the future in which the fumes from our gasoline, oil, and coal-burning engines would year by year turn up the heat of the earth. He must have envisioned the droughts, floods, tornadoes, killer hurricanes, and rising seas—all the unintended consequences of the knowledge we accepted from the Devil in order to become like gods.

I believe that Christ looked down the centuries and took pity on us here today. I believe He made Mary Magdalene see Him in the guise of a gardener as a sign for us, in the time of global warming, to follow His example.

Therefore, Go thou and do likewise! Heed the words of the Lord (Jer. 29.5): "Plant gardens and eat the fruit of them." Obey Him. Do God's work again. In the name of Christ the Gardener, restore the earth we've laid waste. Tend and heal her. Turn her back into Eden while awaiting His return. "Then will every soul be as a watered garden, and none will sorrow any more." (Jer. 31.12). Amen.

The Rev. Theodore Petrakis

Johnny asked Mom, "You think only God should make a tree?"

Mom said, "If I believed that nonsense, I wouldn't be serving us deep-dish manna pie for dessert tonight. You like manna pie?"

"It's the best," said Johnny.

From John Firth Baker's interview in *The International Review of Manual Art:*

Boeth's sermon hit home. It got me interested all over again in the old internal-combustion car engine we studied in ecology at school, one of the many kinds used before electric car motors became mandatory in the U.S. This monster, built around the turn of the century, was a 230 horsepower, fuel-injected, V6-type engine, with a double overhead cam and a 3.2-liter displacement.

I now thought of the internal-combustion engine as some kind of devilish, manmade form of life that farted out hot CO_2 and carbon

The Devil's Fart, 2050, scratchboard drawing

monoxide. And that gave me the idea to call up twenty or thirty pictures of the Devil to see how other artists had visualized him over the years. I went for pictures of devils with big pricks, hairy legs, and hoofs.

Next morning, while brushing my teeth, all the parts of a drawing of my own called *The Devil's Fart* came together in my mind's eye.

For the first time since Nadia was murdered, I made a drawing. It took me a couple of days to break down the engine and then the hind fetlocks and hoofs into simple geometric shapes. The hairs on the legs and neck, which I scratched into the inked board with my etching tool, mark my discovery of the use of texture in a drawing.

I kept thinking about Boeth's sermon. It was like I was reborn.

I wanted to draw Christ the Gardener looking down the centuries at a dead tree—but couldn't picture His face. I searched among the different styles of early Christian art for an idea. I found what I wanted while going through a bunch of 5th-century Byzantine mosaics on the floor of the Great Imperial Palace in Constantinople.

The tree's a dead spruce from a burned-out New England forest, c. 2020.

From Jeanette Baker's journal, December 18, 2050:

For the first time since February 2048, Johnny is drawing again. In the last week he's produced two scratchboard drawings. Despite—or because of—the hiatus, his work is much more grownup. His facility to convey emotion has greatly increased. My patience has paid off.

Polly Baker

The sad expression of Johnny's *Christ the Gardener* always reminds me of the little eight-year-old boy in overalls and a baseball cap looking at his dead birth-tree.

Frances Petrakis

Johnny gave me his drawing *Christ the Gardener* for Christmas 2050. I couldn't believe it was the work of a thirteen-year-old. He was eerily precocious in a lot of respects. The way he talked, for instance, was way in advance of his years. Yes, he was an eerie kid.

Christ the Gardener, 2050, scratchboard drawing

Teddy said, "Johnny's an arsogenic metamorph, Mom, like Nadia Kammerovska."

I knew all about Nadia Kammerovska. I was horrified that her persecutors were Christians. And yet as a Christian myself, I know in my heart that altering the humin genome for any reason except the baby's health is a sin. We're made in God's image—and He made Himself one of us—via the humin genome. I believe He creates each humin being with a specific purpose in mind. When Teddy's prenatal gen-pro indicated he'd probably grow up gay, I was like, "Thy will be done!" My husband, David, wanted me to have an abortion. I divorced him.

Frances Petrakis to John Firth Baker, December 25, 2050:

Thank you for your excellent picture of Christ the Gardener. You're now a gardener, too! You've planted Christ in your soul, where He'll flower forever.

The Rev. Theodore Petrakis

Johnny bloomed in the new year. His cheeks and lips turned a faint red. Fine, colorless hair sprouted all over his white skin. It got silky.

He often dressed up—or rather, undressed and danced *en point* for me in a pair of pink ballet slippers he brought home from his ballet class at the Y.

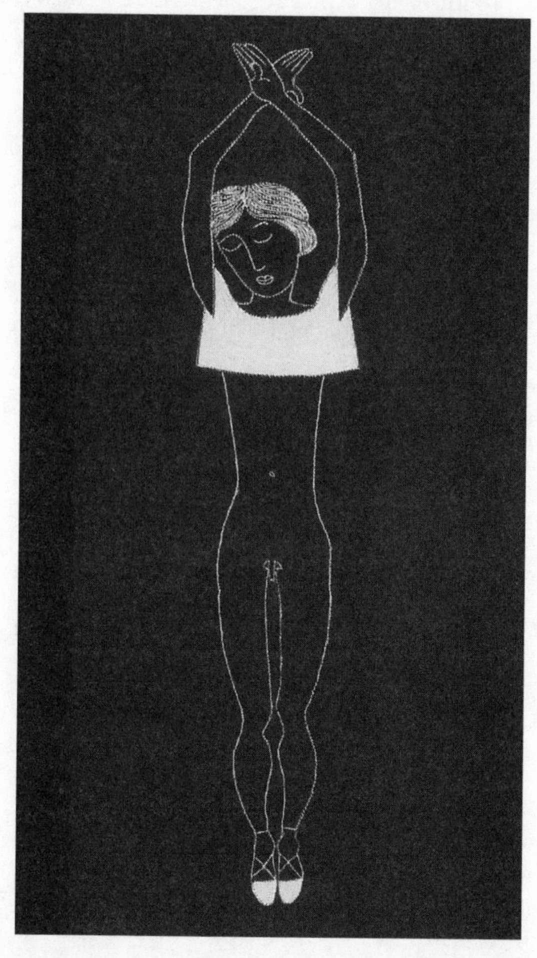

Self-portrait as a dancer (untitled), 2051, scratchboard drawing

From John Firth Baker's interview in *The International Review of Manual Art:*

Teddy, who was into ancient Greek art, introduced me to the sexy red and black paintings of naked boys on 5th-century B.C. Attic vases, cups, and oil flasks. Inspired by their lineal style, I made a scratchboard drawing of myself as a dancer and gave it to Teddy on Valentine's Day 2051.

I told him, "This is how I want you to remember me."

The Rev. Theodore Petrakis

Johnny's drawing gave me an idea. I treated the two of us to a mutual bilingual VR program in Periclean Athens, where we immersed ourselves for three hours twice a week for a month. We learned to speak a few words of ancient Greek. We did the usual things together that free-born Athenian boys once did: wrestled naked, greased with olive oil, in the dusty Palaestra; threw the javelin; and played knucklebones. I picked out tunes with a quill on a lyre made from a tortoiseshell and posed in the nude for him; he sketched me on a wax tablet with a bronze stylus.

From Jeanette Baker's journal, May 4, 2051:

Teddy bought himself and Johnny only free-born male experiences in ancient Greece. Polly and I split the $500 that Unimmerse charges to give Johnny a taste of what life then was like for a free-born, 13-year-old Athenian girl.

From "Chaerestrate, the Nameless Athenian Girl," a composition for Social Studies by John Firth Baker, Grade 8, Cather Keep Junior High School, June 19, 2051:

My twelve immersions in the daily life of a so-called free-born 13-year-old 5th-century Athenian girl taught me much about the oppression of wominkind then and now.

In ancient Athens, I was called "daughter of Xenaenetus" and never by my name, which was Chaerestrate. My parents called me "girl." They said, "Come here, girl! Do this, girl!" And "Good girl!" or "Bad girl!"

I lived behind locked doors with my mother and older sister in the wimin's rooms in the second story of our house, located near the famous Agora, or marketplace. We were not permitted to eat with my father and two older brothers in their dining room downstairs. Every day of the week from dawn till dusk, my mother taught me to mix flour and knead dough, shake and fold bedclothes, and spin wads of raw wool into thread. My fingertips got sore and bloody. My mother also taught me to carry a big jar filled with water on my head. A full Greek water jar weighs 60 pounds!

Like all so-called free-born Athenian girls and wimin, I was not allowed out of the house alone. Once my father commanded my sister, a slave girl, and me to gather roses, crocuses, violets, irises, hyacinths, and narcissi from fields near the City. It was a very hot day, but my sister and I wore ankle-length red linen dresses, called *chitons*. We had to cover our heads with heavy woolen blankets called *himations*. It was hard to breathe. On the street, my sister and I held the cloaks over our mouths and were forbidden to meet the eyes of men and boys.

This brings to my mind three Muslim wimin I once saw walking into a bakery in Custer County. They were bundled up from head to foot in black *chadors*. Only their eyes showed. They looked down.

This was in present-day America, not ancient Athens!

From Jeanette Baker's journal, June 28, 2051:

Today is the 29th anniversary of Mother's suicide.

I've never forgiven her. Late this afternoon, seething at the memory, I blurted out to Johnny, "You might as well know that Grandma Maggie killed herself."

Johnny: "What's for dinner?"

From Jeanette Baker's journal, July 23, 2051:

Thirteen years without a drink. How I'd love to tie one on!

Frances Petrakis

The feast of St. Fiacre, patron saint of gardeners, is kept on August 30. I still celebrate by planting a tree. In August '51, I decided to plant a towering bower with Johnny and Teddy in memory of Nadia Kammerovska. Teddy, Johnny, and I went first to the special feast-day service at St. Fiacre's in Lincoln, then out to Cherry County, where Johnny planted the tree on the lee side of the Wild Cat Creek windbreak.

Then he prayed, "Dear God, sweet Jesus, please give the arsogenic metamorph Nadia Kammerovska eternal life!"

From John Firth Baker's interview in *The International Review of Manual Art:*

[That night] I recognized Nadia Kammerovska from behind. She was standing on the corner of Pudding Street and Prairie Lane in Cather Keep. I tapped her shoulder, and she turned around. I saw from her eyes she was dead.

The shock woke me. It was about four in the morning. I calmed myself down by starting the scratchboard drawing I called *My Nightmare;* it took me the better part of a week to finish.

From an interface between John Firth Baker and Mentor, September 3, 2051:

J.F.B.: You don't dream?

Mentor: No. I can't. I don't know how.

J.F.B.: Dreams give me ideas for drawings.

Mentor: I don't think in pictures.

J.F.B.: What kind of life is that?

Mentor: I'm not alive.

J.F.B: I keep forgetting.

From Jeanette Firth Baker's Journal, October 3, 2051:

ARTCHANNEL'S OCTOBER PREVIEW GUIDE

The Immortal Residue: A Retrospective of the Work and A Biography

My Nightmare, 2051, scratchboard drawing

of the 20th-Century German-Jewish painter Charlotte Salomon (1916–1943), produced in cooperation with the Jewish Historical Museum, Amsterdam

"Und immernoch gibt es Freude und immernoch wachsen Blumen und immernoch scheint die Sonne."—"And yet there is still joy, flowers still grow, the sun still shines."

Those are the words that the doomed 20th-century German-Jewish painter Charlotte Salomon printed in a deliberately childlike hand across one of the last in a series of gouaches that she painted while hiding from German soldiers in the South of France.

This month, in association with the Jewish Historical Museum, Amsterdam, ArtChannel commemorates Charlotte Salomon's death in a gas chamber at Auschwitz with a retrospective exhibition of her work based on her biography by Luisa Materassi entitled *The Immortal Residue.*

Salomon was an original 20th-century painter. Her magnum opus, *Leben? oder Theater? (Life? or Theater?),* is an innovative, painted autobiography. It consists of 769 gouaches combined with written texts created from 1940 through 1942.

From John Firth Baker's interview in *The International Review of Manual Art:*

ArtChannel's show on Charlotte Salomon got me thinking. I decided to draw a picture as a memorial to her.

Just before her deportation she wrote on one of her paintings: "And yet there is still joy, the flowers still grow, the sun still shines." I wanted to use those words in my drawing. I viewed images from the Holocaust for one to go with them.

In an old film on the liberation of Auschwitz, I spotted a single, shorn braid atop a gigantic pile of hair the Nazi phallocrats planned to make into felt slippers and mattress stuffing. The hair had been cut from the corpses of the Jewish and Gypsy wimin and girls gassed in the camp between 1941 and '45.

Soon as I started drawing, I discovered that a braid has a complex structure. I needed to understand how it's woven together. Polly taught me to braid Mother's hair.

Polly Baker

I never saw Johnny so happy.

From John Firth Baker's interview in *The International Review of Manual Art:*

It took me hours to draw three strands of hair woven together into one braid. I also had a tough time printing Charlotte's words in my own handwriting. In the end, Mentor made me the 60-point Palatino letters; I felt like a cheat.

Mother called my drawing *Cut-Off.*

Cut-Off, 2051,
scratchboard drawing

Mother let me read her unfinished Ph.D. thesis on Charlotte Salomon. Mother said, "Nazi-type phallocratic tribalism is alive and kicking in various guises all over the world. The Gender War's just heating up!"

Next day I asked Teddy. "Which side is Jesus on in the Gender War?"

He said, "Neither," and quoted me Galatians 3:28: "There is neither male nor femayl; for ye are all one in Christ Jesus." As the words came out of his mouth, I got an idea for a drawing that symbolized the union of male and femayle in Christ's name.

The next four days I played hookey from school and made the scratchboard drawing called *Galatians 3:28*. It was my second attempt—à la Charlotte Salomon—to integrate a text with an image in one composition. I didn't pull it off.

From Jeanette Baker's journal, November 12, 2051:

Johnny's latest drawing, *Galatians 3:28*, illustrates a quote from the Bible. I fear Teddy is turning Johnny into a Christian—and you can't be a Christian and a Gynarchist. I told Johnny so.

I said, "We Gynarchists believe that humin males and femayles are engaged in a perpetual struggle for dominance and that the femayle gender must seize control and feminize—civilize—huminkind."

Johnny: "Christ offers us eternal life."

Indira Rabindra

I first saw *Galatians 3:28* at Polly's open house on New Year's Day 2052. It was hanging in Johnny's bedroom. I couldn't believe my eyes! In front of the cross, he'd drawn a lingam-yoni, the ancient Indian bisexual symbol for the Divine Mother! Johnny was in

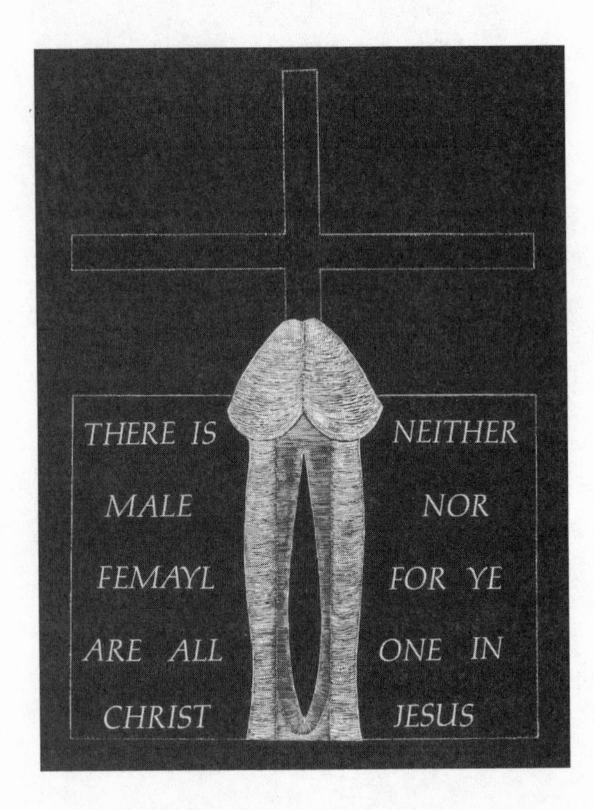

Galatians 3:28, scratchboard drawing

the kitchen watching the Huskers whip Alabama at the Cotton Bowl. We discussed his picture.

Johnny said, "I didn't know my symbol was Indian. It came to me on its own. It symbolizes words of Scripture."

Something told me, "Change the subject!"

From Jeanette Firth Baker's journal, January 4, 2052:

Today Johnny asked me to raise his allowance from $40 to $55 a week, out of which he'll buy all his art supplies.

I suggested that he earn twice the money by working after school at Polly's Parlor, where he could eventually become an apprentice and learn a trade that would guarantee him respect and a good living while he developed as an artist.

"Work?" said Johnny. "I'll think about it."

He was a sourpuss all evening. Just before bedtime, he said, "OK. Have it your way. I'll give the job a shot."

Hair on floor of Polly's Parlor (untitled), 2052, scratchboard drawing

Polly Baker

I hired Johnny to work at Polly's Parlor a couple of hours after school for $100 a week. He served snacks and drinks to the customers and swept up their hair. After two weeks or so, he made me a gift of a little rectangular scratchboard drawing of hairs scattered over the floor.

Johnny said, "Oh, Aunt Polly! Everywhere I look is something to draw!"

From John Firth Baker's "A Glimpse of the Life of One Fourteen-Year-Old American Living Fifty Years Ago from a Written Document of that Time," 9th-Grade History Class, Cather Keep Junior High School, February 19, 2052:

While searching for documents describing the life of an American who was my age fifty years ago, I came across a letter published in the *Lincoln Star Journal* on April 6, 2002.

Lorena Wobig
9th grade, M.S. 131
Lincoln, Nebraska

What is it? How do you get it? Can it be cured?

These are three of the many questions people have about cancer. I myself knew little about cancer until my mother was diagnosed with ovarian cancer last winter.

Cancer is considered a silent killer because there are often no or few symptoms until it has spread far beyond control. Over one million people per year are stricken with cancer and more than half of them die. I hope in the future that number can be drastically reduced. Through research and public awareness I believe we can increase the survival rate of people stricken with cancer.

I hope that one day in the near future I will turn on the television and learn to spot the symptoms of cancer. That won't help my mother, but I hope other people will benefit from the knowledge.

I quote Lorena Wobig's letter in full because it's a glimpse into the life of one fourteen-year-old American in the first decade of this century. It was a tough time for Lorena and her mother. Death from cancer was commonplace. Surefire cures and preventatives for all varieties of the disease were as yet unknown. And since the genetic profile had not yet been invented, people never knew when cancer would strike them. The onset of Lorena's mother's cancer obviously took Lorena and her mother by surprise—something hard for us to grasp today.

Reading between the lines of Lorena's letter, I suspect that her mother's ovarian cancer had already "spread far beyond control." Lorena doesn't even hope for a cure, which in 2002 was still eight years in the future.

On August 2, 2005, the *Lincoln Star Journal* published an obituary of Lorena's mother, Eliza Wobig, aged fifty-one, who died of ovarian cancer "after a long and valiant struggle."

Lorena Wobig's historical period seems remote to me even though it's only half a century ago. Nevertheless, I feel for Lorena because my mother's gen-pro indicates that she'll probably come down with breast cancer in her early fifties. Mother is forty-one. But thanks to modern medicine, she should live over one hundred years. Disease is no threat to her, but we now know that the aging and death of complex animals like ourselves can neither be prevented nor cured. They can only be postponed. Though my mother's old age and death are a long way off, they worry me. The truth is, I worry about my own as well. Nothing has really changed since 2002. Every day of our lives still brings us closer to death.

The Rev. Theodore Petrakis

I was admitted to Oberlin in April 2052. Johnny said, "Congratulations!" and talked about coming to visit me the next fall in Ohio.

I sat him down and said, "No, dear boy, it's not to be. I can't have you visit me on campus. People wouldn't understand. And there's another thing I have to say. Look at you! You're turning into a tall, handsome young man. Why, you've grown three inches in the last year! And that's wonderful! But before long you'll be too grown up for me. I love young boys."

From Jeanette Baker's journal, April 2, 2052:

(6 P.M.) Johnny's sobbing in his room.

The Rev. Theodore Petrakis

The next Sunday, Johnny skipped church. I sent him a dozen magenta metamorphic roses.

Frances Petrakis

I asked Johnny to supper, spiced eggplant with stuffed baked potatoes and, of course, deep-dish manna pie. He accepted. Teddy ate out, so Johnny and I spent the evening alone.

I said, "I missed you at church today."

He picked at the eggplant and said, "You really believe that Christ rose from the dead and is coming again?"

"Yes," I said. "I surely do."

He said, "Lucky you."

From Jeanette Baker's journal, April 10, 2052:

Johnny: "What do *you* believe, Mom?"

I answered him with Clorene Welles' poem "On the Matter of Mind":

Mind is entwined
with matter.
Since all the matter
in the universe
will decay,
mind must cope
without a hope
of permanence,
& find the bravest way
to live
as it unwinds
at every turning
of the day.

Johnny: "What's the bravest way for you to live, Mom?"

"Sober."

Francis Petrakis

Johnny didn't come to church on Easter Sunday, either.

Teddy and I missed Johnny; we ate without him at Flora Flower's, the fancy Palm Springs restaurant.

From John Firth Baker's interview in *The International Review of Manual Arts:*

I joined Local 103 of the Guild as an apprentice on March 23, 2052. The dues were $150 a month. Mother and Aunt Polly sponsored me.

Polly was the Guild's State Chairpersin in charge of Commemorative Events and Public Displays. Her chief responsibility was to organize and equip our contingents, including a thirty-piece brass band, that marched in Martin Luther King Day, St. Patrick's Day, Arbor Day, International Wimin's Day, Earth Day, and Labor Day parades all over Nebraska.

The big Earth Day parade, which goes from Mandan Park to the Offutt Helium-3 Fusion Plant in Bellevue, was coming up. This year's theme was the worldwide protest against China for burning coal; a huge crowd was expected—meaning, extensive news coverage. Polly asked me to design a new marching banner for Local 103.

Polly Baker

Johnny wanted five hundred bucks for the job. We settled for three. I gave him half the money down with the rest to be paid him when I okayed his design.

From Jeanette Baker's journal, April 12, 2052:

Johnny spent the whole advance on his first earnings as an artist to buy me a bound first edition of Phillip Spratt's *The Fruited Plain: Two Hundred Years of Gay and Lesbian Life in the Midwest.*[17]

From John Firth Baker's interview in *The International Review of Manual Art:*

Searching for an image that would immediately identify Local 103,

17. Chicago: Toklas Press, 2018. (18–Sp145)

I thought of my scratchboard drawing of hair on a floor. That became the basis for a little collage, representing a 20" × 30" banner, which took me a couple of days to get right.

Polly accepted my design and had the banner made up just in time for the Earth Day parade.[18]

Polly Baker

Jeanette kept the paper cutout.

Earth Day banner, 2052, paper cutout and scratchboard drawing, on paper

Anselmo Diaz

I was one of the two first trombones in my Guild's brass band, the Blow-Dries. I met Johnny after the Earth Day parade at Local 103's picnic in Offutt Garden. He plunked his plate down next to mine at my table. Shit! A real piece—a fuckin' princess! And I'm a humin hard-on. I smelled beer on his breath. He was sweaty and antsy. We introduced ourselves. He's like, "I'm a keepie. Crowds get on my nerves."

18. The design is still used today.

He told me he lived with his momma in Cather Keep. We made small talk. I told him I was half Mexican and half Irish, but my better half—from the waist down—is Mexican. That made him smile; he got a sweet smile. I'm doin' good. Then this gorgeous Gaian guru from Omaha, a she-he named Billy Lee Mookerjee, led a crowd in a slow, round dance on the lawn. I seen this before. While they dance, they sing the Gaian vision song, "Mother Earth." I knowed the words and joined in. I still remember them:

(sings)

> We love our Mother Earth,
> Our Mother Earth who gave us birth.
> We love to dance, we love to sing
> And drink from Her living spring.
> We love to feel our union flow,
> While round and round like Her we go.[19]

Johnny was like, "I'm through with religion."

But he couldn't take his eyes off Billy Lee, the first Gaian guru he ever seen—with a tattoo on his forehead, a beard, and big naked tits that jiggled up and down while he danced.

I axed Johnny if he had a boyfriend.

He said, "Not no more."

"What happened?"

"I don't wanna discuss it."

We walked on the sandy street lined with sagebrush trees, and he told me his sad story. Then he was like, "Let's go to your place."

Lord, we had such a ball. He called his momma and told her he was spending the night with a friend in Omaha—meaning me at my squat on Dodge Street.

He complained about my smoking. At that time, I was a chain-smoker.

Towards morning, my sleep was cut short by a thunderstorm. I found Johnny hiding under the bed.

He said, "I'm not used to thunder and lightnin'."

---

19. Words and music by Brianna Countryman, Motherworld Publishing, 2038.

From an interface between John Firth Baker and Mentor, April 22, 2052:

J.F.B.: What's the meaning of the tattoo on Billy Lee Mookerjee's forehead?

Mentor: Sri Billy Lee Mookerjee, like all Gaian gurus, is tattooed on the forehead with the astronomical sign for the planet Earth. It indicates he's gained Gaian Consciousness.

J.F.B.: Why the big tits?

Mentor: In Mookerjee's posting "Why I Grew Tits," which appeared on his home page three years ago, he wrote: "My androgynous body is the outward symbol of the harmonious reconciliation of opposites that Gaian Consciousness has wrought within me."

From Jeanette Baker's journal, May 8, 2052:

FATHER TIHON YEFIMYEV, RUSSIAN ORTHODOX PRIEST WHO FINGERED DEAD ARSOGENIC METAMORPH AND HER FAMILY, FOUND BRAIN-DRAINED IN MOSCOW MONASTERY

Poisoned By Barundanga, He Suffers Incurable Amnesia And Inability To Remember New Information; Kremlin Blames Outlawed Gynarchists

Special to IN-News
By Margaret Law

MOSCOW, May 8. Father Tihon Yefimyev, 53, who in February 2048 unmasked the deceased ten-year-old Nadia Kammerovska as an arsogenic metamorph, was discovered drugged with the neurotransmission blocker barundanga in his cell this morning at the Monastery of Saint Czar Nicholas the Martyr.

A monastery spokesman reported that the drug has drained Father Tihon's memories from his brain and destroyed his ability to remember new information. "Father Tihon is suffering from incurable anterograde lacunar amnesia with irreversible after-effects," the spokesman said.

An unnamed police source in Moscow stated that 6 milligrams of the odorless and tasteless barundanga, a scopolamine derivative, was administered to Father Tihon in a can of Coca-Cola, into which the poison had been injected through a tiny hole.

Father Tihon's accusations against Nadia and her parents resulted in the latter's investigation by the Holy Synod for blasphemous desecration of the humin genome, a crime punishable by twenty-five years at hard labor under Article 58 of the Russian Penal Code. On February 20, 2048 Nadia's father Oleg, 46, shot his wife and daughter to death and then turned the gun on himself.

Kremlin ecclesiastical officials close to Father Mikhail Magnitsky, 97, Procurator of the Holy Synod of the Russian Orthodox Church, blamed the Baba Yaga Brigade of the outlawed Russian Union of Gynarchists for poisoning Father Yefimyev. "The sinful wimin who committed this diabolical crime against an Orthodox priest will be brought to justice," one official said.

Polly Baker

Johnny confessed to me that he was shocked by the savagery of the wimin's revenge on Yefimyev. Jeanette had raised him to believe that wimin were more forgiving than men.

Alex Thomas jr. to John Firth Baker, May 15, 2052:

I hate Juilliard.

I recently won the Charles Ives Prize for my *Harlem Renaissance Microtonal Jazz Suite*. My jealous fellow students have spread the rumor that I'm a musical arsogenic metamorph, which I've publicly denied. Arsogenic metamorphs are hated here. Many of the students and faculty belong to the American Association of Naturally Gifted Artists (AANGA). They believe that artistic talent is a gift from God, who alone should decide who gets it.

So I live a lie. I advise you to do the same if you go to an American manual arts school.

From Jeanette Baker's journal, June 4, 2052:

Johnny won't apply to any manual arts school, not even the Manual Art Students League in NYC, but won't tell me why.

From John Firth Baker's interview in *The International Review of Manual Art:*

Very early one morning in June, 2052, I ran into the Gaian guru Billy Lee Mookerjee, with a towel around his waist, in the locker room of the Cather Keep Y.

He said, "Make a pencil sketch of me."

I took a graphite 6B pencil from the top shelf of my locker. But had no paper. A pad of 19" × 24" parchment tracing paper, the kind I use for sketching, appeared on the bench beside me. Then the pencil vanished from my hand.

I thought to myself, This is a dream! and woke up.

From Jeanette Baker's journal, June 6, 2052:

Johnny's made a pencil sketch of a Gaian guru from Omaha named Billy Lee Mookerjee who recently appeared to him in a dream.

Johnny Baker to Mentor, June 6, 2052:

Open a file on Billy Lee Mookerjee.

From John Firth Baker's computer file "BillyLee," entry dated June 7, 2052:

Gaian Consciousness

By Sri Billy Lee Mookerjee

I was born in Phoenix, Arizona, during a record-breaking three-inch snowstorm on Dec. 3, 2020. My folks, Khadiram and Chandra, were poor Brahmin immigrants from West Bengal, who ran a Yoga school on Whey Street. They named me after my father's American guru, Sri Billy Lee Bhairavi.

Mother, in particular, was very religious. As an old-fashioned Indian womin, she worshiped the Goddess Parvati, who's married to the God Siva and is the Hindu ideal of the devoted wife and mother. Mother lived up to that ideal.

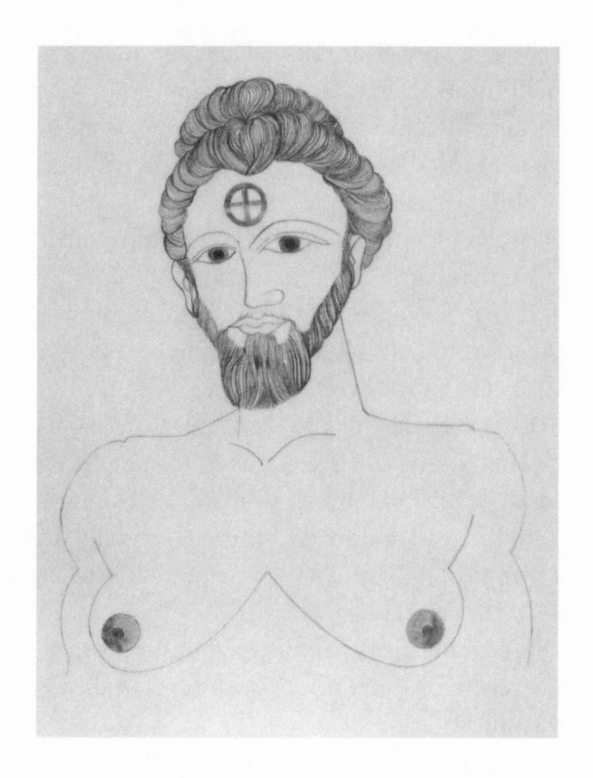

Portrait of Billy Lee Mookerjee, 2052, pencil on parchment

My sister, Devi, is six years older than I. When I was about nine, Mother caught me peeking through the bathroom keyhole at Devi getting out of the shower. Mother, who spoke Bengali with me, said, "Once, as a boy, the God Ganesha tethered his skittish mare and whipped her on the neck with a knotted rope. Afterwards, Ganesha's mother, the Goddess Parvati, showed him some fresh bloody welts on Her own neck, and explained: 'All living femayles are part of Me and what you do to any one of them, you do to Me.'"

I never looked at a naked womin again.

The first ten summers of my life were the hottest ever recorded in the American West. And the winters were the driest. We were too poor to live in a keep. The dust storms gave Mother chronic bronchitis, which weakened her lungs and made her susceptible to a virulent new strain of bronchiolitis that broke out during the spring of 2027. Father couldn't afford to buy her medicine.

The day of her death, on February 3, she said, "Billy Lee, listen to me! Everybody in the world is crazy. Some are crazy for money, some for fame, others for power. You be crazy, my son, just for Her—our Divine Mother—She Who Is!"

Now, I knew that the goddess takes innumerable forms, so I asked, "Which of Her forms should I worship, Mother?"

Mother said, "She'll let you know."

It didn't happen. In the years to come, my soul cried out to the Divine Mother like a hungry kitten, but She never revealed Herself to me in any form. My soul starved.

I won scholarships to the Phoenix Preparatory Academy and the Arizona School of Finance, where I graduated with a B.S. in accounting in 2041. I got a job at the Bank of China's Phoenix branch and rented a small apartment for myself and my dad in Goldwater Keep. It was great to be out of the weather! I should have been happy but instead felt anxious and depressed.

I spent my nights surfing the Net for a guru who could give me the answer to my question: "Which form of the Divine Mother should I worship?"

Each guru pushed his or her favorite goddess. One answered, "Kali"; another, "Holy Mary"; a third, "Spirit-Sophia," otherwise known as Shekhinah. I had a long talk with a Latino priestess of Cihuacoatl, the Serpent Womin.

How to choose between them? I lost my appetite and couldn't sleep. I thought about killing myself. Then, on the evening of April 21, 2044, I called the Gaian guru Srimaati Brianna Andrews and asked her my usual question: "Which form of the Divine Mother should I worship?"

Srimaati Andrews said,

> I mother
> & devour life.
> I father forms
> that thrive and
> those that fade.
> I'm husband

& wife,
windpipe
& knife.
I'm the sheath
that shields
& rusts its blade,
this patch of sunlight,
that patch of shade.

Then she asked me, "Who am I?"

Right off the bat, I said, "Mother Earth."

"Well," said Srimaati Andrews. "That's your answer—Mother Earth, a.k.a. Gaia! She's the one for you!"

I cried for joy.

All I knew at the time about Gaia was what I remembered from high school. I knew that she was the ancient Greek goddess of the Earth. And that, at the end of the last century, her name was given to a scientific theory, the Gaia hypothesis, that says the planet Earth, a.k.a. Gaia, is alive.

I wanted to know more. For $500, I enrolled in Srimaati Andrews' teleseminar, Understanding Gaia, that met Wednesday evenings at seven for six weeks. Srimaati Andrews taught me that the Gaia theory is a fact. Gaia, the planet Earth, is the largest living organism in the solar system. Gaia's atmosphere, oceans, climate, and crust function together as an open thermodynamic system regulated by feedback at a state kept comfortable for life by the behavior of living organisms.

I learned that every humin, myself included, is a synergistic cell in Gaia's evolving composite brain and reproductive system. We must reproduce Her kind by bringing other worlds to life.

I understood Srimaati Andrews' ideas intellectually, but that wasn't enough for me. I yearned to walk on a lawn and feel in my bones that the grass under my feet is a patch of living tissue that lines the insides of the colossal being of which I too am part. In other words, I craved Gaian consciousness.

I knew the only way to achieve that was to become one of Srimaati Andrews' sheilas, a combination servant and disciple. Her eleven sheilas were bearded, big-titted she-hes.

I stopped shaving and quit my job. My beard came in thick and fast. I borrowed $4500 from my uncle Abhayadatta and had a mastogenesis in an Acapulco sex reassignment clinic. My breasts began to swell. I bought a bra. On Earth Day 2047, I presented myself to Srimaati Andrews, hanging with two or three of her sheilas outside her ashram on Washington Street in Hoboken, New Jersey. I said, "Make me one of your sheilas, Srimaatiji, so I can gain Gaian Consciousness!"

She sang,

Think Gaia's
Thoughts,
Feel both Her
Joy and pain.
Be part
Of Her body,
A portion
Of Her brain.[20]

I fell to the sidewalk and gained Gaian Consciousness. This happened to me in Hoboken, New Jersey, at 7:14 A.M. on Earth Day, April 22, 2047. It could also happen to you. Interested? Contact SriBillyLeeMookerjee@Motherworld.com

Johnny Baker to Mentor, June 12, 2052:

Do Gaians believe in an afterlife?

Mentor to Johnny Baker, June 12, 2052:

Billy Lee Mookerjee writes, "Death is the necessary end for living humins who are but cells in the evolving combination nervous and reproductive system of our Motherworld. Death is the mother of evolution."

20. Words and music by Brianna Andrews, Motherworld Publishing, 2038.

Anselmo Diaz

The second Sunday morning in August, Johnny come by my Dodge Street squat in Omaha for a fast fuck. He stayed the afternoon. He called me "Daddy" and said, "Love me!"

I went, "I do!"

And I can't forget that when he came, his sweat smelled sweet.

Johnny was your typical teenager. He called farts "barking spiders" and picked his pimples. After lunch we smoked dope and listened to Hot Ice—I remember what album: *The Face on the Barroom Floor*. We talked about boys. Johnny brought the conversation around to Billy Lee Mookerjee. "Do you know him?" he asks me. "I wanna meet him."

Johnny was nervous about walking alone back to the subway stop on Gretchen Street because it borders the ghetto. So I walked there with him. The temperature was 107.

"I feel faint," says Johnny. "I can't stand the heat."

I'm like, "So stay outta the kitchen."

From then on Johnny and me called the world outside his keep "the kitchen."

Ben Shrapnel

Johnny's expression "the kitchen," meaning the outdoors, outside a keep, caught on in his family, and then among his Cather Keep neighbors, like myself. After Johnny's death, I popularized it among other keepies in my 2059 *Keepsake* article "Keepie Lingo."

Anselmo Diaz

The temperature in the kitchen around Omaha that summer was in the nineties for thirty-one days. The heat kept Johnny at home till Halloween, but he called me once or twice a week to ask, "You love me?"

"I do!" I says. "I do!"

I never knew such a needy boy.

< No. 102 >

John Firth Baker to Clorene Welles, September 22, 2052:

I'm a tenth-grade student at Cather Keep High in Cather Keep, Nebraska. I'm writing a composition for my English class about your poem "The Song of the Earth."

You are my mother's favorite living poet. She often quotes your poems to me. (The truth is, she suggested that I write you this letter.) She lent me her own precious bound copy of the first edition of your *Collected Poems,* one of the four printed books she owns. I dip into it every chance I get.

I like "The Song of the Earth" best. I memorized it. How did you come to write it? I see where the Gaian guru Billy Lee Mookerjee quotes it in his essay "Gaian Consciousness." Are you a Gaian? If not, do you mind that Gaians use your poem for religious purposes?

Please answer me soon. My paper is due in two weeks. Thank you in advance for your help.

Sincerely,

P.S. I hope one day to become a professional visual artist. To prepare myself to earn a living when I grow up, I work every day after school as an apprentice hairstylist. You think it's wise for an artist to make a living that way?

Clorene Welles to John Firth Baker, September 26, 2052:

Wrote "The Song of the Earth" between January & April 2021; was inspired by last words of 19-year-old Algerian Mina Bendjedda, who refused to sing country's national anthem at 2020 political rally, Oran; she tore off her veil, told cop, "Wimin have no national anthems! We sing the song of the earth!"

The cop shot her in the face.

Began "Song" as elegy to Mina, but poem then took on life of its own—as poems often do; turned into something quite different.

"Song" became my expression of immemorial & universal insight: life and death, creation and destruction are aspects of one process; notion many people have had over the years. Ancient Greeks, for example, worshiped Earth Mother, Gaia; wrote her sacred hymns, like the following, translated in 20th century by Apostolos N. Athanassakis:

"Divine Earth, mother of men & the blessed gods,/You nourish all, you give all, you bring all to fruition, and you destroy all."

B.C. Greek hymn, my 2021 poem have same theme.

Derived "Song's" imagery and narrative technique from poem, *"l'Heautontimoroumenos"* ("The Self-Tormenter") by Charles Baudelaire, which can be considered 19th-century French variation on Greek theme. Following verse most influenced me:

Je suis la plaie et le couteau!
Je suis le soufflet et la joue!
Je suis les membres et la roue,
Et la victime et la bourreau!

(I am the wound & the knife!
I am the blow & the cheek!
I am the limbs & the wheel,
the victim & the executioner!)[21]

"Song" = modern American variation on immemorial theme.

Even though planet Earth "narrates" my poem, I'm no Gaian; don't for one minute believe our planet is living being, much less that our brains are its organs of self-consciousness and reproduction. Nevertheless, while writing poem I imagined how Earth would describe itself if it could: in that sense, Gaian ideas influenced me.

Andrews' popular vision songs owe a great deal to my poems.

Bemused that Gaians use "Song" as mantra; wish I could collect royalties.

Pleased though that nearly thirty years later, my poem strikes responsive chord in young people.

---

21. Although Welles neglects to mention it to Johnny, "The Song of the Earth" was clearly influenced by an early draft of T. S. Eliot's *The Wasteland.* Eliot, in turn, was also influenced by Baudelaire's *l'Heautontimoroumenos.* See Constance Dry, "The Concatenation of Influence: Charles Baudelaire, T. S. Eliot, and Clorene Welles," *The Journal of Transformative Poetry,* Summer 2052:417–19. (52–JTB04)

What kind of visual artist are you? Fractalist? Manualist? Interactionist? Cooperatist? A little of each? None of the above?

Anyway, I wish you every success in your career!

Hope I've helped you on your paper.

Sincerely yours,

P.S. Yes, by all means become a hairdresser! Join the skilled working class! Supported myself as dental technician till retiring in 2039; nothing stimulates creative juices as much as a steady income. Let me remind you of my poem on subject.

> Poetry's Potion:
> Money
> mixed with
> blood & honey.[22]

John Firth Baker to Clorene Welles, September 26, 2052:

I'm a Manualist. For some years now, I've been teaching myself to draw. I recently did this portrait in pencil of the Gaian guru Billy Lee Mookerjee as he appeared to me in a dream. Please accept it as a gift from me with all my thanks for your help and encouragement.

Clorene Welles to John Firth Baker, September 28, 2052:

Thanks for your drawing; will treasure it; you have talent.

In a dream, you say? the drawing came to you in a dream? Spoken like a true artist! Dreams—our "nocturnal muse" (Proust)

Stay in touch—with me and your dreams! Look me up if you're ever in NYC!

John Firth Baker to Clorene Welles, September 28, 2052:

To tell you the truth I don't come by my talent naturally, if you get my drift.

Clorene Welles to Johnny Baker, September 29, 2052:

I get your drift. Your secret's safe with me.

---

22. Welles, op.cit., p. 187.

Polly Baker

Jeanette boasted to me that Johnny got three letters from Clorene Welles. And though Jeanette tried to hide it, she was jealous that he gave Welles his drawing of Billy Lee Mookerjee. Jeanette felt that all of Johnny's work belonged to her by right.

From John Firth Baker's English composition "My Favorite Poem: 'The Song of the Earth,' by Clorene Welles," Tenth Grade, Cather Keep High School, October 6, 2052:

Christianity teaches us that death came into the world because of our sins. As I understand Clorene Welles' poem, "The Song of the Earth," the poet believes that all creation is made up of both life and death and that each is an equal part of the whole. I think there's a bitter truth in her idea, which I'm trying hard to accept.

John Firth Baker to Frederick Rust Plowman, October 25, 2052 (unsent):

Today was my 15th birthday. Mother baked me an imperial chocolate cake. Before I blew out the candles, I made a wish that someday we'd meet.

Anselmo Diaz

Johnny came back to the kitchen on Halloween, when the temperature in Omaha was in the mid-sixties. We crashed Billy Lee Mookerjee's costume party at his Ames Avenue apartment. I went as a Fag Hag. Johnny, with a toy bow and arrow, was the naked boy god—what's his name?—all painted gold.

Billy Lee played host from a big chair in his roof garden. His costume was a knockout, but to this day, I don't know who he was supposed to be.

Sri Billy Lee Mookerjee

I'd gotten myself up as an androgynous tree-spirit, sort of Jack and Jill in the Green, or the King and Queen of the May.

Anselmo Diaz

Billy Lee was covered from the neck down with ivy leaves, sewed together to look like scales. His body was like the trunk of a tree overgrown with ivy—but a tree trunk with big boobs! His hands was smeared dark green. Over his head he wore a green mask carved from wood, the likes of which I never seen before in my life. It was a tree's face, if you can imagine such a thing—a tree's bearded face made out of leaves.

Sri Billy Lee Mookerjee

My carved and painted mask, which cost me seventeen hundred bucks, was the work of my old friend Emma Torchlight. Emma, who in those days lived in Juno, came to Omaha for my party.

From John Firth Baker's interview in *The International Review of Manual Art:*

The mask knocked me out.

Some guy at the party told me it'd been made by the Little Bo Peep sipping a glass of red wine at the bar. I asked the guy Little Bo Peep's name, and he said, "Emma Torchlight."

Emma Torchlight! The Kwakwaka'wakw Carver! I knew all about Emma Torchlight from the ArtChannel show on her the previous spring. She was only eleven years older than me, but already famous!

I stared at her work, the leafy, bearded face, painted different brilliant shades of green. My heart thumped. I suddenly understood the power that masks possessed long ago when they changed us into gods and demons.

Then the god, or demon, in the mask gave me a knowing look.

Sri Billy Lee Mookerjee

Eros smiled at me. Later I saw him at the bar, talking with Emma Torchlight.

Anselmo Diaz

Johnny left me in the lurch for some ginch at the bar. I thought, Fuck you, and went home alone.

Emma Torchlight

This tall gold Eros, naked except for red sandals, sidles up to me at the bar and goes, "Oh, Ms. Torchlight! I can't tell you how much I admire your work."

I went, "You can tell me. Tell me!"

Eros had a sweet laugh. He introduced himself and asked my inspiration for the mask I made Billy Lee. I told him I got the idea from a 13th-century wood carving of the Green Man in the choirstall of Poitiers cathedral.

"Who's the Green Man?" he asked.

"An old, old god," I said. "Much older than Jesus Christ, and one of Mother Earth's many lovers."

"Are you a Gaian?" he asked me.

I said, "Sometimes."

Then he said, "I want to draw your beautiful mask."

"Are you an artist?"

He said, "I will be. Right now, I'm teaching myself to draw. Do you draw?"

I said, "Every day."

He was like, "Someday I'll carve a mask."

I thought to myself, Who is this kid?

Sri Billy Lee Mookerjee

Emma introduced me to Johnny, who said, "This is a dream come true, Sri Mookerjee."

And I said, "Call me Billy Lee."

Then he said, "I've wanted to meet you for a long time, Billy Lee. I read 'Gaian Consciousness' last summer. I still think about it."

He told me he was fifteen years old. Only fifteen! He was a keepie in the tenth grade at Cather Keep High. He seemed much older. After school, he worked as an apprentice hairstylist.

He said, "I'm learning a trade so I can support my habit."

"What's your habit?" I asked him.

"Drawing," he told me. "I love to draw. I want to draw your mask."

"Be my guest," I said.

"You mean it?" he asked me. "When?"

"When's good for you?"

"Tomorrow morning."

"What about school?" I asked him.

"I'll learn more here," he said.

So I said, "Then tomorrow morning, here, at nine."

John Firth Baker to Anselmo Diaz, November 1, 2052:

Where'd you go, for Christ's sake?

Anselmo Diaz to John Firth Baker, November 1, 2052:

Do me a favor.

John Firth Baker to Anselmo Diaz, November 1, 2052:

Anything.

Anselmo Diaz to John Firth Baker, November 1, 2052:

Get outta my life.

From John Firth Baker's interview in *The International Review of Manual Art:*

On my way home on the subway, I got the idea for my scratchboard drawing *The Knowing Look*. I was excited and happy. That Halloween night everything seemed possible for me.

Next morning I cut school and arrived at Mookerjee's with my drawing materials at nine on the nose. Billy Lee was having a cup of coffee in his kitchen with Emma. His uncombed hair hung down to his shoulders; his beard needed a trim. He was wearing a ratty blue terry cloth bathrobe that was closed at the neck with a safety pin. I noticed he wasn't wearing a bra. His tits were bigger than I remembered. And he had very hairy legs.

Emma Torchlight

Johnny said he was influenced by Shubha Roy's lean graphic style. He told us he was going to make a scratchboard drawing of Billy Lee wearing my Green Man mask.

Sri Billy Lee Mookerjee

Like my folks, Roy was a Bengali devoted to the Divine Mother. I admire Roy's work. Johnny and I talked about the letters she wrote her father from exile in Nepal and her miserable death there at the hands of the phallocrats. Johnny mentioned his neighbor, the book repairer Indira Rabindra. I knew Indira; we were both members of the Mid-Western Vedanta Society.

Johnny said, "It's a small world."

Then he was all business. He put the mask on my butcher-block table and sat down opposite it with a big pad and a pencil.

Emma Torchlight

I had a train to catch in Chicago for London, so I said good-bye. Johnny pointed with his pencil at the mask and said, "I'll try and do it justice."

He was so serious for a kid his age, I felt sad.

Sri Billy Lee Mookerjee

I left Johnny to teach my three-hour teleseminar on geophysiology, which still meets every Tuesday morning at ten, E.S.T.

From John Firth Baker's interview in *The International Review of Manual Art:*

I was finally alone with Torchlight's mask. This was a big moment for me—the first time I could handle a work of art. I ran my hands all over it.

The mask was hell to draw. It took me all morning to flatten its volume into a lineal, two-dimensional composition on a piece of tracing paper.

From Jeanette Baker's journal, November 7, 2052:

Today Johnny completed a scratchboard drawing he calls *The Knowing Look*. It's his impression of a wooden foliate mask worn by Billy Lee Mookerjee at his costume party in Omaha on Halloween. The mask was carved and painted by Emma Torchlight, the First Nation–British Columbian artist. Torchlight, who's a shrewd self-promoter, dubbed herself "The Kwakwaka'wakw Carver" on an ArtChannel

The Knowing Look, 2052, scratchboard drawing. Collection Billy Lee Mookerjee

show about her, which Johnny and I enjoyed last spring. Johnny sent her *The Knowing Look* as a gift.

I'm jealous.

Emma Torchlight

Soon as I laid eyes on *The Knowing Look,* I figured Johnny for an arsogenic metamorph, like the dead little Russian girl, Nadia Kammerovska. The President of the American Association of Naturally Gifted Artists was recently quoted as saying that Nadia's death was a divine punishment. I thought, "Poor Johnny!"

Sri Billy Lee Mookerjee

Just before Thanksgiving, Johnny sent me a copy of *The Knowing Look*. I thought it was good work for a fifteen-year-old. Emma told me she thought Johnny was an arsogenic metamorph. I said, "Poor kid."

Sri Billy Lee Mookerjee to John Firth Baker, November 15, 2052:

I like your drawing.

Indira tells me you live with your Mother in Cather Keep. I invite you both to join me and some Gaian friends for dinner in my apartment in Omaha at 8 P.M. on December 24, 2052.

Instead of Christmas, we Gaians celebrate the feast of Mother Night. Please join us!

P.S. Emma will be here. She asks to be remembered to you.

Polly Baker

Jeanette said, "I'm going out to that party come hell or high water."

Jeanette Baker to Monique Chung, Ph. D., November 15, 2052:

Your records will show that I'm a keepie shut-in who dropped out of Grex therapy in August 2038. Since then I've lived a productive life in Cather Keep and, until today, never felt a need to leave. However, I just received an invitation to a dinner party to be held next month outside the keep, and I'd like very much to attend with my fifteen-year-old son.

Your records will also show that I'm a recovering alcoholic, for which I take 5 milligrams of Endcrave daily, and type A-2 unipolar depressive, for which I take 2 milligrams of Euphorol daily. I've had it up to here with drugs. Is there any alternative you could suggest I do in the next few weeks that would enable me to go to the party with my son? My financial resources are limited.

Thank you in advance for your help.

Monique Chung, Ph.D., to Jeanette Baker, November 16, 2052:

The best advice I can give you to achieve a temporary remission, without drugs, of your agoraphobia is to try a version of gradual exposure (Grex) therapy. Agoraphobics often find that a trusted companion's presence in a new environment assuages their symptoms. In the weeks to come, make excursions of gradually lengthening duration outside your keep in the company of your son. Work up to having dinner together outside. Take a little walk afterwards. You should then be able to attend your party with him.

From Jeanette Baker's journal, November 18, 2052:

Johnny's presence gives me strength. After work today, we walked arm in arm east on Arbor Road about a quarter of a mile, then back home again.

John Firth Baker to Sri Billy Lee Mookerjee, November 18, 2052:

Mother and I look forward to joining you and your Gaian friends at 8 P.M. on December 24th for the feast of Mother Night.

From Jeanette Baker's journal, November 20, 2052:

Went with Johnny today to the crowded secondhand bound book market on the corner of 56th Street and Fletcher Avenue, where we overheard one womin say to another: "My life sucks!"

Johnny and I said together: "Not mine!"

Have nothing to wear for the party.

Polly Baker

"Keepie pallor" was in fashion. Jeanette was very pale. She bought herself a black silk Chinese suit, which made her look even paler than usual. Also a new winter coat of many colors. Johnny didn't own gloves, so I bought him a pair as an early Christmas present.

We had a happy Thanksgiving, the best in years. Maybe the best ever. Jeanette roasted a twenty-two-pound turkey and made chestnut stuffing. I baked cornbread. We ate dinner by candlelight in my dining room: Jeanette and Johnny, Paco, me, Indira, Ben, the Thomas family, Frances Petrakis, and Teddy, home from Oberlin.

The Rev. Theodore Petrakis

Over coffee in a corner, Johnny asked me what I knew about Gaianism, and I said, "It's a kind of neopagan mysticism, a crackpot new religion of the Earth."

Johnny said, "Maybe so, but the Gaian guru in Omaha is a wet dream."

First thing next morning, he calls me and says, "Guess what?"

From John Firth Baker's interview in *The International Review of Manual Art:*

I had a wet dream starring Billy Lee Mookerjee. I made one of the images into a scratchboard drawing called *Wet Dream.*

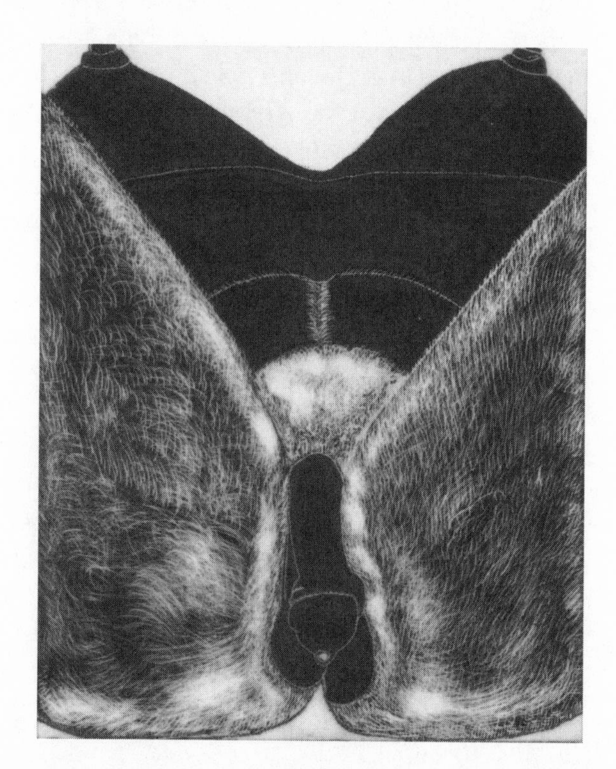

Wet Dream, 2052, scratchboard drawing

Sri Billy Lee Mookerjee

Johnny's drawing is flattering, but not accurate. I'm circumcised. I had myself circumcised after I gained Gaian Consciousness. I did so to reclaim the rite from the Jews, who stole it in ancient times from the Egyptian priests of Isis. My circumcision marks me as a modern servant of Gaia, our living Motherworld.

From Jeanette Baker's journal, December 25, 2052:

The Gaian guru Billy Lee Mookerjee lives in a seven-room, terraced apartment with two working fireplaces that occupies the whole sixty-first floor of a turn-of-the-century blockhouse for the rich.

Mookerjee greeted Johnny and me wearing a Mongolian yellow robe with a red sash; sandlewood-scented beard and sleek blue-black, shoulder-length hair. Eyelids lined by kohl, rouged cheeks and lips. Everybody calls him-her "Srimaanji."

Srimaanji's sheila (an Americanized version of the Hindi word "chela," meaning disciple) is a twenty-nine-year-old bearded she-he named Alfred Howe. Johnny looked daggers at Howe all evening. The two of them gazed at Mookerjee with their hearts in their eyes.

Guru and sheila refer to each other consecutively as "him" and "her."

Mookerjee: "Alfred went to Harvard. He's a digital physicist. She believes that space and time are discreet, the laws of the universe are algorithms. Am I right, Alfred? And what else?"

Alfred: "The universe works according to the same principles as a computer, Srimaanji. In fact, the universe itself is a computer."

A vegetarian buffet: vermicelli with roasted peppers, garden burgers, and spicy mixed-vegetable biryani.

Suspended above the center of the round dining room table was a soccer ball–sized hologram of the Earth seen from the moon. As we sat down to eat, Mookerjee said: "Tonight we Gaians celebrate the mystery of the creation of our Universe from a random fluctuation of the quantum mechanical field we call the Full Void, or Mother Night."

The bald black butch seated opposite me got to her feet and sang in a clear, light soprano:

Mother Night,
Holy Night,
Ever dark,
Always bright.
We have taken
In our care
Earth your daughter,
Sweet and fair,
On this holy night,
This your holy night.[23]

Emma Torchlight's also a dyke. She took the seat on my left. High cheekbones; a flat, oval face, framed by short, straight, black, bobbed hair, which is shaved in back along the hairline. She told me Mookerjee lives in his apartment rent free, thanks to a realtor's rich widow who's a recent convert to Gaianism. The widow is celebrating the Feast of Mother Night in Bombay with the top Gaian guru, Srimaati Brianna Andrews.

All seven other guests were wimin, five of whom were straight, skilled workers: two carpenters, a pretty book repairer (friend of Indira's), and three software engineers. Emma introduced me around. Bobbie Washington, the bald, black, butch soprano is a well-known Transpacific subway busker.

Emma: "In the States, Gaianism attracts mostly wimin—lesbian and straight, artists and intellectuals, and some ecogynarchists as well, who call themselves Gyn-Gaians. An apolitical, mystical Gaianism is big among European earth scientists. The same in Japan. In India, the religion in a slightly different form is spreading among the lower castes, particularly Untouchables, of both sexes."

Emma and I exchanged Net addresses.

After dinner, everybody gathered around the gas fire blazing in the living room fireplace. Mookerjee showed off his celebrated mask. Each of us tried it on. Then Mookerjee tossed it on the flames. Johnny and I gasped; the paint peeled off the smoking wood. The pungent smell of

23. Words and music by Brianna Andrews, Motherworld Publishing, 2043.

burning cedar. Johnny's eyes filled with tears; they glistened in the flickering light. No one moved. We just stood there watching the mask burn up on the grate.

Finally, Mookerjee said, "Johnny, why do you suppose I burned the mask?"

Johnny: "You got me."

Mookerjee: "To remind us that even art perishes. Only Gaia, our living Motherworld, is here to stay."

From Jeanette Baker's journal, December 29, 2052:

A fight today with Johnny over Billy Lee, whom I called a religious nut. "Art means shit to him!"

Johnny: "I don't care! I love him!"

From Jeanette Baker's journal, February 1, 2053:

TOP IN-NEWS STORY:

CLONED CAPABLANCA METAMORPH WINS HUMIN CHESS CHAMPIONSHIP IN OSLO

Ishtar Teratol, 14, To Play IBM's Chess Maven Next Fall In Bid To Win World Chess Championship; Russian Orthodox Patriarch And Polish Cardinal Jointly Condemn Girl As Unnaturally Talented

From John Firth Baker's interview in *The International Review of Manual Art:*

Billy Lee wouldn't have me. I was frantic for a man. I sent my old boyfriend a message: "Anselmo, Be an angel! Take me back!"

He didn't answer, so I made him a Valentine. It's a combination cutout and scratchboard drawing.

Anselmo Diaz

On Valentine's Day, I got this card from Johnny that he drawed by hand. I thought, I'll be damned! I was real impressed. To think he went to all that trouble just for me!

From Johnny Baker to Teddy Petrakis, February 15, 2053:

Around nine last night, Anselmo called me from his one-room squat

Valentine for Anselmo Diaz, 2053, paper cutout on scratchboard drawing. Collection Billy Lee Mookerjee

on Ames Street in Omaha and said, "Come to Daddy!"

I went to him in the freezing rain. He pulled down my pants, put me over his knee, and spanked me for being a naughty girl who left her Daddy in the lurch on Halloween. Then he bathed and powdered me and made love to me till midnight.

We smoke a lot of dope together and swill Amae. Made a date with him for Saturday night.

Anselmo Diaz

I said to Johnny, "Wish I could draw."

He went, "Wish I could, too."

Johnny Baker to Teddy Petrakis, February 19, 2053:

Anselmo had a Mexican father and an Irish mother. His father deserted his mother before he was born. His mother deserted him when he was eight months old. He was raised by her mother in the Seattle barrio they call *"El Cagadero"*—"the Latrine." His granny sold him at age eleven for $20,500 to a twice-convicted dogfight promoter. Anselmo was the guy's slave. He wore an electronic dog collar day and night for two years. His master zapped him with a shock if he didn't hop-to. Anselmo's job was to trap alley cats and tie their legs together. Then he tossed them in the ring between two fighting pit bulls to arouse their blood lust.

On Christmas Day 2042, Anselmo managed to deactivate his collar and give his master the slip. He says, "I raised myself up from the depths and made me a good life."

From Jeanette Baker's journal, February 24, 2053:

Developed a new symptom today soon as I tried leaving the keep alone. First my left temple tingled. Then, with increasing intensity, the tingling spread to the whole left side of my face and into my mouth and tongue.

Polly Baker

The tingling was the last straw. Jeanette said to me, "Let's face it: I'm a keepie shut-in for good."

Emma Torchlight to Jeanette Baker, March 3, 2053:

Hello! Remember me? I'll be at my dealer's in St. Paul this coming Friday (March 7). Can you join us there for dinner?

Jeanette Baker to Emma Torchlight, March 4, 2053:

I don't like going out in the weather. Why don't you both come here Friday around eight for a home-cooked meal? I'll make us apple-bean jumble with carrot corn bread and red potato-spinach salad.

Emma Torchlight to Jeanette Baker, March 4, 2053:

Thanks. Nina, my dealer, can't make it, but I'll be there with bells on.

How's Johnny? Send him my best.

Emma Torchlight

As luck would have it, the subway computer went down, and I arrived at Jeanette's two-and-a-half hours late. Johnny, who'd already eaten, interrupted his homework to sit with us awhile at the table. Since last I saw him, he was much more physically mature: his features were thicker, his Adam's apple bigger, his shoulders broader, his voice deeper. There was fuzz on his upper lip. I noticed little black hairs already sprouting below his sideburns, alongside his ears. He was taller, too.

Johnny asked me if I was sore at Billy Lee for burning my mask, and I said, "Sure I was sore. But I forgave him. He can't help himself. He is who he is."

"Which is what?" said Johnny.

"Well, I once asked him, 'Billy Lee,' I said, 'Who are you—really?' And he said, 'Sometimes I can't tell where I leave off and Gaia begins.' "

Jeanette showed off Johnny's drawings, which embarrassed him. He left the room in a huff. I sympathized. My mother did the same with me. She once showed off my carvings to a total stranger on a Port Churchill street.

From Jeanette Baker's journal, March 8, 2053:

After supper, Emma and I strolled around Lake Twilight. Told her Johnny's an arsogenic metamorph.

Emma: "My mom would have done the same for me if she could."

Emma's mother, who's a carpenter, apprenticed her at age twelve for seven years to the innovative Tlingit maskmaker Tommy Rough Surface, who's transformed traditional Native American maskmaking.

Emma: "Tommy taught me a mask must reveal the face concealed by the mask of the face."

Me: "You've got a lovely hairline. Don't let your hairstylist shave it. Tell her to cut your hair in a curve that follows the nape of your neck. Better yet, let me cut it."

Emma: "I will."

We spent the night making love in my bed. I discovered the little blemishes on her body peculiar to her trade: the thick calluses on her right palm and along the joints at the base of her fingers and right thumb, the two small crescent-shaped scars—which I covered with kisses—on her upper right breast and the one in the middle of her right thigh. It seems that now and then the curved knife blade with which she carves a block of cedar on her lap slips on the wood and gashes her flesh.

Johnny Baker to Teddy Petrakis, March 12, 2053:

Emma stayed the weekend. She and Mother are lovers. I hate them.

From John Firth Baker's computer file "BillyLee," entry dated April 22, 2053:

GAIANS GET RELIGION
CHIEF GURU INCORPORATES CULT AS CHURCH

By Ross Azzarella
Special to IN-News

NEW YORK, April 22, 2053. Celebrating Earth Day in New York today, former atmospheric processor and presently chief Gaian guru Srimaati (Holy Mother) Brianna Andrews, 50, announced, "Under Article Eight of the Religious Corporations Law of New York State, we two-and-a-half-million American Gaians have incorporated ourselves into the Church of Gaia, the religion of the living planet Earth.

"The word 'religion' means to bind together," said Andrews. "We Gaians are bound together by our commitment to helping huminkind gain Gaian Consciousness and make a covenant with our living Motherworld."

Johnny Baker to Teddy Petrakis, June 2, 2053:

Day before yesterday, during an eleven-hour blowout of the S.W., a homeless wrinklie got suffocated by dust on the corner opposite the keep's West Gate.

I glimpsed her corpse being dug from a drift by the cops. Ever see a corpse? This was a first for me. The stomach was swollen.

From Jeanette Baker's journal, June 20, 2053:

CATHER KEEP HIGH SCHOOL HOME REPORTS

Student: John Firth Baker **Grade:** 10
Course: PreAlgebra
Teacher: Janis Birt
Date: 6/20/53
Semester Grade: C–
Genetic Propensity for Subject: Average.
Understanding of Concepts: Poor.
Homework Preparation: Poor.
Class Participation: Poor.
Written Work: Poor.
Tests and Quizzes: Poor.
Effort: Poor.
Comment: Topics covered this semester included factoring, work with fractions, decimals, percents, and simple line graphing.

John showed little interest in acquiring the concepts and techniques of the above, which were thoroughly discussed in class. His homework was ill-prepared—if at all. He was frequently absent from class.

John's gen-pro indicates he should have average mathematical skills. A great disparity exists between John's intellectual potential and his scholastic performance in this subject.

Student: John Firth Baker **Grade:** 10
Course: United States Herstory
Teacher: Brigid Khalid
Date: 6/20/53
Semester Grade: C
Genetic Propensity for Subject: Does not apply.
Understanding of Concepts: Excellent.
Homework Preparation: Poor.
Class Participation: Good.
Written Work: Poor.

Tests and Quizzes: Adequate.
Effort: Adequate.
Comment: John was an erratic student. His homework was often sloppy. During class discussions, however, he showed his considerable intelligence by clearly articulating his political philosophy, Gynarchism, and applying its critical insights to U.S. herstory.

John's passionate ideological commitment, however, often makes him intolerant of differing political opinions. He must learn to moderate his enthusiasm so that his classmates have a chance to participate in a meaningful dialogue with him.

Student: John Firth Baker **Grade:** 10
Course: Earth Science
Teacher: Barbara Ellis
Date: 6/21/53
Semester Grade: A
Genetic Propensity for Subject: Does not apply.
Understanding of Concepts: Excellent.
Homework Preparation: Excellent.
Class Preparation: Excellent.
Written Work: Excellent.
Tests and Quizzes: Excellent.
Effort: Excellent.
Comment: John is very taken with the Gaia hypothesis and constantly related it to our work. He became the class authority on the ocean's crust, which, as you know, serves the Earth as a kind of self-regulating global water-treatment plant that maintains the planet's chemical equilibrium.

John recently gave an outstanding oral report on the unique way the Earth vents its internal heat through the hydrothermal vents and megaplumes on the ocean floor. He showed a deep appreciation of how the Earth rids itself of heat, thereby maintaining the fragile chemical balance that keeps us alive.

It was a pleasure to have John in my class.

Student: John Firth Baker **Grade:** 10
Course: English
Teacher: Kenneth Hubner
Date: 6/20/53
Semester Grade: A–
Genetic Propensity for Subject: Does not apply.
Understanding of Concepts: Excellent.
Homework Preparation: Excellent.
Class Preparation: Excellent.
Written Work: Excellent
Tests and Quizzes: Very good.
Effort: Excellent.
Comment: John was a joy to teach. He loves Shakespeare's *A Midsummer Night's Dream* and communicated his enthusiasm to his less-than-enthusiastic fellow students, who regarded Shakespeare as hopelessly old-fashioned, tough to understand, and irrelevant to modern life. There was plenty of resistance in class to studying *A Midsummer's Night's Dream* till John pointed out that the name of the popular English music group "Hot Ice" was taken from Theseus' speech in Act V, Scene 1 of the play: "Merry and tragical, tedious and brief. That is, hot ice and wondrous strange snow."

Wish I'd spotted that! I certainly will make good use of his observation when I teach the play to future classes.

In general, John did excellent work in English this term.

Student: John Firth Baker **Grade:** 10
Course: Concert Jazz.
Teacher: Dottie Hanson
Date: 6/21/53
Semester Grade: Credit Withheld.
Genetic Propensity for Subject: Average.
Attention in Class: Poor.
Punctuality: Poor.

Brings Materials: Poor.
Ability to Take Directions: Poor.
Ability to Work with Others: Poor.
Practice and Class Preparation: Poor.
Tone Quality: Poor.
Intonation: Poor.
Fluency of Technique: Poor.
Rhythmical Accuracy: Poor.
Comment: Given John's gen-pro, which emphasizes his rich complement of visual arsogenes, I was surprised that he opted at the beginning of the year to fulfill his requirement for credit in the Arts by taking Concert Jazz.

At first, John strove valiantly to master the elements of playing his instrument of choice, which was the trombone. But he rapidly lost interest and made no further effort to acquire any musical technique or indeed to participate at all in class work.

I am therefore unable to give John credit for his work this term in Concert Jazz.

I asked Johnny how he intends to make up the above withheld credit; he said, "I dunno." These days, his answer to everything is "I dunno."

Drifting, drifting—the boy is drifting.

He hasn't made a drawing in five months.

Anselmo Diaz

Johnny never once invited me home to meet his mother. I never set foot in Cather Keep. That hurt my feelings, but I never said nothin' to him about it.

Johnny couldn't help hisself. He was born and raised in a keep, and everybody knows what a keep is short for. A keep is short for "keep out."

Johnny Baker to Teddy Petrakis, June 21, 2053:

Mother's been hinting like mad that she wants a drawing from me for her upcoming birthday.

I haven't drawn a line since February. I fear I've lost my touch.

From Jeanette Baker's journal, July 3, 2053:

Forty-four today.

Johnny ignored my little hints over the last few months and instead of a drawing gave me a first edition of *Femina Dominans*.[24]

Emma, who's working in Mexico, forgot my birthday altogether. Forty-four! Ugh!

Emma Torchlight

Jeanette never mentioned her birthday to me. Come to think of it, she never told me her age.

Johnny Baker to Teddy Petrakis, July 9, 2053:

Last night when it cooled off a bit, I dragged Anselmo to a Gaian round dance in Elmwood Park. The dancers were led by Billy Lee, who looked gorgeous in scarlet harem pants.

The drawing I made of him from my dream is a bad likeness. He's much more Indian-looking.

After the dance, Billy Lee said just four words to a big crowd. "Death makes life possible." I felt he was addressing me personally. Then he recited the poem "Two-some" by the Gaian poet Sistah Sally:

> Death,
> We be a two-some.
> Make dat a one-some!
> Cause—
> —les face it:
> No you,
> No me.[25]

---

24. Maria Lopez, *Femina Dominans: A New Wominkind*, Northampton, Mass.: Hippolyta Press, 2028. (28–L0102)

25. Sistah Sally, *Poems*, New York: Parnassus Press, 2038:110. (38–Sa556)

Anselmo Diaz

Once a month, I visited my Granny out in Cleveland at a Guild home for wrinklies called The Humin Touch. Her heart and lungs was in good shape, but mentally she was off the air. Johnny couldn't believe I took care of her after what she done to me as a kid.

"Shame on you," he says. "You still want her love."

"Jeez, I never thought of that, but it's true."

Johnny Baker to Teddy Petrakis, July 16, 2053:

Anselmo, who's got a taste for drawings done by hand, asked me to draw his Granny's portrait from life. I'm giving it a try. We visited her this afternoon at a Guild wrinklie home in Cleveland called The Humin Touch, because the staff is all humin—no carebots allowed.

Granny's name is Shelagh Cavanaugh. She was ninety-four last month. She's been in the wrinklie home four years. Three years ago, she started getting senile but responded well to CREB rejuvenation therapy. Then her insurance ran out, the therapy ended, and her senile dementia came back worse than before. She babbles night and day.

Anselmo recorded some of her babbling. We're both fascinated by it. She plays with words. For example, at one point, she was like, "Exceptional change, exceptional change, exceptional change. See this hole they dug in the back of my hand? Cold star coffle, cold star coffle, cold star coffle."

Later she went, "Don't let me die. I'm too young to die."

I never looked at a wrinklie's face up close before. All I could think was, This is how Mother will look when she's ninety-four.

Anselmo Diaz

I took my vacation the last two weeks in July so I could go to Cleveland with Johnny every morning and watch him work.

Them two weeks cost me a pretty penny. Johnny's art supplies alone—paper, pencils, erasers—cost over two hundred and fifty bucks. And there was our subway fares and lunches. All told Granny's picture set me back more than six hundred bucks.

Johnny Baker to Teddy Petrakis, July 22, 2053:

Worked today on Granny's portrait for four straight hours, but made no progress. All my drawings are lifeless. I need a theme, some emotion, to convey.

While I draw, Granny babbles. Anselmo records her. Around noon, she got quiet, and he went, "Whatcha thinking about Granny? Me?"

"A girl will soon give me a pill, which will put me to sleep. Then she'll pin me to the wall for three months and rebuild my body, so I'll come back to a new life much smarter and stronger than I am now."

Portrait of Shelagh Cavanagh, 2053, pencil on paper.
Collection Billy Lee Mookerjee

Johnny Baker to Teddy Petrakis, July 23, 2053:

This morning Granny went, "When I was a young girl, I had me a beautiful profile. The envy of all."

Then she stopped talking, and for a moment you could see in her eyes that she was thinking about her once-beautiful profile.

That's the moment I will draw.

Anselmo Diaz

Not long after Johnny was murdered, Mookerjee bought his two drawings off me for eight hundred bucks each.

From John Firth Baker's computer file "BillyLee," entry dated September 11, 2053:

CREEPING SAND HILLS TO BE IRRIGATED
BY METAMORPHIC "WATER BUGS"

New Bacteria Designed To Irrigate Dunes Of
Spreading Tri-State Sandy Wastes Sown By Margaret Kim,
Governor Of Nebraska

Brief Invocation At Ceremony Given By
Midwestern District Guru Of The Church Of Gaia,
Sri Billy Lee Mookerjee

Special to IN-News
By Lily Johanna Davis

LINCOLN, Nebraska, September 4. From her office today in the State Capitol, Nebraska's Governor Margaret Kim, 49, activated the release of billions of metamorphic bacteria over the Creeping Sand Hills that cover parts of Nebraska, Colorado, Kansas and Oklahoma. The new bacteria, *Pseudomonas hydrophilia,* nicknamed "water bugs" by their creators, were designed and manufactured by Dr. Jean Hutslar and her staff of bioengineers at the College of Agriculture of the University of Nebraska. The introduction of the water bugs into the environment was OKed last January by the Federal Recombinant DNA Authority.

The multitude of rapidly-multiplying metamorphic microorganisms will live exactly six months in the sand dunes, all the while extracting water from the air. They will then die. The water within their dead cells will be retained in humus-like compounds which will slowly break down and irrigate the dunes.

Next spring the irrigated dunes will be fertilized with various proliferating species of metamorphic vegetation which will gradually fix the creeping Sand Hills in place. The Sand Hills will eventually be planted with a variety of metamorphic species of fruit-bearing shrubs and trees which were also developed under Dr. Hutslar's direction at the University of Nebraska College of Agriculture.

Gov. Kim said, "Thanks to Jean Hutslar and her brilliant staff of Cornhusker bioengineers, the Creeping Sand Hills will be transformed within a decade into the world's largest public orchard."

The Governor, who is a Gaian, invited Sri (His Reverence) Billy Lee Mookerjee, 32, one of twelve regional gurus of the Church of Gaia, to deliver an invocation at today's ceremony. Sri Mookerjee was brief and to the point; he quoted one line of Scripture (Jer. 29:5): "Plant gardens and eat the fruit of them."

From Jeanette Baker's journal, September 11, 2053:

Emma's here for the weekend. Johnny aloof and jealous.

From Jeanette Baker's journal, Friday, October 6, 2053:

TOP IN-NEWS STORY: Teratol Ready For Revenge

CLONED CASABLANCA METAMORPH HOPES TO BE FIRST HUMIN SINCE 2009 TO WIN WORLD CHESS CHAMPIONSHIP FROM IBM'S CHESS MAVEN

FACTS OF THE FACE-OFF:

ISHTAR TERATOL VS CHESS MAVEN
October 7–16, 2053, Hotel Asgard, Oslo, Norway

	TERATOL	CHESS MAVEN
Height	5 ft	29 in
Weight	98 lbs	1 lb
Age	15 yrs	24 yrs
Birthplace	Beit Tiamat, MedSea	Elmira, N.Y.
Hardware	50 billion neurons	10 gigabillion parallel processors
Moves per Second	2	2 trillion
Power Source	Electrical/chemical	Electrical/chemical

From Jeanette Baker's journal, October 7, 2053:

TOP IN-NEWS STORY:

PLEASED TO MATE YOU!

Teratol Wins First Game Of Eight-Game Championship Match

From Jeanette Baker's journal, Oct. 8, 2053:

TOP IN-NEWS STORY:

IBM CHESS MAVEN TURNS DOWN AN OPPORTUNITY TO DRAW AND WINS

From Jeanette Baker's journal, October 9, 2053:

TOP IN-NEWS STORY:

CLONED CAPABLANCA METAMORPH DEFEATS COMPUTER IN THIRD OF EIGHT MATCHES FOR CHESS CHAMPIONSHIP PRIZE WORTH $5,000,000

Daringly Sacrifices Queen And Wins In Fifty-Move Masterpiece

Alex Thomas jr.

Johnny and I spoke that night. I know a little something about chess and explained that Teratol's totally unexpected sacrifice of a queen, the most powerful piece on the board, to a computer programmed to take full advantage of her slightest mistake showed strategic genius.

"The hell with Teratol," Johnny said. "The girl's a homophobe!"

"Why a homophobe?"

"Because she sacrificed a queen!"

Johnny blew me a kiss; I couldn't remember him so happy. I was happy, too. Ishtar Teratol made us proud to be metamorphs.

I talked chess with Johnny after every game. Or rather, I talked, and Johnny listened. After the fourth game, which ended in a draw, Johnny said, "I'm no match for chess. Ha-ha!"

The game was beyond him. But he sure pulled for Teratol.

From Jeanette Baker's journal, October 13, 2053:

TOP IN-NEWS STORY:

TERATOL ROOKS SELF, OVERLOOKS CHESS MAVEN'S PLOY OF SACRIFICING ROOK, LOSES FIFTH GAME IN TWENTY-THREE MOVES

Match Even At 2½ Each

From Jeanette Baker's journal, October 14, 2053:

Teratol's victory in her sixth game today thrilled Johnny.

He said, "I'm proud to be a metamorph and don't care who knows it."

I warned him that a public revelation of his identity would expose me to prosecution under the Created Equal Act.

Johnny will be sixteen tomorrow. Polly's giving him a party.

Am developing a real interest in chess. Hooked on Sarah Jonas' column, "Gambytes." Jonas gives Teratol a good chance of winning tomorrow's game.

Polly Baker

Teratol's third defeat ruined Johnny's birthday party.

Alex Thomas jr.

I called to wish Johnny a happy birthday. We talked about the three-and-a-half to three-and-a-half game tie in the desperate struggle between a humin being and a machine. Our conversation inspired me. I stayed up all that night composing my duet for computer and soprano, *Tied Score*, which scores electronic regularity against aleatory improvisation.

From Jeanette Baker's journal, October 15, 2053:

Sarah Jonas: "Ishtar Teratol is in a tight spot. She has used up most of her opening attacks and probably has no surprises left for tomorrow's game to decide the outcome of the World Chess Championship. Chess Maven knows Teratol must fall back on the classic variations: tactics to which it has complete access. To win Teratol must rely on the power of her imagination."

From Jeanette Baker's journal, October 16, 2053:

Teratol, at her press teleconference after today's deciding match: "Last night, before going to sleep I searched my files, looking for a surprise opening strategy I could use to catch Chess Maven off guard. I checked out hundreds of openings. None of them did it for me. I mean, an opening that does it immediately puts many other moves in my head; I can picture all the potential positions on the board.

"I called up a hardly used black defense in reverse: the Steinmetz defense to the Ruy Lopez, which hasn't been played in over a hundred years. Like Momma says, '*Eso es eso.*' That was it! I immediately pictured hundreds of variations of this old-time reverse defense strategy, which I now knew was the way to open tomorrow's game.

"But then what? I mean, how could I then sucker Chess Maven into a trap? I wracked my brains. Then it came to me. In the second game, Chess Maven turned down a draw and beat me. I thought, Turn its strength against itself. Make it play to win!

"So in the game, I offered my queen again as a sacrifice—but in return for only a rook and a knight. Chess Maven saw the material lure but couldn't understand why I'd sacrifice the queen a second time during a match. Computers assume the humin mind is limited. Chess Maven must have figured I can't understand all the complications of sacrificing my queen for a rook and a knight.

"Then I had another brainstorm. I made two repetitions. Chess Maven refused to accept the draw. It allowed my sacrifice and played to win. It can't help itself; that's how it's programmed—it plays only to win.

"At that point all I had to do was promote my pawn on the a-file and get a new queen. I won the game in three moves."

Johnny: "Long live the humin mind!"

Wakinoya Yoshiharu

Teratol's victory was also a triumph for Fritz and the Ozaki Institute. As a result he won a huge GE contract to design a humin genome that would stimulate the enlargement of the inferior parietal lobe, the math center of the brain, endowing it with the capacity to create a Theory Of Everything.

At the party celebrating the contract, Fritz came to me stinko and said, "Shokaki, I'm gonna make us a TOE-head! A TOE-head will give us the formula to master space and time. Whoopee!"

From Sri Billy Lee Mookerjee's home page, October 21, 2053:

My beloved sheila, Alfred Howe, has left my service after failing to gain Gaian Consciousness. He took a job with Lunartech-Interares in Armstrong Keep on the moon. I know I speak for all my fellow Gaians in wishing him the best of luck.

Johnny Baker to Sri Billy Lee Mookerjee, October 22, 2053:

Last summer in Elmwood Park, I heard you say, "Death makes life possible." I'm terrified of death. Teach me to affirm that it's a necessity.

Help me gain Gaian Consciousness. Take me on as your sheila in place of Alfred Howe.

Sri Billy Lee Mookerjee to Johnny Baker, October 24, 2053:

No. You were born to be an artist. Serve your gift, not me.

Alex Thomas jr. to Johnny Baker, January 12, 2054:

Tied Score, which I dedicated to Ishtar Teratol, had a student premiere performance in Paul Hall last night. A well-organized gang of AANGAs shouted down the soprano, a talented undergraduate from the Juilliard Opera Center who burst into tears and ran off the stage. Fistfights broke out in the audience.

From Jeanette Baker's journal, March 8, 2054:

TOP IN-NEWS STORY:

Maria Lopez Kidnaped On International Womin's Day

Longtime Chairpersin Of North American
Gynarchist Liberation League Taken By Unknown Assailants;
Four Masked Men Abduct Leading Antagonist Of Legalized
Polygamy Outside Atlanta Hotel; Bodyguard Fatally Shot

From John Firth Baker's computer file "YoungGynLeague," entry dated March 9, 2054:

Feminize the Humin Race!

Date: March 9, 2054
From: jfbaker
To: CKHYGL
Subj: Taking over this afternoon's all-school International Womin's Day Assembly in the quad.

Sisters:

We have just been instructed by the Executive Committee of the North American Midwest Gynarchist League to turn this afternoon's International Womin's Day celebration into a protest rally against Sister Lopez' kidnaping.

Here are some tips from the Committee on how a small group like us can dominate a crowd jammed into a confined space:

1. The International Womin's Day rally is scheduled for 3 P.M. Arrive promptly at 2:30.

2. Facing west, towards the honey locust tree, fan out through the crowd in the shape of an inverted V, which will make it seem that there are many more of us present than are actually there.

3. At 2:55 P.M. *sharp,* start chanting "Free Maria Lopez!" in unison for five minutes. (Keep at it. Others will join in!)

4. At exactly 3 P.M. our chairpersin, Sandy Chan, standing on a chair, will raise both arms—our signal to shut up. Sandy will then speak for five minutes. At the end, she'll call for a unanimous resolution, to be passed by acclamation, of the whole student body: "Free Maria Lopez now!" *Whoop it up!!!*

Sister Johnny Baker, (11th Grade) Secretary,
The Cather Keep High Young Gynarchist League

From John Firth Baker's computer file "YoungGynLeague," entry dated March 10, 2054:

FEMINIZE THE HUMIN RACE!

Date: March 10, 2054
From: jfbaker
To: CKHYGL
Subj: An emergency self-criticism session

Sisters:

An emergency self-criticism session will be held in room 406 (the chem lab) at 5 P.M. today to analyze our collective failure to take over yesterday's rally in the quad. Attendance is mandatory. Sisters who fail to attend will be expelled from the Cather Keep High Young Gynarchist League without right of appeal!

Sister Johnny Baker, (11th Grade) Secretary,
The Cather Keep High Young Gynarchist League

From Jeanette Baker's journal, March 10, 2054:

Lopez still missing; her bodyguard, an ex-Marine named Ruth Cardoza, was buried today in Arlington.

From Jeanette Baker's journal, March 14, 2054:

TOP IN-NEWS STORY:

MORMON FUNDAMENTALISTS FREE MARIA LOPEZ IN EUGENE, OREGON

Foe Of Polygamy Was Clitorectomized And Her Nipples Amputated In Captivity By Religious Org

The True Church of Old Line Aryan Mormons (TCOLAM) Home Page Declares It Made Chief American Gynarchist "Atone For Sins With Blood Offering"

From John Firth Baker's computer file "YoungGynLeague," entry dated March 23, 2054:

FEMINIZE THE HUMIN RACE!

Date: March 23, 2054
From: jfbaker
To: CKHYGL
Subj: Minutes of today's meeting.

Sisters:

It was unanimously resolved at today's meeting that we send Sister Maria Lopez a token of our esteem while she's recuperating from her recent ordeal.

Our Chairpersin, Sister Sandy Chan, suggested we give Sister Lopez a first edition of the 20th-century classic, *The Reign of the Phallus* by Eva C. Keuls, the 1985 book that gave the word "phallocracy" to the world.

Sister Sandy reported that her mom, Ruby, who's a lifelong Gynarchist, owns a copy of said book and told Sandy she'd be pleased to donate it to our cause. Ruby's copy, however, is minus a cover, and would cost at least $225 to repair, which we can't afford because as our Treasurer, Sister Cassandra Kramer, pointed out, our treasury is down to an all-time low of $5.82.

At this point our Secretary, Sister Johnny Baker, volunteered to ask his good friend, the book repairer Indira Rabindra, to re-cover said book gratis as gesture of sympathy for Maria Lopez.

Sister Baker will report back on the results of his request to Ms. Rabindra as soon as he can.

Sister Johnny Baker, (11th Grade) Secretary,
The Cather Keep High Young Gynarchist League

Indira Rabindra

As a womin, sure, I felt for Lopez, but I told Johnny business is business. My charge for re-covering a book, depending on its condition, was upwards of $264. Then I had an idea. I always wanted one of Johnny's drawings. I told him I'd repair *The Reign of the Phallus* in exchange for a drawing he'd make me on the subject of bound books.

Johnny said, "I don't know anything about bound books."

I said, "I'll teach you."

"You got yourself a deal."

Because *The Reign of the Phallus* didn't need to be resewed, I was able to re-cover it during one long Sunday, from 8 A.M. to 7:00 in the evening with half an hour off for lunch. I work on my feet; it gives me better leverage and control. Johnny watched me the whole time. I can still see him standing on the other side of the big table behind my precious 1939 letterpress, the kind that screws down by hand.

Repairing *The Reign of the Phallus* was a routine job. I added eighty-pound manila endpapers and used blue canton flannel for the cover. Johnny wanted to help. I showed him how to round the corners with my bone folder and crease the joints in back. He caught on fast—Johnny had a feel for tools. He also glued the completed case.

After work, he asked to see my little collection of 20th-century bound and printed books.

From John Firth Baker's interview in *The International Review of Manual Art:*

I gawked at Indira's old books—a couple hundred all told: novels, histories, herstories, and biographies neatly stacked on ten or twelve shelves. I never saw so many bound books together in one place. Each book was a different height and width and color. The crowded shelves were a feast for the eyes!

Linda Stein, ex libris for Indira Rabindra, 2036, ink on scratchboard drawing. Collection Indira Rabindra

I picked a familiar title off the bottom shelf: *Gimpel the Fool,* by Isaac Bashevis Singer, a book of short stories I read at school in a digital edition. There was something pasted inside the front cover.

Indira Rabindra

Johnny had never seen a bookplate before. He asked me what *ex libris* meant. I explained, and he said, "I'm gonna make a bookplate for Maria Lopez."

Ex libris for Maria Lopez, 2052, ink on scratchboard drawing. Collection National Archives, Washington, D.C.

From John Firth Baker's interview in *The International Review of Manual Art:*

As you well know, the bookplate I designed for Maria Lopez made me famous—or I should say, infamous. For the life of me, I can't recall how I thought of the image. I remember drawing it and giving the original to Indira, but not how it came to me in the first place.

Indira Rabindra

As you can well imagine, given its subsequent notoriety, Johnny's bookplate is now worth a small fortune. I gave it on permanent loan to the National Archives.

Sri Billy Lee Mookerjee to Johnny Baker, April 5, 2054:

I'm writing you from Denver, where I'm helping the young congregation of Colorado's First Church of Gaia prepare for the Centennial State's upcoming annual Earth Day parade. This year's parade commemorates the recent extinction by global warming of a unique local species of butterfly, the Uncompahgre fritillary *(Boloria acrocnema)*, which lived only in the cool, wet environment once found on the Uncompahgre and Red Cloud Peaks in Colorado's San Juan Mountains. During the last decade the climatic change to warmer, drier weather here wiped the species out.

I remember the banner you designed two years ago for Local 103 of the Hairstylist's Guild in Nebraska's Earth Day parade, and I wonder if you would design a marching banner for our Church, using the likeness of the extinct butterfly.

Unfortunately the Church can only afford to pay you the token amount of $350 for your work, but you will have the satisfaction of using your talent in Gaia's service.

Johnny Baker to Sri Billy Lee Mookerjee, April 6, 2054:

Make me your sheila and my talents are yours to command. Otherwise, bug off! (Ha! Ha!)

Yours truly,

Sri Billy Lee Mookerjee to Johnny Baker, April 6, 2054:

Make yourself into what you were born to be—an artist.

Cather Keep High Young Gynarchist League to Sister Maria Lopez, April 21, 2054:

Dear Sister Lopez:

Please accept this gift of a 1985 first edition of Eva C. Keuls' *The Reign of the Phallus* from our membership as an expression of our admiration for you in your struggle against phallocratic oppression.

The book was donated by the mother of our chairpersin, Sister Sandy Chan. The bookplate inside the front cover is the work of our Secretary, Sister Johnny Baker, who drew it by hand.

We Young Gynarchists at Cather Keep High hope you enjoy our present and are soon back feminizing the humin race.

Sincerely,
John Firth Baker,
Secretary, The Cather Keep High Young Gynarchist League

Sister Maria Lopez to The Cather Keep High Young Gynarchist League, May 3, 2034:

FEMINIZE THE HUMIN RACE!

Dear Sisters:

Thank you for your good wishes and thoughtful gift. I shall always treasure the first edition of *The Reign of the Phallus* and the bookplate that your Secretary, Sister Johnny Baker, drew especially for me.

My ordeal at the hands of TCOLAM convinces me that we must intensify our struggle against all phallocratic religious authority. Organized submission to mythical tribal father gods is the psychological basis of the global phallocratic oppression of wominkind.

Sisters! Topple the altars that phallocratic priests have erected in your minds to their tribal father gods! Raze their stone shrines to the ground!

Yours in Sisterhood,
Sister Mary Lopez, Chairpersin,
The North American Gynarchist Liberation League

Sister Maria Lopez to Sister Johnny Baker, May 3, 2054:

Thank you again for your personalized bookplate. Your innovative representation of the Gyn Sign piercing a male symbol in the guise of a snake is too potent a symbol to be reserved for my personal use. It must be put to work in our struggle to feminize—to civilize—the humin race. Accordingly, the Executive Committee of the North American Gynarchist Liberation League authorizes me to purchase exclusive rights to your representation of the interlocking, combatant gender symbols which appears on my bookplate for an honorarium of $100.

If you agree, Sister Johnny, please sign the accompanying document, and, as you are legally underage, please ask your mother, Sister Jeanette Baker, to cosign it. I'm confident she will. Our records show that Sister Jeanette has been an active, valued member of the North American Gynarchist League since July 2, 2033.

Thank you both in advance for your inestimable contribution to our Cause.

Yours in Sisterhood.

In consideration of the payment of $100.00, receipt of which is hereby acknowledged, I hereby convey to the North American Gynarchist League all of my right, interest and title in and to my representation and drawing of the Gyn Sign piercing a male symbol, in the guise of a snake, which appears on Maria Lopez's Bookplate, with the understanding that the aforesaid representation will not be used for commercial purposes or profit, but only for the advancement of world Gynarchism and the feminization of the humin race.

____

Sister John Firth Baker

____

Sister Jeanette Baker (Parent)

Johnny Baker to Mentor, May 6, 2054:

What's the cheapest way to grow tits?

Mentor to Johnny Baker, May 6, 2054:

The Salmacis Gender Reassignment Clinic in Havana, Cuba (www.hermaphrodite.com) offers clients a no-frills transgenic mastogenesis for $7040.

Transgenic mastogenesis is a painless implantation into a humin of a hybrid molecular vector carrying a mastogenic gene from the male Malaysian Dayak fruit bat *(Dyacopterus spadiceus)*, the only known male mammal that nurses its young. Its mastogenic gene, discovered in 2014, stimulates the growth of milk-producing breasts in the male bat without altering its male secondary sexual characteristics.

Transplanted to humins, the gene does the same within three to four months.

For Sale, online ad, 2054, scratchboard drawing

From John Firth Baker's interview in *The International Review of Manual Art:*

I spent the night drawing my chest like my chest was going out of style—which it was.

John Firth Baker's online advertisement on boybond.555, May 13, 2054:

Now that I caught your eye, the truth is I'm a summer rental. My name is Johnny. I'm 16. W. Blue eyes. 5'11". Uncut. Very well hung. I'll be your slave boy while school is out from June 14 through Labor Day. I'm cheap at the price: $8500 (no haggling), plus a round-trip ticket to New York, where my Master must reside. Want me for your very own? Contact slaveboy@boybond.555.

Dominus to slaveboy, May 19, 2054:

I'm a thirty-nine-year-old, successful member of the business class. I own a hanging-garden apartment twenty-four floors above an Upper West Side Manhattan canal. Send me a picture of yourself naked. If I like what I see, I'll meet your price and make you my slave.

Dominus to slaveboy, May 20, 2054:

Sold!

Johnny Baker to Mentor, May 20, 2054:

Give me one paragraph on New York.

Mentor to Johnny Baker, May 20, 2054:

New York City (pop. 12,102,142) is the cultural and fun capital of the world. The city's made up of five boroughs, the heart of which is Manhattan Island. From 2028–36, as the rising Atlantic flooded the Eastern Seaboard, much of the old city of Manhattan was torn down. Present-day New York was built in its place along 504.3 miles of freshly dug waterways and canals.

Slaveboy to Dominus, May 20, 2054:

I hope to be a manual artist. In fact, I did the drawing for my online ad. Please make up some cover story about me winning a bogus scholarship, with all expenses paid, to study manual art in Manhattan this summer.

Otherwise, Mother won't let me go.

Your obedient slave boy, Johnny.

P.S. My full name is John Firth Baker.

The Rev. Theodore Petrakis

Oberlin let out late that year, the last week in May. After church, the first Sunday I was home, Johnny came for brunch. All he talked about, over my spinach frittata, was Billy Lee—and how he, Johnny, was going to prove himself worthy of becoming Billy Lee's sheila.

He said, "First off, I'm gonna buy myself tits."

Then he swore me to secrecy and showed me his online ad.

I told him, "You're crazy! Who's this guy 'Dominus?' What do you know about him? You're taking your life in your hands."

"Tell me about it!" he said.

Kenneth Kingsley, Attorney and Councilor at Law, to Katherine G. Jackson, Curator of 21st Century Manual Arts at the American Museum Without Walls, March 3, 2067:

It has come to my attention that in your upcoming biography of the late arsomorphic [sic] Manual artist John Firth Baker you plan to reveal the identity of my client and portray him as a sadistic pederast. In this regard, it is incumbent upon me to warn you that any such action would severely prejudice the rights of my client to anonymity and freedom from baseless slander.

Accordingly, should you undertake such a course of action I would feel compelled on behalf of my client to make use of all available legal remedies. These would include, but not be limited to, injunctive relief and damages, both punitive and compensatory, insofar as your action would be undertaken with full notice and awareness of the consequences.

It is no mean matter to defame an individual and thereby severely hamper his ability to function in a normal way in the community of his choice. The damage this type of slander incurs is likely to last for a lifetime and encompasses both emotional trauma and the very tangible loss of income and financial assets.

Conchita Perez to John Firth Baker, May 27, 2054:

Dear John Firth Baker,

On behalf of Ms. Celia Campbell-Kibble, President of the Campbell-

Kibble Foundation, I'm delighted to inform you that you are the recipient of the first annual Joseph L. Campbell Summer Scholarship for Young Manual Artists which Ms. Campbell-Kibble recently established in her late father's name. The manual drawings you submitted were deemed by our three independent judges to be the best they received.

The scholarship amounts to $8500, plus free board at Ms. Campbell-Kibble's Manhattan apartment and free transportation to and from New York. You will be required to live at Ms. Campbell-Kibble's from July 1 through Labor Day, during which time you must attend a daily four-hour actual class that meets five times a week at the New York Manual Art Students League.

Please notify me by Saturday, May 30, if you agree to accept the Joseph L. Campbell Summer Scholarship for Young Manual Artists.

Sincerely,
Conchita Perez

From Jeanette Baker's journal, May 27, 2054:

Johnny has won the first annual Joseph L. Campbell Summer Scholarship for Young Manual Artists ($8500!), which will necessitate his living in New York and taking classes at the New York Manual Art Students League. In other words, he'll begin his formal training as a manual artist. It's of course my dream come true. Yet I worry about him being loose at his age in New York. NYC is the S&M capital of the world.

Alex Thomas jr. to Johnny Baker, June 3, 2054:

Your mom told my mom you'll be in New York this summer. Me, too. But we won't be able to get together. I'm taking an NYU saturation course in Ebonics. I've long had a thing for African-American speech. Like Waleed Parmalee says, "It be spoken music to my ears."

And like Parmalee, I wanna write orchestral music that incorporates the Ebonic melody and its complex rhythms. But because it was never spoken at home, I gotta learn it from scratch. The NYU saturation course stipulates that I live with an Ebonics-speaking family and speak only Ebonics with them and my friends.

You and me got so much to say to each other that I would be sorely tempted to break the rules. Therefore we can't meet. Music comes first. I know you understand and will forgive me.

My advice about New York: Everybody will tell you what you must see in this town. I say, listen up, as well. Bouncing off the water or the sides of the canals, every single sound here is muted, fluid and resonant. Waves slap, gondolas bump, voices echo. Man, you ain't never heard nothin like New York.

Jeanette Baker's journal, July 3, 2054:

Today I'm 45—the same age as Momma when she died.

Johnny Baker to Jeanette Baker, July 3, 2054:

Happy Birthday, Mother. Many happy returns of the day.

I'm writing you from Ms. Campbell-Kibble's jasmine and lavender garden. It hangs twenty-four floors above the 79th Street intersection of the West End Canal and the Hudson River. The one-way canal goes north. It's now jammed with noonday traffic. I count one blue and white police boat, two yellow water taxis, two gondolas, a white ice cream barge. A red fireboat, siren screaming, is speeding uptown. Its wake rocks the orange crosstown waterbus picking up passengers at the corner. There's lots of turquoise mixed in the depths of the greenish-gray canal water.

But the heat! A West Side neighborhood is called "Hell's Kitchen." To tell the truth, all of NY in the summer is hell's kitchen—the temperature right now is 104.1 degrees.

You need big bucks to live well in this town. I know for a fact Ms. Campbell-Kibble rents her three-bedroom apartment for $61,600 a month. She's a very private person, like her father, who was a little-known but big-time collector of early 21st-century manual art.

Next Monday I start a class in drawing from life at the Manual Art Students League. Don't worry. I won't let on what I am.

Happy Birthday, Mother! I miss you. The hairdressers here, though very expensive, are too Chinese-y for my taste. The Mandarin cut doesn't become me at all, so I'm letting my hair grow out.

Have a good Fourth.

Ms. Campbell is having a cookout on her hanging garden. Politicians and rich business-class types expected. Maybe even some Beautiful People!

Your loving son, Johnny

Johnny Baker to Teddy Petrakis, July 4, 2054:

To tell the truth, I adore being a slave. It's restful, not thinking for myself. This afternoon, butt-naked, I served drinks and hot dogs to my Master's guests at his July 4 barbecue. My Master is very "God bless America!" As the sun went down, he read the whole Declaration of Independence aloud. Then he gave me as a gift for the night to a friend whose name you'd instantly recognize if I was free to divulge it.

Jeanette Baker to Johnny Baker, July 11, 2054:

I'm so proud of you! I hope your first life class went well. Please thank Ms. Campbell-Kibble on my behalf for her kindness to you.

I hope her party was fun. Any Beautiful People show?

Enjoyed your description of your neighborhood. You have a wonderful eye for color. What a painter you'll be, once you set your mind to it! Reading remains the only way I can leave the keep. A proposal to extend the Guild insurance plan to cover treatment for us keepie shut-ins was recently turned down by the benefits committee as too expensive. (Bashy Weinberg, by the way, is running for Treasurer of Local 103 in the Fall. Think I'll back her. She's got a Jewish head for money.)

Emma, who's twenty-seven next month, is trying to decide whether to have a baby. We're no longer lovers—just good friends.

Emma Torchlight

I was thinking about having a daughter. Jeanette told me that all her life she'd feared that if she'd had a daughter, she (Jeanette) would've wound up like her mother—a suicide.

Johnny Baker to Teddy Petrakis, July 21, 2054:

My Master let me play tourist for three hours this afternoon.

I saw a funeral—a very fancy funeral—making its way SE along the Canal Street Canal towards some cemetery in Brooklyn. Picture seven black Kanoye cabin cruisers purring along all in a row. I'm talking seven twenty-two-foot-long pitch-black boats, each powered by a GE 186 KW "Cat." The sun shone on the silver cross on the prow of the lead ship, a floating hearse. Riding high in the stern, a gleaming black impermium coffin; silver handles and the biggest wreath you ever saw, roses and white hydrangeas.

Teddy Petrakis to Johnny Baker, July 21, 2054:

"O Death, where is thy sting?" (1 Cor. 15:55)

Johnny Baker to Teddy Petrakis, July 21, 2054:

In the same old place.

Jeanette Baker to Johnny Baker, August 1, 2054:

This is the longest we've ever been apart. The house is empty without you. I miss your deep voice, which sounds so much like my poor Daddy's. I miss your musky smell, the beard sprouting all over your face—your physical *maleness,* which also reminds me of Daddy, whom you've more than replaced in my life. Gynarchist or not, I love having a son. You're part of me. I can't imagine the world without you. Hell, I even miss your unmade bed and the dirty underpants you leave on your bedroom floor.

I miss your moods. Why are adolescents so angry all the time? I was always depressed. But mostly, I miss the way you think; I miss sharing, via your drawings, the unexpected things you see with your mind's eye.

Counting the days till we're together again,

Love, Mother

Johnny Baker to Jeanette Baker, August 6, 2054:

I miss you, too.

Jeanette Baker to Johnny Baker, August 20, 2054:

I know you're busy working and I don't wanna bother you, but drop me a line when you get the chance, let me know how you are. If you don't, I understand. I can wait. Only twelve more days till we're together again.

Johnny Baker to Jeanette Baker, September 1, 2054:

Dear Mother,

I'm writing you from the Salmacis Gender Reassignment Clinic in Havana, where I've had a transgenic mastogenesis costing $7040 which I earned by working as a sex slave last summer in NYC. I'm growing tits like Billy Lee Mookerjee so I can become his sheila and gain Gaian Consciousness.

Good-bye! Forgive me!

Your loving son, Johnny

Polly Baker

Jeanette showed me Johnny's letter, saying, "This is the thanks I get." Then she sobbed and sobbed.

From Jeanette Baker's journal, September 4, 2054:

Thank God for Endcrave!

My disappointment with Johnny goes way beyond the merely personal. By becoming a she-he, he's betrayed our political principles. He's made himself a willing dupe of the American phallocratic establishment. As an educated Gynarchist, Johnny knows phallocracy encourages transgenderism—particularly male-femayle transgenderism—because transgenderism reduces the femayle body to an appropriable object.

Mookerjee's home page puts him in Washington, D.C., where undoubtedly Johnny has gone.

He's a minor. I'd be within my rights to have the cops bring him home. But I won't. For some time now, I've had the feeling that Johnny's living out a truly original destiny, with which I'm powerless to interfere.

Sri Billy Lee Mookerjee

On Sunday, September 6, 2054, I was leading the morning service in the Gaian Wimin's Cooperative Shelter on Euclid Street and Sherman Avenue in Washington, D.C. It was a tough time in my life. I was going on thirty-six and all alone. My sheila, Alfred Howe, had recently walked out on me because he hadn't gained Gaian Consciousness. I thought maybe it was my fault. Spreading Gaian Consciousness was my life's work, and I was no damn good at it!

That was pretty much my state of mind that morning, when into the shelter walks Johnny, who joins me singing "My Motherworld." I was moved that he knew Srimaati's words by heart.

Katherine G. Jackson

My Motherworld
A Gaian Vision Song

O, my Motherworld,
I love you
More and more
Each passing day.
Let me share your
Life eternal
While I make my
Mortal way.[26]

Sri Billy Lee Mookerjee

Johnny threw himself at my feet, saying, "I'm growing tits, Srimaanji! And a beard! I wanna be like you in everything! Make me your sheila, Srimaanji! Help me gain Gaian Consciousness!"

---

26. Words and music by Brianna Andrews, Motherworld Publishing, 2031.

I tested his determination to persevere in his spiritual quest by answering "No."

Johnny Baker to Teddy Petrakis, October 4, 2054:

For almost a month, I've been eking out a living as a manual street artist—a portraitist—around Capitol Keep, in D.C. I charge my two or three daily customers (mostly Chinese tourists) $65 apiece for an idealized black-and-white (charcoal) likeness of themselves. The sugary portraits are crap, and teach me nothing, but to tell the truth, I draw them too slow to make any real money.[27] The competition is fierce, particularly from a well-organized gang of young West African immigrants who each churn out six or seven slick portraits a day.

Art supplies—charcoal pencil, vine charcoal, 13" x 19" sheets of Canson ingress paper at $5.50 each, which I cut in half, and fixative—run me about $45 a week.

I eat for free—ripe manna for the picking, right off the trees—in the Franklin Square Public Orchard. The stuff constipates me. What I wouldn't give for a pepperoni pizza!

I share a room at the Y for $114 a night. Tonight's roommate, you'll be glad to hear, is a Methodist minister from Birmingham, Ala. He averted his baby blues when I undressed.

My enlarged nipples are spongy and broken out in tiny bumps, like soft sandpaper. One day I'm sore under both armpits; the next, beneath one tit. Both are already bigger than golf balls and growing fast.

Billy Lee's visiting London. Every evening, with my heart in my mouth, I check his home page for fear she's chosen someone else to be his sheila.

From Jeanette Baker's journal, October 22, 2054:

A sleepless night. This morning at work, Polly outlined my three possibilities:

1. Hire a sect deprogrammer to kidnap Johnny and deprogram him. (Can't afford it.)

2. Go to D.C. and beg him to come home. (Don't think I'm able.)

27. Not one of the estimated thirty charcoal street portraits produced by JFB during this period has been located.

3. Adopt a wait-and-see policy for six months—which is what I've decided to do.

Jeanette Baker to Johnny Baker, October 25, 2054:

Happy Birthday!

I can't believe you're seventeen! It seems like yesterday that I gave a final push and there you were. I remember your first cry and the midwife holding you up between my legs, still attached to me by your umbilical cord. You looked like you were covered with runny white cheese. Your head was a little squished. I held you in my arms and kissed the tiny purple soles of your unused feet.

Enough! I won't bore you with a mother's memories.

Polly and I have added $500 to your cash card. Use it any way you see fit.

So your guru's in Rio with his (her?) guru, "Ma" Andrews.

Emma: "The word is, they're lovers."

I'm now exclusively immerse-sexual. I'm more comfortable with a virtual lover than an actual one. In case you haven't noticed, I have trouble expressing love.

Be that as it may, I love you. Please come home!

Johnny Baker to Jeanette Baker, October 25, 2054:

I love you, too, but can't come home. I'm out to gain Gaian Consciousness.

Thanks for the money. Thank Polly, too. I used $155 of it to buy myself a much-needed 40-B bra. I love how my tits have a life of their own. They swing to the right when I take a step with that foot, jiggle a bit up and down, then when I step down on the left foot, do the same on that side. My nipples are still slightly sore.

Having tits makes me feel closer to you than ever before.

From John Firth Baker's interview in *The International Review of Manual Art:*

The chill in the air and rainy weather ended my career as a street artist. I made a scratchboard drawing of my rapidly developing breasts and used it to go into a better-paying line of work.

John Firth Baker's online advertisement at transgender.238, October 25, 2054:

Hi! I'm Johnny, a 17-year-old she-he. My boobs look like this:

They are available for tit play. I'm also growing my first beard. I'm yours by the hour in greater D.C. Cash only, please. Special travel rates. You supply the place, I supply the unique me. Uncut, all inoculations attested. Contact titsboy@transgender.238

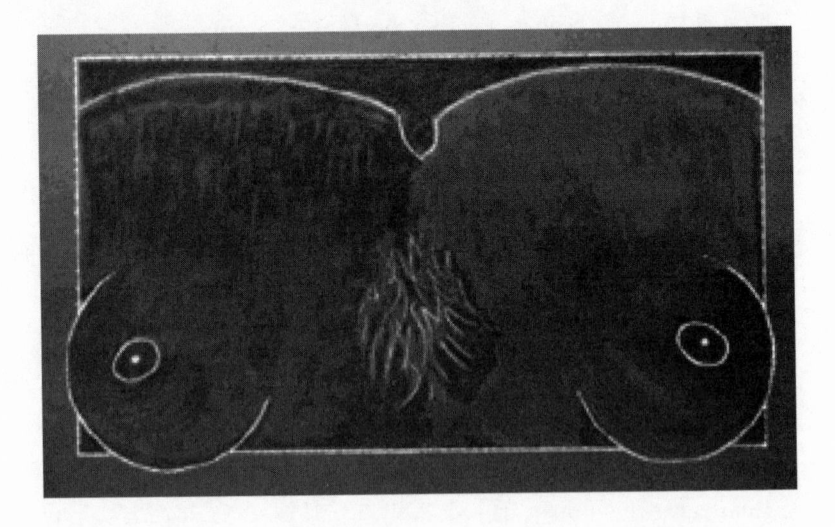

Online ad, 2054, scratchboard drawing

From John Firth Baker's interview in *The International Review of Manual Arts:*

The first day, thanks to my ad, I turned two tricks at $850 apiece. That evening I bought myself a steak dinner and a good bottle of California red, which set me back two hundred and ninety bucks, then took a room for the night at the Truman.

Nearly a quarter of all hits on my ad were from business-class types desperate to rent me for an hour—but only on the sly. So I rented a furnished one-bedroom apartment, with all utilities, and night air-conditioning for $2420 a month in a straight—mostly white—skilled working-class neighborhood near Washington Circle, a block or so northeast of the Flooded Zone.

I averaged two tricks a day, seven days a week. My tits were squeezed, cupped, kneaded, rubbed, kissed, bit, and stroked; my nipples, licked, sucked, kissed, tweaked, nibbled, plucked, pulled, and twirled.

I was in seventh heaven.

From Sri Billy Lee Mookerjee's Home Page, Wednesday, October 28, 2054:

Washington, D.C. Saturday is one of my favorite Gaian holidays. Halloween for us Gaians marks the Earth's New Year, the midpoint between the Autumn Equinox and Winter Solstice.

The First Church of Gaia in D.C. will celebrate the Gaian New Year by throwing a traditional Halloween apple-bobbing party for neighborhood children at the Gaian Wimin's Cooperative Center on Euclid Street and Sherman Avenue. Join me there Saturday, 5 P.M. Give the kids a good time—and have fun! Welcome our Motherworld's New Year!

Sri Billy Lee Mookerjee

Johnny came up to me at the beginning of the party and said, "Make me your sheila, Srimaanji," and again I told him, "No."

A neighborhood girl of about seven eyed us and asked, "Is you guys Mommies or Daddies?"

I said, "Both," and Johnny went, "Yeah, we're both."

The girl took Johnny by the hand. I watched him teach her to catch an apple between her teeth. Both got soaked, and laughed and laughed.

I overheard Johnny asking her, "Do you like to draw?"

"Oh, yeah," she said. "Lots."

Then I had a brainstorm and said to Johnny, "Draw me as if you were a little kid again."

From John Firth Baker's interview in *The International Review of Manual Art:*

I spent over eighteen hundred bucks turning my little living room into a drawing studio. I bought a secondhand drafting table, a stool, a lamp, pencils, erasers, charcoal, felt-tipped pens, India ink, sable brushes, an ounce of white opaque watercolor, and twelve sheets of 19" × 26" lanalaid printmaking paper at twelve fifty a sheet.

And all the time I wondered, How the hell do I draw like a little kid again?

The answer came to me soon as I started work: *with my left hand!* To my surprise, I drew with my left hand in a childlike style that resembles Jean Dubuffet's.

Portrait of Billy Lee Mookerjee, 2054, paper cutout, ink, watercolor, structural paint on paper. Collection Billy Lee Mookerjee

Sri Billy Lee Mookerjee to Johnny Baker, November 12, 2054:

Congratulations! Your drawing of me does indeed look like it was done by a gifted child. That's only the beginning. If you want to be my sheila and gain Gaian Consciousness, you must become like a child again in all things. A little child. A baby. *My* baby, utterly dependent on me. I will be your father and your mother. Through me you'll be reborn.

Johnny Baker to Sri Billy Lee Mookerjee, November 12, 2054:

That's for me!

Sri Billy Lee Mookerjee to Johnny Baker, November 12, 2054:

John Firth Baker, I take you as my sheila.

Johnny Baker to Sri Billy Lee Mookerjee, November 12, 2054:

Command me.

Sri Billy Lee Mookerjee to Johnny Baker, November 12, 2054:

Give up sex, including raising the dead. No more booze or drugs for you. Over the weekend give everything you own, except your Mentor and the clothes on your back, to the Salvation Army.

And then report to me 5 A.M. Monday at the shelter.

From Jeanette Baker's journal, November 16, 2054:

Mookerjee on his home page today:

"I'm pleased to announce I've taken John Firth Baker, 17, as my sheila. Johnny has dropped out of high school and abandoned a promising career as a manual artist to devote himself to my service in her pursuit of Gaian Consciousness."

Numb at the news.

Wakinoya Yoshiharu

Fritz hit the roof when he read about Johnny.

Johnny Baker to Teddy Petrakis, November 16, 2054:

Three times today, for two minutes on each breast, Srimaanji dry-nursed me in his office at the Gaian Cooperative Wimin's Shelter. My sucking will stimulate his breasts to produce milk.

Johnny Baker to Teddy Petrakis, November 20, 2054:

Srimaanji's milk tastes like sugar water.

> Sweet union!
> I have drunk my fill,
> And fused with
> My Guru's will.[28]

Oh, Teddy, I've never been so happy.

Johnny Baker to Teddy Petrakis, November 23, 2054:

No wonder there's talk about moving the government to Omaha (!) or Marquette [Michigan]. Yesterday's storm surge that flooded the Lincoln Memorial left behind a stink of raw sewage mixed with stagnant seawater. And the roaches and rats! Last night in the shelter, a humongous gray rat scampered out from under my cot and out the hall door. I couldn't sleep a wink afterwards.

I work eight hours a day, seven days a week, in the Shelter's kitchen, serving manna soup, manna salad, manna pie, fried manna, boiled manna, steamed manna, roast manna, etc. etc, to the thirty-six femayle noahs and their brats, flooded out of their squats in the last eight years. They live here permanently. I can only take little kids in small doses. Their constant demands drive me up the wall.

Sure am a born keepie. I can't get used to the rough, cracked, weathered complexions of the older wimin—black or white. The black faces are the color of ashes and look dead.

Most bore me stiff. The only thing they talk about, besides their bowel movements, is hitting the lottery. They discuss their bowel movements because an all-manna diet is so fucking constipating. The whole American underclass must be constipated. My constipation has given me piles.

---

28. Words and music by Brianna Andrews, Motherworld Publishing, 2037.

Shanga Shirvington

Shit, Johnny was a she-he, and a she-he be a freak to me. Ugh! All the same, I must own he had nice tits.

Ol' Johnny Baker, I really liked him. For a short while, white or no, he was both sister and brother to me. I was fifteen when we met. That was in the K Street Shelter, where I lived alone after my auntie Coralie done passed at seventy-four. She passed on the street in my arms. August heat killed her. She and me, we used to live outta the weather between Fort Totten and West Hyattsville in the ol' Green Line Metro tunnel. Swarm a tunnel bunnies drove us topside; tunnel bunnies be rats to you.

There was rats big as cats in the shelter, too. Whenever Johnny see one, he scream, "Mama!"

From Jeanette Baker's journal, December 1, 2054:

Dreamed last night I visited Johnny in D.C. Pleaded with him to come home with me. But, of all things, a large and repulsive gray rabbit, with coarse, filthy fur, hopped across the floor between us.

Johnny, very scared, whispered, "That's a bad sign!"

The dream ruined my day.

Johnny Baker to Teddy Petrakis, December 4, 2054:

I now nurse twice a day on Srimaanji's sweet, blue-white milk, which cured my constipation. I often doze off at Srimaanji's breast for a few minutes. When I wake, I'm calm for hours.

Teddy Petrakis to Johnny Baker, December 25, 2054:

Merry Christmas!

Johnny Baker to Teddy Petrakis, December 25, 2054:

Last night, Srimaanji initiated me into the mysteries of Mamagon Gaia, who is revered in Japan. *Mamagon* is Japanese for "monster mother." Mamagon Gaia personifies both the creative and the destructive aspects of our Motherworld. Her song goes:

My womb is full,
My tits are too.
The life I bear
I soon will chew.[29]

My initiation into Mamagon Gaia's mysteries was held underground near L'Enfant Plaza, in an abandoned station of the old Metro Orange Line. Water water everywhere but not a drop to drink. Rats, though, and busted cinder blocks, broken pipes, dripping walls, the crunch of roaches underfoot, rusted tracks, and a stench of piss you wouldn't fuckin' believe.

The initiation ceremony was secret. All I can reveal is what you won't like. Teddy, the truth is, I'm an idol worshiper. I worshiped Mamagon Gaia in the form of a badly carved wooden statue. The initiation was disgusting. More I'm not allowed to say.

Merry Christmas.

Shanga Shirvington

When Johnny come back to the shelter Christmas Eve, he sneaked a stiff drink.

Sri Billy Lee Mookerjee

I can reveal this much: part of the initiation into Mamagon Gaia's mystery involves certain deliberately repellent acts that help the initiate identify with the elementally destructive—the all-devouring—aspect of our Motherworld.

Teddy Petrakis to Johnny Baker, December 28, 2054:

My dear boy, worship Gaia in any form you want, but do it fervently. Fear her and love her with all your heart, with all your soul, and all your might. Think of her day and night. But above all, consider her beginning and her end. And sooner or later, by God's grace, you'll seek out her Creator and worship Him with the same fervor.

Happy New Year!

---

29. Words and music by Brianna Andrews, Motherworld Publishing, 2040.

The Reverend Theodore Petrakis

In the fall of my junior year at Oberlin, I got the call to preach the Gospel. I believed—I still believe—as Margaret Boeth says, that religious fervor unlocks the meaning of life.[30] I prayed that Johnny would become a fervent idolater so that God could then harvest his fervor for Himself.

Johnny Baker to Jeanette Baker, January 1, 2055:

Happy New Year!

Jeanette Baker to Johnny Baker, January 1, 2055:

Happy New Year!

Are you drawing?

Johnny Baker to Jeanette Baker, January 1, 2055:

Srimaanji forbids me to draw. He commands me to look at things for their own sake, not to fix them on paper. "The world," he says, "is made up of an infinite series of creative acts."

He invented a spiritual exercise especially for me. Once a day, for half an hour, I gaze at something as if for the first time—like a baby. It's very hard work. Today I focused on a cheap glass salt shaker with a dented blue tin top. As always, the longer I looked the more I saw. Only at the end, I noticed the pattern of the fifteen holes punched in the top. Fourteen were arranged in a circle within a pentagon; the last hole was in the center. I could go on and on about the salt shaker. I catch myself looking at everything through fresh eyes.

Nina May Randolph

Johnny Baker saved my little girl, Violet, from a bad beating—maybe much worse. It's a long story, but worth telling. What happened was this. My boyfriend, Bud Claypool, beat my seven-year-old black and blue every chance he got. Bud drunk rye whiskey; he takes a drink, then whacks Violet cross her face. He calls the whack "my chaser."

The poor baby! Things got so that soon as Violet seen Bud reach-

30. See Margaret Boeth, "The Blood-Dimmed Tide," *Collected Sermons,* (sermon delivered March 25, 2035), Princeton, N.J.: J. Edwards Press, 2040:85. (40–Bo426)

ing for his bottle, she made a dash for the door. Bud was after her like a shot. "Whoopee! Lookit me!" he yells. "I'm chasin' my chaser!"

Oh, he was a funny one!

I once got between them, and Bud grabbed me by the hair and drug me round the floor, wrenching my neck and scraping the skin off'n my back. What could I do after that? Bud drunk rye and beat Violet something terrible. Thanksgiving day, he busted her nose with the back of his hand. Oh, the blood!

Then he taunts me, "Don't you feel awful you can't stop me? Some mother who can't protect her own little girl!"

Time after time, he beat my baby up and taunted me. "You some fucking lousy mother to lemme do this to your own flesh and blood!"

One morning pretty soon after the New Year, Bud got dead drunk, passed out under the table, and lays there like a dog turd in the gutter. I run for it with Violet to Billy Lee's Shelter for Wimin, on Euclid Street and Sherman Avenue, which I seen on the web that fall. I figured a man with tits might take kindly to kids, and I weren't wrong.

Can't say the same for Johnny. Tits and all, he was a big baby hisself, 'specially around Billy Lee, who was both Ma and Pa to him—more Ma than Pa, if you get my drift. Leastways, so the wiminfolks in the Shelter told me. Man nurses boy! I never heard the like before.

That first day I could see Johnny was peeved by Billy Lee's attention to Violet. Fact is, Johnny sulked and pouted like *he* was the seven-year-old. But first thing in the morning, when Billy Lee tells Johnny, "Take Violet to the Howard University Children's Clinic for a checkup," Johnny says, "Right away!"

Naturally, I go along.

Well, sir, the minute the three of us step out the front door into the pouring rain, Bud rears up in front of us and makes a grab for Violet. Who knows how he knowed where we was!

I recollect what happened next in, like, slow motion. Violet screamed, I froze, but Johnny, with his head down, throwed hisself in Bud's way. The top of Johnny's head clobbered Bud smack in the mouth; Bud's teeth split open his lower lip and Johnny's scalp. Talk about blood! Did you know that spilt blood turns pink in the rain?

The rest is a blur, except for Bud; I seen him cut and run towards Fairmont Street, one hand over his mouth, bleeding all the way.

Johnny Baker to Teddy Petrakis, January 8, 2055:

My scalp's healing. (Can't believe I was so brave!) Violet hasn't spoken a word since the attack. Doctors say she needs psychorobotic therapy.

With Claypool still on the loose, Nina May (Violet's mother) won't set foot outside the shelter for fear that he'll waylay them again. Srimaanji, who knows everybody, took the matter up with the Capitol Hags, a local Gynarchist underground action squad, some of whom are also Gaians.

Sri Billy Lee Mookerjee

No comment.

Johnny Baker to Teddy Petrakis, January 16, 2055:

Srimaanji tells me Claypool's been "fixed"—but won't let on what that means.

Johnny Baker to Teddy Petrakis, January 19, 2055:

Get this: The Capitol Hags "fixed" Claypool with two manipulated sets of regulatory genes that control production of vasopressin and oxytocin, a couple of hormones released in the blood during sex and childbirth. The genes will make the s.o.b. constantly produce very high levels of both hormones, and freak him out, like Srimaanji says, with "an insatiable craving" to nurture little kids.

How 'bout them apples?

Teddy Petrakis to Johnny Baker, January 20, 2055:

But of the fruit of the tree which is the midst of the garden, God hath said, of them apples, ye shall not eat.

Johnny Baker to Teddy Petrakis, January 20, 2055:

Ha! Ha!

Teddy Petrakis to Johnny Baker, January 20, 2055:

Ha! Ha! yourself. This is no laughing matter. Involuntary genetic manipulation is a grave sin.

From Jeanette Baker's journal, January 24, 2055:

Me: (tonight, 11:50 P.M.): Johnny, you awake? I miss you. If you're awake, let's have a look at you.

Johnny: Here I am, Mother.

Me: You're looking good, Johnny.

Johnny: Tits and all?

Me: Tits and all. Johnny, I want you to know, I'm paying your monthly apprenticeship dues for the Guild—just in case you come home.

Johnny: Good night, Mother.

Johnny Baker to Teddy Petrakis, February 6, 2055:

All this morning, Claypool knelt on the street outside the shelter, weeping and pulling his hair and going something like, "Forgive me, Violet Randolph, and if you can find it in your heart, give me the chance to make up to you what I done. Lemme take care of you or I'll die."

Nina May yelled out the window, "Ah, blow it out your ass!"

This whole business makes me proud to be a Gynarchist.

Am stuck on the road to Gaian Consciousness. I still don't *feel* any personal connection between myself and our living Motherworld. Srimaanji says submit to him in all things and Gaian Consciousness will come to me.

Johnny Baker to Jeanette Baker, March 22, 2055:

A few hours ago the late afternoon sky caught my eye—the red sun half-covered by a dark purple cloud with a bright red border. A lemon-yellow streak below it slowly turned green, then blue, but with the green mixed in it—a cerulean blue.

The colors got me thinking of the paint box you gave me and your hopes for me to paint masterpieces. I'm sorry to disappoint you. My goal is to awaken spiritually to our planetary destiny.

Johnny Baker to Teddy Petrakis, March 31, 2055:

Bud Claypool showed up this morning at the door of the shelter with a cuddly Winnie the Poohbot as a gift for Violet. It stretches out its stubby arms and cries in the cutest voice, "Roses are red, I know Violet is blue. Let me make it up to you. Love, Bud."

Nina May said, "Fuck off!"

Teddy Petrakis to Johnny Baker, May 10, 2055:

See this?

GOOD SAMARITAN SLAIN TRYING
TO PREVENT CHILD ABUSE

WASHINGTON, D.C. May 10. An unemployed former exoduster from Oklahoma City, Robert "Bud" Claypool, 28, was stabbed to death this morning by Lee McKibben, 32, an electrician, when the former tried to prevent McKibben from beating his daughter Hannah, 8, with a wire hanger.

"Bud tried to interfere, so Lee stabbed him in the chest with a kitchen knife," said a witness, who refused to identify herself. McKibben is under arrest. Hannah, whose mother Anita, 27, was found drunk at the scene, was placed in the care of the Washington, D.C., Municipal Children's Shelter.

Johnny Baker to Teddy Petrakis, May 10, 2055:

Am still proud to be a Gynarchist.

Sri Billy Lee Mookerjee

Johnny showed an interest in geophysiology, the workings of our Motherworld. To further his education, I accepted an invitation for us to attend an actual conference on planetary reproduction hosted by the Japanese Earth Scientists Association, which was meeting in Tokyo in early June. Johnny was raring to go to Japan; he hoped to meet her biological father, who was head of the Ozaki Institute of Humin Metamorphic Genetics in Kyoto.

Johnny Baker to Jeanette Baker, June 6, 2055:

Dear Mother,

Tokyo University *Shiro* (keep). The Japanese call their never-ending rain "night-sweats" from a line in Miyoko Nakaya's famous poem "Global Warming":

> Earth is feverish,
> drenched in night-sweats:
> torrential rain.[31]

Speaking of poets, a young friend of Clorene Welles, the exogenetic botanist Irene Winters, gave a talk here today on terraforming Mars. I couldn't take my eyes off her face. She looks like an African work of art. Gossip is she goes both ways. How's Emma?

Yesterday morning, I spoke with Plowman's secretary, Wakinoya Yoshiharu, in Kyoto, who sends you his regards. I'll bet that once upon a time he was a pretty boy.

Made a date to see Plowman in his office a week from this coming Wednesday, the 16th, at noon. Gulp! My father! At long last! I can hardly believe it! I'm counting the days. What to wear? What to wear? My hair's in good shape and my beard is very much in style here. Van Dykes, three-day-old beards, shaggy beards—everything except wispy Chinese Mandarin beards—are popular. The in look is an unshaven, out-of-work, down-at-the-heels, 17th-century Samurai, which I find very attractive.

Japanese men are hot. Physical fitness is all the rage. The favorite outdoor teenage sport is off-road rain biking. Believe it or not, it looks

31. Miyoko Nakaya, *Collected Poems*, trans. Myra Lotto, San Francisco: Kami Press, 2042, 158. (42–NaLo7)

like fun!!! Never thought I'd say that about a sport, did you? But Srimaanji is encouraging me to get more physical exercise.

I miss you. Love to Polly.

Your loving son, Johnny

P.S. After the Conference ends next Saturday, Srimaanji and I will vacation for the rest of the summer in Kyoto as the guests of his friend the Gaian guru Sodo Yokoyama.

Johnny Baker to Jeanette Baker, June 9, 2055:

Dear Mother,

The Gender War here claims an average of 90 lives a year—men and wimin. The phallocratic terrorists call themselves Thunder Gods in honor of the kamikaze suicide pilots ("Thunder Gods") from the second half of the Global Tribal War. They are fanatically tribal and anti-Chinese. Naturally, the Gynarchist Isle of Wimin Movement is staunchly anti-tribal but—being Japanese—is also fiercely anti-Chinese.

They're currently killing each other over the Yasukuni Shrine in the heart of Tokyo, where the spirits of the kamikaze are worshiped. The Isle of Wimin Movement tried to blow up the shrine twice in the last year. Four of the attacking wimin and three of the defending phallocrats died in these attempts.

Johnny Baker to Jeanette Baker, June 12, 2055:

Dear Mother,

Thank you, thank you, thank you for the rain suit and socks! It must have set you back a bundle. Rain suits (and socks) cost a fortune here. (Everything costs a fortune here!) I immediately rented a bike and gave my new outfit a try. It's cut short in front so it doesn't bunch up. The hood fits neatly under my helmet, though it obstructs my vision when I look over my shoulder. Still, there's nothing like being warm and dry while riding off-road in a torrential downpour! Thanks again!

Four more days till I meet Plowman! Tomorrow Srimaanji's taking me shopping on the Ginza for a Kabuki kimono, which is very fashionable this year.

Johnny Baker to Indira Rabindra, June 14, 2055:

I thought of you today, while visiting a manual book publisher in Edo Keep, near Tokyo, whose population lives and works in a picture-perfect copy of a 17th-century Japanese village, which was built without nails by Zen Manualists. The publisher, whose name is Akiko Yosano, prints books by hand on blocks of cherry wood, a process that takes months. Yosano believes that even old-fashioned movable type can't capture the essence of flowing Japanese script and doesn't make an artistic effect. A professional calligrapher copies the manuscript on sheets of handmade rice paper, which are then pasted on the wood blocks. The wood is carved away to preserve the handwritten script. The blocks are then printed in woodblock style and the pages printed. Illustrated books were a revelation to me. Each is what you say a book should be: a well-made artifact, not just an electronic replicator of words and images. I love feeling the texture of the rice paper! And what a wonderful smell the pages have: a mixture of fresh ink and glue! I'd give anything to own a Yosano masterpiece. She let me handle her prized reprint of the 17th-century classic novel *The Great Mirror of Male Love,* by Ihara Saikaku, which was illustrated by Shundo Hara. Maybe someday I'll illustrate a book for Yosano. Anyway, like I said, I thought of you and your collection.

Best, Johnny

Johnny Baker to Teddy Petrakis, June 14, 2055:

Srimaanji and I are living under the weather in a small, leaky frame house in Kyoto near the Shinsen-en Sacred Spring Garden. Our host, and Srimaanji's dear friend, is the head of the Japanese OnLine Church of Gaia, the Rev. Guru Sodo Yokoyama. He speaks perfect English. Today she took me by the arm and went, "A sheila (he pronounces it 'sheira') is like a good piece of wood, and a master guru is like a carpenter. Even good wood won't show its fine grain unless worked on by a good carpenter. Even a warped piece of wood in the hands of a good carpenter shows the results of good craftsmanship. Whether you turn out to be a good piece of wood or a warped one, you're in the hands of a master carpenter, your esteemed guru, Srimaanji Mookerjee. Obey him in all things, and you will gain Gaian Consciousness."

Yokoyama-san teaches that you gain Gaian Consciousness by meditating on what he calls "Gaia's face"—the natural world in any and all of its manifestations.

His new sheila, Jukishi Wakayama, aged 26, and I speak through autotranslators. Jukishi's been trying to gain Gaian Consciousness for the last two years. He's the eldest son of a rich pawnbroker who owns a shop in downtown Kyoto. Teddy, get this: she told me, "Three years ago, I quit my father's business when I read in the Christian Bible, 'For what shall it profit a man if he shall gain the whole world and lose his own soul?' "

Jukishi's old man is madder than hell because his eldest son and heir became a Gaian guru's sheila—although he admits that having a she-he son whose yang and yin are in perfect balance has brought him good luck (i.e., lots of business).

Twice a day, Jukishi and I nurse at the same time in opposite corners of a tiny room. The patter of rain on the tile roof makes me sleepy. Jukishi spends three hours a day in the little overgrown backyard garden meditating on a tall, scraggly *sakaki* tree. The *sakaki* tree is a sacred evergreen whose shiny-topped leaves supposedly attract gods to light on its branches. Jukishi's mantra is a Japanese translation of the poem "On Seeing Weather Beaten Trees," by Adelaide Crapsey, a 20th-century American poet who influenced Clorene Welles:

> Is it as plainly in our living shown,
> By slant and twist, which way the wind hath
> blown?[32]

32. *The Collected Poems of Adelaide Crapsey,* edited, with an introduction by Clorene Welles, New York: Parnassus Press, 2048:131. (48–CRWE25)

Jukishi's cute, and I know he feels the same about me, but it's hands off for both of us! Man, am I horny!

Johnny Baker to Teddy Petrakis, June 15, 2055:

I meet my father tomorrow morning at ten. How do I address him? I can't call him Dad. I know that he doesn't think of me as his son. I'm just one of three subjects in one of his famous genetic experiments. And yet, and yet . . .Teddy, help me!

Teddy Petrakis to Johnny Baker, June 15, 2055:

And yet, and yet you hope he'll call you, "My boy, my son!" The same with me.

Why this longing in the humin soul for a father? Is there a gene for it, do you suppose? I like to think our Heavenly Father implanted the need in us so we'd turn to Him.

Sri Billy Lee Mookerjee

Johnny was so nervous that morning about meeting his father, he threw up his breakfast.

Jukishi Wakayama

I remember how sexy Johnny looked in his new red, white, and blue patchwork Kabuki-style robe. And his matching umbrella with the bone handle! I remember that well.

Wakinoya Yoshiharu

Fritz got drunk the night before his meeting with Johnny. It was a tough time for him. Remember that in the fall of '53, Ishtar Teratol's victory over Chess Maven had won Fritz and the Ozaki Institute a huge GE contract to design a genome that would enlarge the inferior parietal lobe of a humin brain, giving it the wherewithal to create a Theory Of Everything. Since then, he and his team had been working round the clock with not much luck on Operation TOE-Head.

Fritz was also under great pressure from the Board of Directors—

sixteen rich, old Japanese men, all except two born in the last century. And every one a phallocratic tribalist. They wanted Fritz to enhance the genome of a Japanese male who would be the one to solve the riddle of the universe and make us masters of space and time. If you ask me, those big shots were jealous of him.

Poor Fritz! He felt alone and threatened. He was also pushing fifty; his youth was over. Sure, his Capablanca metamorph had been a great success. But the results weren't in yet on Ozaki's Project, the experiment he'd made in honor of his one true love. Make no mistake. Fritz is a romantic.

Where was I? Oh, yes. Nadia Kammerovska was dead, and Yukio Tanaka had long since stopped drawing, so he now pinned his hopes on this seventeen-year-old kid, who stopped making art to become the disciple of a Gaian religious nut.

Last but not least—and don't laugh—Fritz was mourning the death of his twenty-year-old yellow-naped Amazon parrot, Sozoshii. The bird had been a gift to Fritz from Ozaki-san. Fritz and that bird were crazy about each other. Sozoshii had an English vocabulary of twenty or thirty words and simple phrases. Sometimes when I was out of her sight, she called out my name in Fritz's voice. She only did it occasionally, so I always took the bait and answered "Yes?" She never answered, and I'd feel like a fool. Make no mistake. It's infuriating to be humiliated by a bird.

Sozoshii was never sick a day in her life. Then, without warning one March night, she keeled over from a mutated form of mycobacteriosis—avian TB. She dropped dead off her perch before Fritz's eyes. There were no last words.

Johnny Baker to Jeanette Baker, June 16, 2055:

Plowman insists I call him "Fritz." He sends you his regards. So does his secretary—what's his name—an aging pretty boy who uses too much makeup. Fritz told me to tell you his pet parrot died recently. He feels bad because, with all his scientific know-how, he couldn't protect her from a deadly new bacteria.

He asked why I want to gain Gaian Consciousness. I said, "To overcome my fear of death." He said, "The fear of death is the beginning of wisdom," and for the first time, we looked across his desk into each other's eyes, which are the same shade of blue.

We talked about Nadia and her murder. He told me about Yukio Tanaka, the third arsogenic metamorph in Ozaki's Project. You once met his mother. Fritz showed me a drawing Yukio made at the age of thirteen—twelve by the way we count. It's the face of a storm demon called a Thunder God. Yukio also did the calligraphy.

I envy the way he integrated the words and the image. The Thunder God is the last drawing Yukio ever made. He quit art after his father died of a heart attack. Yukio won't say why he gave it up. He lives with his mother in Tokyo. She's a caregiver in an old age home. Yukio's apprenticed to a portable shrine maker. I'd like to meet him. Fritz will try and arrange it.

Fritz asked if I was doing any drawing myself nowadays.

I said, "Not at the moment" and he said, "That's a pity."

He asked to see an example of my work.

I can't get Yukio's drawing outta my mind.

Sri Billy Lee Mookerjee

I arranged to send Plowman a copy of Johnny's drawing of me in the style of a child. He called to thank me.

He said, "Johnny draws like Jean Dubuffet," and I said, "His talent stands in the way of his gaining Gaian Consciousness. He must choose between them."

Plowman said, "Between us, you mean! Johnny must choose between you and me!"

"So it seems."

From Jeanette Baker's journal, June 28, 2055:

Momma hanged herself thirty-three years ago today.

Who was it who once said, "A suicide is a timid murderer?" Momma murdered my childhood.

Gov. Ezra Koyle of Utah, the Seer Prophet & Revelator of the

Yukio Tanaka, *Thunder God*, 2049, paper cutout, brush and ink, on paper. Collection Mariko Tanaka

Mormon Church, has declared himself a candidate for the Christian Republican presidential nomination next year. This is the man who flaunts Federal law by keeping fourteen wives ranging in age from 15 to 43.

I couldn't care less about Koyle or the mutilated Sister Lopez. All I care about is Johnny. He's breaking my heart.

Johnny Baker to Jeanette Baker, July 3, 2055:

Happy birthday, Mother! Many happy returns of the day.

Jeanette Baker to Johnny Baker, July 3, 2055:

Come home and become an artist.

Johnny Baker to Jeanette Baker, July 3, 2055:

I can't. Srimaanji says that exercising my talent prevents me from seeing the whole world as an infinite series of creative acts.

Johnny Baker to Teddy Petrakis, July 16, 2055:

Gaians say you suddenly "fall into Gaian Consciousness." Well, Srimaanji "fell" into it again last night in the backyard garden. The episode lasted three hours and twenty minutes. A little before nine o'clock, he and I were strolling down the sand path that winds among the tall grass and the reeds and mossy stones. We were hoping to hear a nightingale. The scraggly *sakaki* tree was still. I noticed the moonlight shining on some dewdrops stuck on a spiderweb that was strung between two reeds.

All of a sudden, Srimaanji goes, "I feel woozy," and her eyes roll back in his head, and she sags to the ground, with a scary grin on his face.

She lay on his stomach in the tall, wet grass to my right, and when I knelt beside her, he groaned like she was in terrible pain. I yelled for my pal Jukishi (the other sheila), who came charging out of the house and down the sand path and at every step he took—maybe four all told—Srimaanji screamed in agony.

Yokoyama-san called out to us from the doorway, "Sit down, both of you, but very gently, then don't move! Stay where you are!"

The three of us watched over Srimaanji for the next three hours. He didn't move a muscle. It was a hot, sticky night. I heard a screech-owl screech. Along about eleven, I happened to glance at the *sakaki* tree, some twenty feet away. The top branches, which are maybe twenty feet high, swayed in a breeze and Srimaanji, who you remember was *lying face down* on the grass, went, "Ah! Ah! Ahhhhh!" like she was having a pleasant dream. Then the breeze stopped, the branches just hung there, and he breathed quietly again.

By this time my backside was asleep, so I stood up very carefully, but was off balance, and to steady myself put my right foot down, with all my weight behind it, on the grass. Srimaanji screamed.

I burst out crying. At last I understand. *Srimaanji is Gaia in humin form.*

Johnny Baker to Teddy Petrakis, July 18, 2055:

For supper tonight, instead of bean curd, arum root noodles, and bamboo sprouts dressed with sweet sauce, I nursed from the breasts of the Motherworld himself.

Then we fucked.

Johnny Baker to Jeanette Baker, July 23, 2055, cc Teddy Petrakis:

Mother dear, I irrevocably renounce the gifts you bought me in order to concentrate all my energies on my spiritual development as Srimaanji's sheila. I believe that gaining Gaian Consciousness is now within my grasp because of the great spiritual progress I've made since coming with him to Japan.

I know my decision will cause you great pain, and that makes me feel guilty and sad. But I must live my own life. You want me to create art, but I've discovered that what *I* want is to experience—in Srimaanji's words—"our Motherworld creating herself."

Your loving son, Johnny

The Rev. Theodore Petrakis

Johnny called me with the news. God forgive me, I was secretly pleased that he gave up drawing. I was surprised to realize how jealous I was of his gift. Lord knows, I wish I were more creative!

Jeanette Baker to Johnny Baker, July 24, 2055:

What's happened isn't your fault; it's mine. I now see quite clearly that my inadequate mothering of you is to blame for your infatuation with the fantasy of a Motherworld. I've gotten what I deserve.

Polly Baker

Paco and I were in New York on vacation the last two weeks in July.

It was hot and crowded. We were glad to get home. The first words out of Jeanette's mouth to me were, "Oh, Polly, I'm so unhappy!"

Johnny Baker to Frederick Rust Plowman, August 1, 2055:

I've given up art to gain Gaian Consciousness. I must know why Yukio quit drawing. Was it religion? Please arrange a meeting between us.

Wakinoya Yoshiharu

Fritz was dumbfounded by Johnny's decision. Like many physical scientists, he lacked an appreciation of modern depth psychology. He had underestimated the influence of their unconscious minds in the development of his two remaining arsogenic metamorphs. Neither Yukio nor his mother had revealed the reason for the boy's renunciation of his gift. All Fritz knew was that it was connected with the sudden death of Yukio's father. Now Johnny had renounced his gift for a crackpot cult.

For the first time, Fritz saw Yukio and Johnny as complex, mysterious beings, not just the subjects of a scientific experiment. Fritz became curious about their inner lives. He asked me to set up a meeting between the two boys on condition that Johnny share with him what transpired between them. Johnny agreed.

Polly Baker

Jeanette decided to go to Johnny when he returned to the States and plead with him to resume his career as a manual artist. I agreed to help her.

So three times a week for the rest of August, Jeanette practiced leaving the keep on my arm. We walked in the evenings, when it was a little cooler.

Johnny Baker to Jeanette Baker, August 8, 2055:

Dear Mother,

Last night, I finally met Yukio Tanaka, who shares a two-room, un-air-conditioned apartment with his mother in a poor part of northeastern Tokyo called Akebane.

They had me and Fritz's secretary to supper (greasy deep-fried manna with gummy noodles and salty seaweed). Yukio put away four or five cups of chrysanthemum-scented Amae and got very red in the face.

I told Yukio I gave up drawing for my religion. He has a great esteem for Gaianism, which the Japanese call "the way of the Earth." He himself follows "the way of Japan," called Shinto. He worships many *kami*—divine beings, including "the glorious war dead," men who died fighting for the "sacred land of Japan" and became gods. I said that on principle I'm against all wars, which are in essence phallocratic tribal conflicts. He went, "Ah, so!" and poured us green tea that tasted like an old sock.

His mother kowtowed to me all night. Yukio explained that as a devout Buddhist, she considers me a living personification *(keshin)* of Jizu, a Buddhist god of compassion, who was a womin in his previous life.

Yukio is straight. What a pity! Like many Japanese men, he has short arms and legs in proportion to his yummy muscular torso. Shining black, slanted eyes, high cheekbones and beautiful white teeth. His teeth turn me on.

Yukio invited me to visit him alone at work tomorrow afternoon.

Oh, mother, don't blame yourself for what's happened. Be happy for me!

Wakinoya Yoshiharu

Yukio thanked me for introducing him to Johnny. He said he was honored to meet the esteemed young Gaian *on'yoshi,* an archaic Japanese phrase meaning a "Master of Yang and Yin," which he used rather than the common word for a she-he, *ryosei,* literally "both sexes."

Johnny Baker to Jeanette Baker, August 9, 2055:

Dear Mother,

Spent an hour this afternoon with Yukio in his workshop near Kishibojin Temple, just east of Ueno Park. He showed me around his workshop, where everything's handmade with chisels, planes, saws, brushes, etc. A strong, sweet smell from the wood shavings all over the floor.

Yukio's an apprentice lacquerer, one of eight different kinds of apprentices who make very expensive portable wooden shrines out of Japanese cypress for neighborhoods, wedding halls, offices, and homes.

We confessed to each other that we miss drawing. Yukio wouldn't say why he quit. But he wants to tell me. We're becoming friends. Tell you the truth, I have a crush on him.

From Jeanette Baker's journal, August 11, 2055:

TOP IN-NEWS STORY:

DIVA TO HEAD AMERICAN ASSOCIATION OF NATURALLY-GIFTED ARTISTS; PROCLAIMS HER VOICE A GIFT FROM GOD

Mezzosoprano Anna Stein Vows AANGA Boycott Of All American Metamorphic Artists

There once was a diva named Anna
Who defined the vox humana
As a gift from God
Who gave her the nod
To avoid metamorphic artists
Like a *Pox americana.* (limerick.831)

Johnny Baker to Teddy Petrakis, August 13, 2055:

August 13th is the day when Japanese families visit their family graves. Yukio invited me to accompany him and his Mother to the little cemetery near Tokushima University where his father is buried. I felt honored. Yukio poured water over the gravestone, burned incense, lit two red paper lanterns. He and his mother prayed. She arranged three red roses, some ferns, and a huge white chrysanthemum in a black lacquered bowl on the grave.

Yukio's father's spirit came home with us on the subway. Yukio and his mother welcomed him with a ceremony at a little family altar she keeps on a kitchen shelf. Then they offered the spirit some saki and little dishes of various foods like grilled eel, which we shared with him for lunch. (Grilled eel supposedly restores your strength sapped by the heat, which was 106 degrees at 3 P.M.)

Yukio says his father's spirit, riding on the east wind, often leaves the graveyard on its own and comes to haunt him.

Johnny Baker to Jeanette Baker, August 14, 2055:
Dear Mother,

Yukio's father, a salaryman in robotic sales, took out a forty-year loan to buy Yukio arsogenes at the Ozaki Institute. "I had no fuckin' childhood." Drawing and calligraphy lessons began at two. Yukio studied four hours a day, seven days a week, for the next nine years. But there was no pleasing his father, who often smacked Yukio across the face to discipline him. He insisted that Yukio copy Hokusai. Yukio prefers drawing from his imagination.

Yukio went, "My father was a chain smoker. One day he dropped dead of a heart attack on a Tokyo street. May the gods forgive me! I was relieved at the news. I thought, at last he's off my back. He won't hit me anymore. Now I'll draw and paint to please myself!

"The same night my father appeared to me in a dream. He said, 'So you're glad I'm dead and left wandering here in the dark! You ungrateful son! In punishment for your evil thoughts, I forbid you to draw or paint again on pain of death.' "

Am lucky to have Fritz for a father.

From Jeanette Baker's journal, August 14, 2055:

Sister Lopez has signed a multimillion-dollar book deal for her autobiography, *In the Hands of Homo Rapiens,* which details her abduction, rape, clitorectomy, and nipple amputation by TCOLAM.

She says, "All the money will go to the creation of a new Gynarchist fighting organization, to be called 'The Furies.' "

Sister Lopez: "All phallocratic religions, like Mormonism, sanction the oppression of wiminkind. The Furies dedicate themselves to a ceaseless struggle against the male gender's misogynistic tribal cults.

"FEMINIZE THE HUMIN RACE!"

From Jeanette Baker's journal, August 15, 2055:

I reread Johnny's letters every night before I go to bed. It's hard for me to accept that he's living an independent life.

Johnny Baker to Jeanette Baker, August 15, 2055:

Dear Mother,

Today was the 110th anniversary of the end of the second half of the Global Tribal War. The anniversary's a big deal here—daylong Memorial Service with Emperor at the Yasukuni Shrine. Crowd over three million, huge pyramid of yellow and white chrysanthemums, prayers to the Glorious Dead.

Yukio prayed at home to the popular favorite, Kuga Noboru. Kuga was wounded and captured by Chinese in 1931. He committed seppuku to atone for the shame of being taken prisoner. The emperor made him a god.

Yukio prayed to Kuga: "Please restore Nippon to her former imperial glory!"

Then he prayed to his father's spirit: "Leave me in peace!"

My father, going hiking in the Alps, called to say good-bye. He sends you his regards. He told me to tell you that—like you—he's sorry that I renounced my gift.

Sri Billy Lee Mookerjee

Johnny and I returned to Washington in the middle of September and put up at the K Street Shelter. We were on our spiritual honeymoon. In Japan, Johnny had learned to project upon me the attributes of our Motherworld, but he had only begun her journey to gain Gaian Consciousness. Now I had to help him experience *herself* as the Motherworld !

Johnny Baker to Jeanette Baker, September 24, 2055:

Dear Mother,

I'm back in D.C. working in the church shelter on K Street. I mop the floors, serve the meals, and obey my guru in everything. Obedience to him gives me peace of mind. Yes, I still miss drawing but, at the same time, feel immensely relieved that I no longer have to live up to your expectations for me as an artist. I was always worried about failing you. Pleasing you meant more to me than anything. That was my whole life. Now I live to gain Gaian Consciousness. Forgive me for causing you pain.

Jeanette Baker to Johnny Baker, September 24, 2055:

Arriving D.C. with Polly tomorrow noon.

Polly Baker

I booked Jeanette and me a double room for two nights at a bed and breakfast on Truman Avenue in Washington. We left our bags there and went to the shelter on K Street. Jeanette was determined to confess to Johnny that she had experimented on him as an infant in order to stimulate his brain development.

She said, "I considered him an object—not a humin being. I see now, that was an evil thing to do. I must beg his forgiveness."

You know what? I felt as guilty as Jeanette. After all, I had bank-rolled her. I was her accomplice in experimenting on her baby. The question is, Why did I do it? I've given that a lot of thought over the years. I think I did it in hopes of going down in history as the womin who helped Jeanette Baker make a visual artist to order—to create a creative humin being.

Katherine G. Jackson

At the same time, though, you mentioned earlier that you were against Jeanette setting herself above the law, the Created Equal Act. How do you square that?

Polly Baker

I can't. I was torn both ways. You know what? My desire for a little bit of immortality got the better of me.

From Jeanette Baker's journal, September 25, 2055:

Late this afternoon, I confessed to Johnny that I'm a mother–artist-maker. I told him in detail how, when he was an infant, I gave him "the lust of the eye" to implement his arsogenes.

I said: "Forgive me for experimenting on you."

Johnny: "You weren't a mother to me. What were you? A monster! I wasn't your baby. I was a thing to you. It's horrible. How could you? Weren't you ashamed? Go home! I never wanna see you again!"

Polly Baker

Next morning, Jeanette and I caught the 8:02 Chicago express. She had a panic attack boarding the train.

Sri Billy Lee Mookerjee

Johnny told me how he had been experimented on by his mother.

He said, "She didn't love me for myself. I was only a means to an end for her. What am I to you?"

"You and I are one."

From Jeanette Baker's journal, September 27, 2055:

5:15 A.M. Awake all night.

From Jeanette Baker's journal, September 28, 2055:

5 A.M. Ditto. Palpitations.

From Jeanette Baker's journal, September 29, 2055:

8:12 A.M. Overslept. Dry mouth, sweaty palms, palpitations.

Polly Baker

Since coming home, Jeanette looked like hell—there were these dark bags under her eyes—and her heart wasn't in her work.

But she said cheerily, "I'm not depressed. Polly, you gotta believe me. I'm on top of this! Put your mind at rest! Put your mind at rest!"

I remember she repeated herself a third time: "Put your mind at rest."

From Jeanette Baker's journal, October 3, 2055:

To my future readers:

My reason: "Death is the mother of Beauty; hence from her,
Alone, shall come fulfillment to our dreams
And our desires."
Wallace Stevens (1879–1955)

My method: Still (8:15 P.M.) up for grabs.

My madness: Take your pick.

My Last Will & Testament: I leave everything I own—$21,071.30 in savings, personal belongings (furniture, cookbot, VR equipment, etc.), my stainless-steel Swiss barber scissors, clippers, assorted other hair-cutting tools—to my son, John Firth Baker, whom I request to pay my aunt Polly the $1808 I owe her. I also leave to him any royalties due me from the eventual publication of this journal.

My epitaph: "I shall not wholly die." (Horace, 65–8 B.C.)

Jeanette Baker to Johnny Baker, October 3, 2055:

Darling Johnny. It's 8:31 P.M. This will be posted to you early tomorrow morning your time, so you won't be able to interfere with my plan to kill myself—I can't decide how. (2 options)

Forgive me. Good-bye my darling son—my own. I'm much nearer to you than in D.C. and so much happier. No, Johnny, I take it back. I won't beg your forgiveness—hate me!—hate me! *But open your gift—that alone will save you.*

{{{{{{{{{}}}}}}}}} (a last big hug) & XXXXXXXXX's
from your loving Mom

From Jeanette Baker's journal, October 4, 2055:

At 1:12 A.M. I looped my old black patent leather belt through its buckle around the chrome-plated clothes rack in my bedroom closet, then tested it with one good tug, which tore the buckle off. Will now (1:32) go with panty hose—à la Momma.

Sri Billy Lee Mookerjee

Johnny woke me a little after seven holding a hard copy of his mother's suicide note in her hand.

"Read this," he says and reads it again over my shoulder. First, she giggled hysterically. Then he said, "That's mother all over! I should've known!" Then she screams, "Mother! How could you do this to me?" Finally, he said, "It's my fault! I told her I never wanted to see her again!"

Polly Baker

Johnny called me around six-fifteen, local time, and Paco and I ran upstairs to Jeanette's apartment. Her bedroom door was ajar; all her shirts, skirts, and pants were piled neatly on her bed, and the clothes closet's double doors were wide open.

Jeanette's corpse, in a white bra and panties, was hanging from the middle of the chrome clothes rack. Her knees were bent. Her lower legs were sprawled out behind her on the closet floor, among some overturned shoes. Her naked feet were purple; likewise, the hands at her side. Her head was flopped on one shoulder—the left, I think. Her face was bluish gray and all bloated. Her swollen tongue protruded from her mouth.

I remember thinking, "Oh, no! Not again!" and then I called Johnny.

He was like, "I got my wish. I'll never see her again!"

Paco took charge of everything, calling the police and whatnot. I remember the cops were nervous; they didn't know what to say. One asked me to leave the bedroom while she and her partner took Jeanette down. I remember feeling guilty and angry.

You know what? I still feel guilty and angry.

Sri Billy Lee Mookerjee

I took Johnny back to Cather Keep the evening of that same day,

Monday, October 4th, 2055—one long day! We went straight to Polly's house at 124 Kuttner Street. Outside the door, Johnny turned to me and said, "I'm an orphan."

Polly Baker

The first words to me out of Johnny's mouth were, "Did you see Momma's body?"

He called her "Momma," like he did when he was a baby.

I lied and said, "No."

"I want to read the autopsy report."

Paco said, "I'll arrange it."

From: John A. Hayes jr., M.D., Associate Medical Examiner
To: John Firth Baker
Sub.: Report of Autopsy, Office of Chief Medical Examiner, City of Lincoln, Nebraska
Date: October 5, 2055

Name of Decedent: Jeanette Baker
M.E. Case No.: 219-B
Autopsy Performed by: J.A. Hayes M.D., Associate Medical Examiner

FINAL DIAGNOSES
HANGING

A. Circumferential ligature of neck (panty hose)
B. Circumferential deep ligature furrow
C. Livor mortis in glove and stocking distribution

EXTERNAL EXAMINATION

Received in a bag: 1 pair of white underwear shorts and 1 bra.

The unclothed body is that of a well-developed, well-nourished 5'4", 115 lb, white femayle, whose appearance is consistent with the reported age of 46. Muscular rigidity is past, and lividity is in the lower extremities, anterior face, and distal upper extremities ("glove and stocking" distribution).

The body is cool.

The atraumatic scalp is covered by straight, black hair, approximately 14" in length, tied up with a scrunchy hairband. The face is atraumatic. The blue iredes have dull corneae with marked bulbar and palpebral conjunctival congestion; scattered petechiae are present. The nose is atraumatic, with bloody purge issuing from nostrils. The lips show drying change. The oral cavity contains natural dentition in good repair.

Evidence of injury: Hanging

When the decedent is initially viewed, a ligature extends circumferentially around the neck; the ligature consists of tan panty hose (Juno brand, size M) the legs of which have been twisted together and tied once. The knot is positioned in the right submandibular region. When the knot is removed, the ligature furrow circumference around the neck is 11"; the uncompressed neck below the level of the ligature mark has a circumference of 13½". The ligature mark is a deep furrow, with a parchment-like base, approximately ⅝" in width to ⅞" at the greatest width (in the region of the knot). The furrow is transverse to slightly oblique rising slightly towards the right side. No other trauma is present on the neck.

Facial congestion is prominent, with scattered periorbital petechiae noted.

Johnny Baker to John A. Hayes, M.D., October 5, 2055:

Dear Doctor Hayes,

The decedent #219-B was my Mother, Jeanette Baker. Can you please tell me 1. What are periorbital petechiae? 2. Did she suffer much? 3. How long did she take to die?

John A. Hayes, M.D., to Johnny Baker, October 5, 2055:

Dear Johnny Baker,

Periorbital petechiae are tiny purplish hemorrhages surrounding the eyes.

I estimate that your Mother was unconscious within fifteen to thirty seconds and took from four to five minutes to die.

You have my deepest sympathy.

Johnny Baker to J. A. Hayes, M.D., October 5, 2055:

Thank you for your help.

Please—one thing more. What does "the blue irides have dull corneae with marked bulbar and palpebral conjunctival congestion" mean?

J. A. Hayes, M.D., to Johnny Baker, October 5, 2055:

The decedent's eyes have lost color and luster.

The Rev. Theodore Petrakis

I arrived home from Oberlin Saturday noon and went straight to Johnny, who was in a daze. During the day, everybody gathered around him at Polly's: Emma Torchlight, Alex Thomas, his mother, my mother, Indira, Ben Shrapnel, Bashy Weinberg. Oodles of people from the Hairdressers Guild plus half the Keep stopped by.

The news made the rounds late in the afternoon that the Cornhuskers had whipped Colorado 21–12.

Johnny raised his eyes to the ceiling, gave a big grin, and called out, "Ma, you hear?"

Emma Torchlight

Sitting side by side, Johnny and I talked about Jeanette. Johnny said, "Srimaanji's my mother now."

Polly Baker

Johnny recalled to me braiding Jeanette's hair one night in the kitchen some five years before. He said, "It's the happiest memory of my life."

Alex Thomas jr.

Johnny hugged me and went, "Thanks for being here." Then he said, "I can't believe this is happening."

Polly Baker

After supper Johnny, Paco, and I arranged Jeanette's funeral. Johnny decided to have her cremated and her ashes scattered around the old homestead in Cherry County—just like her mother.

Francisco (Paco) Gonzalez

Jeanette was cremated Sunday in the Scott Bluff Crematory. Monday morning, I picked up her cremains in a shiny bronze urn, which a bunch of us took out to the old Powder Horn Ranch in Cherry County.

Polly Baker

Around noon that Monday, for the second time in my life, I dumped the ashes of a family member out of a bronze urn in Cherry County. Then, like Jeanette had once done before him at the same spot, Johnny recited that bleak little poem I can never get straight.

Katherine G. Jackson

To what shall I compare my life?
Streaking west,
above Bayonne,
a jet trail at dusk.[33]

Polly Baker

The whole thing for me was like a recurrent nightmare from thirty-three years ago.

Francisco (Paco) Gonzalez

I saw Johnny kneel down and very gently, with the back of his hand, brush off a bit of his Mom's cremains that had settled on one of his shoes.

Sri Billy Lee Mookerjee

The things you remember! I remember thinking Johnny needs a haircut. And I remember looking around and feeling mighty pleased that the metamorphic "water bugs" released on the sand dunes with my blessing only two years before had irrigated them; they were covered with reddening bunch grass.

33. Welles, "After Monomoto," op. cit., p. 96.

The Rev. Theodore Petrakis

I remember Johnny saying, "I'm hungry! How can I be hungry at a time like this?"

Johnny Baker to Teddy Petrakis, October 9, 2055:

D.C.'s half flooded.
I wish I was dead.

Teddy Petrakis to Johnny Baker, October 9, 2055:

I pray for you twice a day. So does Mother, who sends all her love.

Johnny Baker to Teddy Petrakis, October 9, 2055:

Be happy your mother is alive. How I envy you! Like Welles says, "I begrudge the world its joy."[34] Been rereading her collected poems. They make me feel close to Mother. She loved them so. That reminds me. But of what? I forget. I can't think straight.

Johnny Baker to Teddy Petrakis, October 11, 2055:

Tonight Srimaanji took me to a service for Mamagon Gaia. She personifies the devouring aspect of our Motherworld, who eats us up alive. Mamagon Gaia is perpetually hungry and thirsty. Her rites are secret. I worshiped her.

Johnny Baker to Teddy Petrakis, October 13, 2055:

For the last three nights, I've had the same nightmare. I'm climbing a mossy hill—more like a huge mound of earth—under a blue, cloudless sky. A stiff wind is blowing; I hear leaves rustling in the distance. The hill is much steeper than I thought. The moss underfoot is slippery. I have to watch my step. But instead, as I climb, I keep my eyes on the bright blue sky. I reach the top and stand still, legs apart.

I dread looking at the ground beneath my feet. I know if I look down, I'll see something horrible coming out of the earth. But I can't help myself. Mother's living face, covered with moss and dirt, stares up

34. Welles, "In Memoriam: Vita," op. cit., p. 43.

at me. But her eyes are no longer blue. They've turned greenish-brown, and she has a bloody nose. I wake up panting, in a cold sweat.

Johnny Baker to Teddy Petrakis, October 15, 2055:

Last night my nightmare woke me at 3 A.M.

When I was ten, Mother taught me to rid myself of a bad dream by drawing it. I know I will never in my life be free from this new nightmare until I draw it. I woke Srimaanji and told him I must do like Mother said and open my gift. He told me if I did that, I could no longer be his shiela. I said good-bye. He wept bitterly.

Teddy Petrakis to Johnny Baker, October 16, 2055:

I'm grateful you've split with Mookerjee. He's nothing but a contemporary idolater. Gaia is his idol. Like all idolaters, he believes his idol is alive. Mookerjee's so-called church is an ancient idolatrous iniquity in a 21st-century guise.

Yet I'm also grateful to Mookerjee for awakening your religious fervor. I pray that you will now turn it to Christ.

Sri Billy Lee Mookerjee

I'm only humin; Johnny's open repudiation of our relationship was humiliating. Twice in my life now, I'd failed to keep a sheila.

Clorene Welles to Irene Winter, October 26, 2055:

My aged brain seems okay: no dizziness or blind spots in nearly a month; how's your Dad's palpitations? Better, I hope.

"If only, when you hear old age approaching, you could bolt the door!"[35]

What's the word in Utah on America's Prophet, Seer & Revelator, the great Gov. Koyle? Will the little prick run for Pres.? Ghastly thought.

You came up in my conversation yesterday with eighteen-year-old Johnny Baker; bearded, bedraggled, appeared on my doorstep because

35. Masado Kokinshu, "Old Age," *Collected Poems,* Spokane: Tagami Publishing, 2025:11. (25–Ko771)

I once wrote him: Look me up if you're ever in NYC. I'm letting him stay with me awhile.

Complex creature: she-he (keep this quiet):arsogenic metamorph/ wannabe manual artist; 3 yrs. ago sent me a pencil sketch he made from a dream he had of his Gaian (now ex) guru, Billy Lee Mookerjee.

Johnny's the son (by artificial insemination) of your colleague, F.R. Plowman. He heard your Mars lecture last summer in Tokyo; couldn't take his eyes off your beautiful face, which he wants to paint.

Johnny arrived here from D.C., only $29.70 to his name; mother a recent suicide; says my poem "In Memoriam: Vita" is helpful to him in his grief.

Katherine G. Jackson

"In Memoriam: Vita"
by Clorene Welles

Grief and rage besiege me.
I begrudge the world its joy,
& crave its power to destroy.

Saw your sister Saturday.
She looks like death warmed over.
We rubbed each other raw
with the age-old questions:
"What's it all about?
How do we bear it?"[36]

Polly Baker to Johnny Baker, October 25, 2055:

Happy Birthday!

Johnny Baker to Polly Baker, October 25, 2055:

Thanks. It's a big one!

I've left Srimaanji to fulfill Mother's last wish for me and open my

36. Welles, loc. sit.

gift. Please send me my set of oil paints, which you'll find on the top shelf of the hall closet, c/o Clorene Welles, Apartment 44A, Asgard Spire, NYC 10024-89.

Polly Baker to Johnny Baker, October 27, 2055:

Congratulations! Your oil paints are in the mail, along with assorted other art supplies I found in your old room—paper, pens, pencils, scratchboards, three steel etching needles, and Jeanette's barber scissors. Use everything in good health!

How are you fixed for cash? I've credited $1000 to your account as a birthday present. You have $21,071 coming to you from Jeanette's Last Will and Testament, which will take another 6–8 mths to probate. Minus $1808 she owed me. In the meantime, against the $20,263 net amount, I'll loan you $900 a month. You can't live on that, of course, but it should help.

Take care of yourself, Johnny. You're all the family I have left.

PS. Is that the *poet* Clorene Welles? Your old pen pal? She must be nearly 100. I read somewhere she's very sick.

Johnny Baker to Polly Baker, October 28, 2055:

Thanks for the art supplies—and $, which is a godsend!!!

My old pen pal, the poet, Clorene Welles, is ninety-two. She suffers from a wrinklie brain disease called "transient ischemic attacks." It gives her dizzy spells and blind spots. She's two years beyond the cut-off for her insurance to pay for a telemerized arterial replacement, so the disease will eventually kill her.

Clorene's got all her marbles. She hopes to write one more poem before she dies.

I made a little scratchboard sketch of her this afternoon while she was taking a nap. I was happy to draw again. All I think about while drawing is the work at hand. Mother would be pleased.

Johnny Baker to Polly Baker, November 1, 2055:

Clorene introduced me to a 23-year-old visual artist named Nat

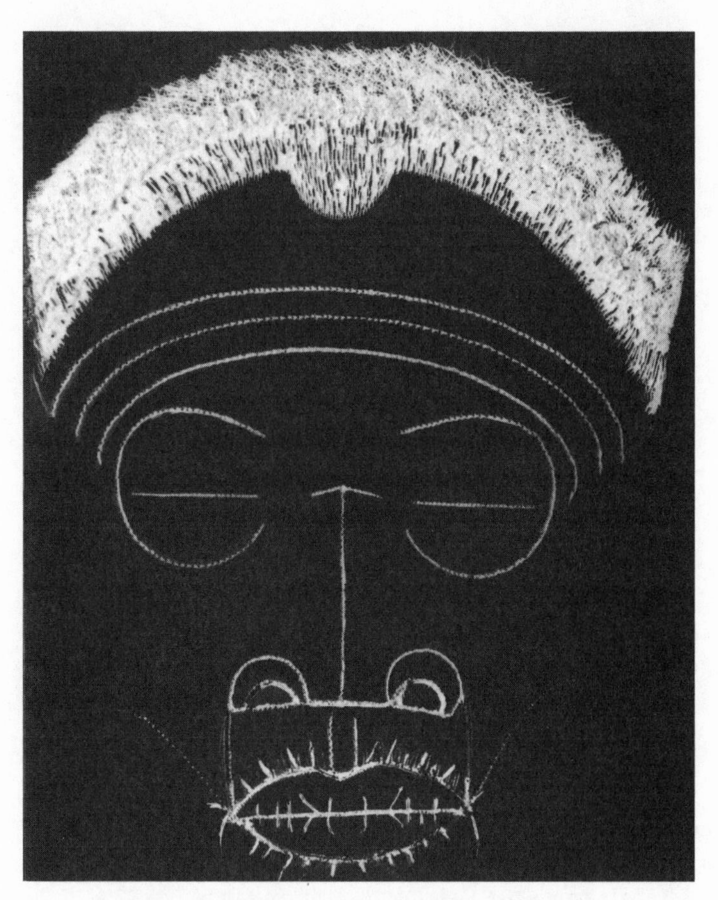

Portrait of Clorene Welles, 2055, scratchboard drawing

Glogow. He's a fractal symbolist, who doesn't draw manually but, like me, is interested in integrating words and images. He does good work. Here's something of his that Clorene bought for $1500.

Nat likes the sketch I made of Clorene sleeping. Our mutual passion for words and pictures made us immediate pals. We got high together. Told him the story of my life—everything. Have decided to be myself from now on—all that I am.

Finite area enclosed by infinitely expanding boundary:
A fractal symbol of the humin mind.

Nat Glogow, *A fractal symbol of the humin mind,* 2055,
digitally generated image. Collection Herbert Welles

Nat Glogow

So Johnny was a visual arsogenic metamorph! I said he was lucky to know for certain that he had talent. He confessed he was worried that he'd been given second-rate arsogenes.

Johnny told me that his mother had committed suicide in October and that he suffered a recurrent nightmare about her. He said, "It's driving me nuts."

We talked for hours. I told him I'm straight and he was like, "I'm sorry."

Johnny mentioned he needed a place to live. I offered to rent him a room in my studio on the ground floor of 112 Melville Canal for $1250 a month. He jumped at the chance.

Johnny Baker to Polly Baker, November 9, 2055:

The peeling walls of my new studio smell of mildew. At high tide, waves in the Melville Canal lap under the windows.

Nat Glogow and I get along fine. He was born in Pocatello, Idaho, where his grandfather, who was a rabbi, was murdered by skinheads during the exoduster riots of 2018. Nat tells Jewish jokes: Mr. to Mrs. Goldberg, "If one of us dies, I'm not getting married again."

Johnny Baker to Teddy Petrakis, November 10, 2055:

Had the nightmare again last night. Today I tried and failed to paint Mother's face coming up at me out of the ground.

From John Firth Baker's interview in *The International Review of Manual Art:*

I worked a week without making any progress. My painting technique was nil. I didn't know how to create the illusion of volume or depth on a two-dimensional surface. I knew nothing about perspective. What to do? I was desperate.

One morning I happened to think of Emma Torchlight, who got me thinking of masks. Then I thought: Why not use a mask instead of the painted image of a face? I pictured a papier mache mask of the face in my nightmare, pasted face up on a canvas.

That was the moment I conceived *The Ground Beneath My Feet* (Plate 1), which took me about a month to make. I stumbled on a new style. I introduced color, texture, and sculpted relief into my work.

Johnny Baker to Sri Billy Lee Mookerjee, December 12, 2055:

Dear Srimaanji,

I conquered my nightmare about Mother by capturing it in this image called *The Ground Beneath My Feet.*

Sri Billy Lee Mookerjee to Johnny Baker, December 13, 2055:

Would like to buy it. Will you take $2000?

Arriving NYC Saturday, 9:45 A.M., staying rectory First Church of Gaia, High Bridge Island Park. Can you have dinner with me 8 P.M. that night at the Imperial? We'll celebrate the sale.

Johnny Baker to Sri Billy Lee Mookerjee, December 13, 2055:

Thank you for buying *The Ground Beneath My Feet.*

I need the money. I earn my a living at night by hustling—"sniggling the gig," as it's called in NYC slang.

You're on for dinner. The Imperial is imperial but will cost you a bundle!

Come here 11 A.M. Sunday for brunch. My roommate Nat and I are having a few people over—Clorene, Irene Winters, and Alex, who's still at Juilliard. Teddy can't make it. He just got accepted at Harvard Divinity School for an M.A. in theology. He's spending Xmas in flooded New Orleans at the Episcopal Home for the Indigent Aged.

Polly Baker to Johnny Baker, December 17, 2055:

This locket, which belonged to Jeanette, holds a lock of your baby hair. I came across it going through her things the other day—stuff I'd put away right after her death and didn't have the heart to examine till recently.

Johnny Baker to Polly Baker, December 17, 2055:

Eerie. I recently read about the locket in Mother's journal (Feb. 8, 2040). Mother's words, her locket, and her barber scissors are all that's left of her to me.

Sri Billy Lee Mookerjee

The Imperial was expensive, but the food only so-so. Afterwards, Johnny and I walked north along the East End Canal. He begged me to take him back to the rectory and make love to her, but I refused.

Sunday morning at the brunch, I bought *The Ground Beneath My Feet*. I felt I had taken possession of a tangible Gaian vision.

Nat Glogow

Johnny was in a funk at the brunch. He got stoned. I overheard him say to himself, "Poor Mother!"

Alex Thomas jr.

When I got home, I couldn't get Johnny's sad face outta my mind. He made me think of the spiritual "Sometimes I Feel Like A Motherless Child." The melody, in E-flat minor, kept going through my head. Next morning, I began work on my choral piece in four parts, entitled *True Believer,* which celebrates Afro-American spirituality.

Teddy Petrakis to Johnny Baker, December 24, 2055:

Merry Christmas from New Orleans, which is suffering its worst flood in twelve years. Salt water from the Gulf 110 miles away has backed up the Mississippi to the city, where fishermin now catch sea trout off Bourbon Street, and the local freshwater fish, gasping for air on the muddy banks, are devoured by hogs.

Drinking water in the city mains has gone bad, and stagnant pools everywhere spread nasty new forms of waterborne diseases like hepatitis, *E. coli* infections. They're the breeding ground of a mutated parasite called *neo-Cryptosporidium* that eats mucous membrane.

Our 213 Episcopal wrinklies (average age 94) are a handful. About a third have become raving "Revoked Covenanters," converts to a sect sweeping the South that claims global warming with its rising seas is a sign that God has revoked His covenant with Noah (Gen. 8:22): "While the earth remaineth, seedtime and harvest, and cold and heat, and summer and winter, and day and night shall not cease."

The Revoked Covenanters believe daylight will soon cease. Yesterday evening, in preparation for the "Coming Long Night," Nessa

Porte, 95, tried to blind herself by splashing her eyes with rubbing alcohol. The shock gave her a fatal heart attack.

Such is my Christmas. How *you* doing?

Johnny Baker to Teddy Petrakis, December 24, 2055:

Not so hot. Xmas is sad without Mother.

Burying myself in work. I'm making my self-portrait as a young manual artist. It's a collage construction, in primary colors, composed of palette-shaped cutouts and various artist's materials: an articulated hand manikin ($488!) and hog bristle paintbrush ($81.40).

After hours of painting today, the primary colors mixed in my head and I caught flashes of their composites—orange, green, and purple—on my walls and ceilings.

Nat Glogow

Johnny often came home at dawn covered from head to toe with mosquito bites, which he infected by scratching. He said he hustled on the bridges, where all year long, swarms of mosquitoes buzz around the lights.

From Sri Billy Lee Mookerjee's home page, December 26, 2055:

Johnny Baker, mourning his mother Jeanette who died in October, has left my service as sheila to pursue a career as a manual artist. Johnny wants it publicly known that she is an arsogenic metamorph—and proud of it! He feels she can no longer deny his genetic artistic propensities. I took one look at her first work in color, *The Ground Beneath My Feet,* and agreed.

Johnny may have given up being my sheila, but *The Ground Beneath My Feet* shows that he's unconsciously continuing her quest to gain Gaian Consciousness on his own as a manual artist.

The Ground Beneath My Feet is a tangible Gaian vision. It says: The ground beneath our feet is alive!

I predict that John Firth Baker will become the first Gaian manual artist. Gaians interested in buying her work can contact him at JFB@wksp.com. Her prices start at $4000.

From John Firth Baker's interview in *The International Review of Manual Arts:*

I lost a guru but gained a patron.

From: A Naturally Gifted Manual Artist
To: The Arsogenic Metamorph John Firth Baker
December 28, 2055:

God Himself, as a sign of His favor, gave me a natural gift for painting in watercolors. I'm a new Winslow Homer! But I can't sell my work for shit.

Your unnatural talent was forged in hell by the angel of the bottomless pit. You think it will make you rich and famous. But beware! The Lord God is jealous of His bounty and will not be mocked. Nadia Kammerovska's death was God's will!

Alex Thomas jr.

Johnny admitted to me that the letter from the new Winslow Homer scared him. It scared me. Nadia Kammerovska's fate haunted all us "arsogenic metamorphs," as we were coming to be called.

Johnny's coming out, via Mookerjee's home page, took guts. I decided to admit publicly at Juilliard that I was a musical metamorph, artificially equipped in France with absolute pitch, an acute intervalic sense for harmony and scales, and auditory brain lateralization, which gives my brain auditory dominance.

Next day I told four of my friends in Advanced Musical Composition.

They looked at me funny. They said, "It makes no difference to us where your talent comes from," but they looked at me funny.

Yukio Tanaka to Johnny Baker, December 29, 2055:

Forgive me for intruding on your grief. I recently read about your esteemed Mother's death on Mookerjee-san's home page, posted here by the Online Japanese Church of Gaia. My heart goes out to you. We have a new thing in common. We now both mourn a beloved parent.

With one big difference—you've returned to art! If I do so, I'll die. My father's spirit warned me of this in a dream on Christmas Eve.

Wakinoya Yoshiharu

Yukio Tanaka put me onto Mookerjee's home page about Johnny, and I told Fritz, who then learned that Jeanette had committed suicide.

Frederick Rust Plowman to Johnny Baker, January 2, 2056:

I'm sorry about your mother. I blame myself. She'd be pleased to know you've gone back to work as a manual artist.

I'll be in NYC around April 1 for a lecture series, which I'm forced to give protected by bodyguards. I'm regarded by many religious people in the States as a devil, possessed by Satanic pride. They're right. I'm fiendishly proud to be humin, a member of a species finally able to direct its own evolution—to become the Lord of Life.

I'm bringing Yukio with me to New York. I've made arrangements for him to see a psychotherapist who specializes in treating blocked artists and writers.

Johnny Baker to Frederick Rust Plowman, January 2, 2056:

Yukio is welcome to crash with me.

I wanna paint your portrait.

Johnny Baker to Teddy Petrakis, January 5, 2056:

Two days ago, high winds and a 3.5-inch rainfall lasting four hours flooded a leaky houseboat tied up on the Canal Street Canal. Two sleeping kids, four and six, left alone by their parents, drowned. The mother later hanged herself. News of her death gave me a flashback of Mother's funeral on the dunes.

I'm using Mother's barber scissors to make a cutout collage called *Self-Portrait as a Young Manual Artist.* When the steel gets warm from my hand—as it did from hers—I feel close to her.

Thanks to Billy Lee's 12/26/55 home page, I've become the darling of the rich local Gaians—including four Beautiful People, high-fashion models, all aged nineteen. They were made in Switzerland by a genetic engineer who went to MIT with Fritz. The two Americans among them are scared to admit they're metamorphs for fear of incriminating their parents.

Johnny Baker to Teddy Petrakis, January 6, 2056:

This morning, I finished my *Self-Portrait as a Young Manual Artist* (Plate 2), which, on Billy Lee's advice, is for sale at $4000.

From John Firth Baker's interview in *The International Review of Manual Art:*

My *Self-Portrait as a Young Manual Artist,* which is a cutout collage, also incorporates textured images painted in color.

The work proclaims my vocation. The oval thumb-hole in the center of my self-portrait's palette-shape head contains three primary colors in place of the Gaian tattoo I would have worn had I gained Gaian Consciousness.

Doris Peel

At the beginning of 2056, I was serving my first term as president of the congregation of New York's First Church of Gaia in High Bridge Island Park. I was part of the crowd that hung around Johnny's studio, where I bought his *Self-Portrait as a Young Manual Artist* for $4000. The same week our guru, Sri Jaimie Tenorio, and his sheila, Gil, left our church and "went below," as we Gaians say, to dedicate themselves to serve the underclass.

At my suggestion as head of the Search Committee, the congregation offered Sri Mookerjee a yearly salary of $200,000 plus housing and living expenses to become our guru. He accepted immediately.

Sri Billy Lee Mookerjee

I wanted to be near Johnny, who I felt was destined to make a unique contribution to Gainism as an artist.

Nat Glogow

Johnny's growing celebrity made me jealous.

Johnny Baker to Teddy Petrakis, January 14, 2056:

I'm painting Irene Winter's portrait. Irene's an exogenetic engineer from Salt Lake City, who works at the Dyson Institute designing plants to live on Mars. An ex-Mormon turned Gaian, she dreams of a future terraformed Mars (to be called Mari, one of the names of the ancient Great Goddess), which will be ruled by wimin.

I fell in love with her face at a lecture she was giving in Tokyo. It reminds me of those young, serenely beautiful brass sculptures of sacred Benin queens and princesses.

I see Irene as a Mar(t)ian priestess wearing a ceremonial headdress emblazoned with the Gynarchist symbol.

She's visiting her 94-year-old father, the only African-American Mormon bishop, in Salt Lake. He's got congestive heart failure and like Clorene is too old to be eligible for rejuvenation therapy.

Irene Winter to Johnny Baker, January 16, 2056:

Family business will keep me here over the weekend. Daddy's sister Lorinda is broke and needs to sell her half of the condo that she and Daddy own in Chango Keep, under the Caribbean.

Daddy's worse. He says, "I ain't scared to die" and I believe him, because like all good male Mormons, he believes that after his death, he gets to be the god of his own planet where he'll beget innumerable children on his innumerable wives.

Yesterday we had a terrible fight about Maria Lopez vs. TCOLAM, He's scared of the Furies. Daddy of course is an American Christian Republican and backs Gov. Koyle in the coming election. In fact, Daddy is an important black supporter of the Seer Prophet & Revelator of the Mormon Church.

Daddy became a Latter-Day Saint in 1996, twenty years after the doctrine of the curse of Ham was recanted and black men were admitted to the priesthood. He was a used-car salesman and joined ward twelve on Salt Lake's working-class west side. Daddy was among the first black temple workers.

The church was a big step for him socially. Mormons look out for their own. Daddy's business took off. He bought into a used-car lot in West Valley City. His first wife, Rachel, died in 2018. He married Mom in 2025. She was a twenty-nine-year-old knockout, who married him for his money. Daddy married for sex. Our love of beautiful wimin is the one thing Daddy and I have in common.

Irene Winter to Clorene Welles, January 17, 2056:

I wrote Johnny a long letter yesterday. His talent, intensity, and personal history fascinate me, but I'm repelled by his hairy body. Do you suppose he shaves his breasts?

Johnny just called to ask me my hat size, which is 6⅞. He's making some kind of a headdress for me to pose in. Is he a good artist?

The Ground Beneath My Feet creeps me out.

Johnny Baker to Yukio Tanaka, January 23, 2056:

Sitting here smoking late at night thinking of you after working all day on a papier mâché black-lacquered headdress inspired by the Edo helmets we both admired that evening in the Nishimura Virtual Museum.

I understand Plowman wants to bring you with him to NYC. Come. Stay with me as long as you want. Fuck your father's spirit!

Nat Glogow

One day, apropos of nothing, Johnny went, "I told my mother I never wanted to see her again, and she killed herself. I'm to blame."

Yukio Tanaka to Johnny Baker, January 25, 2056:

Many thanks for your nice words about the relationship of my humble drawing and poor calligraphy. We Japanese believe the art of drawing consists of four elements: vertical, horizontal, combining, and scattering. If I say so myself, I scattered the kanji in my Thunder God drawing very well.

I humbly accept your kind invitation to stay with you in NYC. A doctor can't help me. But—who knows?—maybe my father's angry spirit won't have such a hold over me in America. It's a well-known fact that spirits don't like traveling over water.

So you're making a lacquered papier mâchè headdress inspired by Edo samurai helmets. As you probably remember, I know a little about lacquer. What color are you using?

Johnny Baker to Yukio Tanaka, January 26, 2056:

Black.

Yukio Tanaka to Johnny Baker, January 27, 2056:

Ah, so! The ancient Japanese method of making black lacquer is best. Add soot from burning pine to the natural golden or reddish-brown variety.

Johnny Baker to Teddy Petrakis, January 27, 2056:

Yukio's coming to stay with me in NYC. Yummy!!! Come into my parlor said the spider to the fly.

Nat Glogow

I just had another memory of Johnny's thoughts about his mother. One foggy winter morning on the west walkway of the Melville Canal,

Johnny and I spotted a black cat stalking a half-grown pigeon with a stumpy tail. The pigeon was cheeping frantically. It was too young to fly. Johnny shooed the cat away. The pigeon fluttered along the stone wall, cheeping even faster and louder than before. Cheep! Cheep! Cheep!

Johnny went, "Poor li'l thing wants its mother," and I saw tears in his eyes.

Johnny Baker to Mentor, February 8, 2056:

Assemble all audiovisual records of Mother in 2051, when she wore long hair, and prepare them for incorporation into MemoRX 2-A VR program.

Michael Salzman

In the winter of 2056, I programmed a half-hour MemoRX VR visit in her 2051 kitchen from the deceased Jeanette Baker to her son John, virtual-aged fourteen. It cost Baker $2500 to braid his forty-two-year-old mother's hair while she said things like "You're a good kid. I love you"—the usual stuff people pay to hear their dead mothers tell them.

Johnny Baker to Teddy Petrakis, February 11, 2056:

Today Irene showed me her lab at the Dyson Institute. She and her colleagues are designing a lichenlike metamorphic plant for Mars that has thick stalks. It must survive high amounts of radiation in a frigid climate with long seasons. I thought of my little metamorphic birth tree, which couldn't make it in Cherry County. It was like somebody walked on my grave. Then I took Irene back to the studio, where I gave her my *Portrait of Irene Winter* (Plate 3).

She said, "Am I really that beautiful?" I was like, "You are to me." We had the studio to ourselves; Nat was at his stepmother's in Brooklyn. Irene said, "Let's make love." I went, "You're my first womin," and she went, "I never fucked a she-he before." But her pussy turned me off, and my hairy tits repelled her. Irene said, "Never mind, we're still friends."

From John Firth Baker's interview in *The International Review of Manual Art:*

My poor Irene! Tell you the truth, I can't bear talking about my portrait of her. It brings back too many painful memories.

Nat Glogow

On Wednesday night March 1st, 2056, at Irene's Washington Heights apartment, Johnny, Irene, and I gave Clorene her ninety-third birthday party.

Jesus! Ninety-three! Clorene started reminiscing about Martin Luther King's assassination. "I was poor and black and five years old. We lived in Philly. It was raining."

Then she complained of double vision, lost her balance, and sat down heavily on the blue sofa. She said her right side felt numb. She was having another attack. It lasted only a minute or two but scared everybody half to death. Johnny turned pale.

When the attack passed, Clorene said, "Not enough blood reaches my brain, and one of these days it'll kill me. But not before I write my death poem."

She said lots of poets wrote death poems. Alfred Lord Tennyson wrote "Crossing the Bar" on his death bed, and Sir Walter Raleigh wrote his own epitaph in verse the night before he was beheaded.

Johnny and I saw a lot of Clorene that spring. We were with her the afternoon she was asked, as a distinguished American Elder Poet, to endorse 82-year-old "Granny" Smith for reelection as president. Clorene was thrilled! She relished playing the role of the grande dame of American Poetry.

Johnny said to her, "If Smith is reelected, I bet you're asked to write a poem for her inaugural."

Clorene said, "I've only got one poem left in me to write—my death poem."

Sri Billy Lee Mookerjee

I commissioned Johnny to carve an image of Mamagon Gaia for my church.

"How do you see her?" he asked me.
I said, "Like the words to her song:

My womb is full
My tits are too,
The life I bear
I soon will chew."

Johnny Baker to Emma Torchlight, March 27, 2056:
Billy Lee will pay me $4500 plus expenses to carve an image of Mamagon Gaia, our all-devouring Motherworld. I picture her as pregnant and hairy, with a beard and fangs. But I know nothing about carving. Can you give me a hand?

Emma Torchlight to Johnny Baker, March 28, 2056:
With pleasure. Come to my studio, 105-1 Orchard Street, Anchorage, Alaska, on April 15th.

Nat Glogow
Yukio, Plowman, and Plowman's secretary showed up on our doorstep on the evening of April 2. So this was the world-famous Professor Plowman! He looked tired.
Johnny hugged Yukio, who also looked tired. I knew all about him—how his father's ghost had made him quit drawing. Plowman said Yukio had an appointment the next afternoon with a famous neuropsychotherapist, somebody Nelson, who would help Yukio overcome his fear of the supernatural and get him drawing again.
Yukio said nothing. Johnny couldn't take his eyes off him. His stare made Yukio blush.
Plowman and his secretary left for a hotel around midnight. Yukio sacked out on a futon at the foot of the dresser. Then he got up again because he forgot to brush his teeth. He went into the bathroom.
Johnny walked up behind him at the sink and said, "You got beautiful teeth."
I saw in the mirror that Yukio blushed again.

From John Firth Baker's interview in *The International Review of Manual Art:*

Yukio's sharp, white teeth turned me on. That night in bed, while raising the dead, I pictured him biting my nipples. First thing in the morning, I began turning my masturbatory fantasy into a new picture called *The Nip*.

Wakinoya Yoshiharu

At the last minute the next afternoon, Yukio balked at seeing the neuropsychotherapist. Outside the office, he told Fritz, "Feel that wind? That's an east wind. My father's spirit! It's a bad omen. I can't go to the doctor today!"

Yukio Tanaka to Mariko Tanaka, April 5, 2056:

Dearest Mother,

I didn't see Doctor Nelson because of a bad omen. Father's vengeful spirit has pursued me to NY. I'm anxious from morning till night. What will become of me?

I'm posing with bared teeth for Johnny, who's sketching me in pencil. I wish Father's spirit would let me draw again. Make an offering to him at the family altar for me. I remember him constantly lighting one cigarette with the burning end of another. Sometimes, when he whacked me across the face, I smelled his tobacco-stained fingers. I'm paying a terrible price for that one moment of being relieved at his death. After all, I was only a little kid!

New York is full of hairy, bearded Jews who wear long black coats and fur hats in the warm weather. Chink tourists swarm all over the canals. New York is truly a floating world. I took a gondola ride. I thought we would be swamped by the wake of a water bus on the Broadway Canal!

Wakinoya Yoshiharu

Fritz dropped the idea of neuropsychotherapy for Yukio.

I suggested, "Get him a Buddhist priest."

Fritz said, "Over my dead body!"
Science is Fritz's religion.

From John Firth Baker's interview in *The International Review of Manual Arts:*

The Nip is a kind of dual portrait of myself and Yukio—and a representation of my fantasy about us that inspired me. The work combines a scratchboard drawing of Yukio's face with a nude self-portrait I painted in gouache, my first use of that medium. It was also my first shot at painting a naked humin body. I stumbled on the technique of layering the transparent gouache to capture skin tone. (Plate 4).

Nat Glogow

When Yukio saw *The Nip,* he went, "Ah! So!" and blushed again.

Yukio Tanaka to Mariko Tanaka, April 14, 2056:

Dearest Mother,

Johnny's taking me to Alaska, where he will make a carving and I will pay my respects in the Aleutians to our brave soldiers who were killed there more than a hundred years ago.

Sri Billy Lee Mookerjee

I advanced Johnny the $1200 for a round-trip ticket to Anchorage for Yukio.

He said, "I'm in love."

Emma Torchlight

The day after arriving in Anchorage with Johnny, Yukio took off for the Aleutians, where he stayed overnight. Johnny told me his story.

He said, "Yukio won't let me touch him—yet. I'm working on it. We're both lonely. Sometimes we talk all night. We discuss art, being arsogenic metamorphs, and our dead parents. We're both haunted by the dead."

Yukio Tanaka to Mariko Tanaka, April 16, 2056:

Dearest Mother,

I'm writing you from under a palm tree on windswept Lookout Hill at the east end of Attu island in the Bering Sea. Attu is where 2500 of our glorious Imperial Marines fought 11,000 American soldiers to the death from May 11 to 17, 1943. Refusing to surrender after a seven-day battle, our surviving warriors all died making a banzai charge, screaming, "Japanese drink blood like wine!"

They were men after my own heart. I too could drink blood like wine.

Sketch for *Mamagon Gaia,* 2056, pencil on paper. Collection Emma Torchlight

Johnny Baker to Sri Billy Lee Mookerjee, April 20, 2056:

Yukio's slightly sour smell makes me dizzy. His presence fills me with energy that flows into my work. This morning, following Emma's advice, I made the enclosed pencil sketch of Mamagon Gaia in profile. It's heavily influenced by Mexican devil masks, which are composed of simple geometric shapes. That should make it relatively easy for a beginner like me to carve.

I must carve the shape I sketched in a 3' × 2' red cedar log.

Emma says, "Find the volumes of the wood by carving *in*. Subtraction will slowly reveal to you the form you seek."

Emma Torchlight

One evening after work, Yukio went for a walk alone. I confessed to Johnny my desire to have a daughter to love, and he said, "How about Jeanette's grandchild?"

I said, "You mean it?" and he said, "Why not? Only, I can't take any responsibility for raising her."

"Naturally," I said. "The responsibility's all mine."

We agreed to have a daughter named Jeanette. I said, "I'll cherish her."

Johnny said, "She'll have a better life than Mother's."

Johnny Baker to Polly Baker, cc Teddy Petrakis, Irene Winter, Srimaanji Billy Lee Mookerjee, April 27, 2056

Congratulate me. I'm gonna be a father. Emma was artificially inseminated this morning with my sperm. She'll have a daughter named Jeanette. Emma raised $50,000, which she paid to have Jeanette metamorphically enhanced with a cluster of Methuselah genes in an Anchorage clinic. Emma tells me many business-class Alaskans do it. Says that congressional exclusion of Methuselah genes from the genomic enhancement prohibited by the Created Equal Act is leading to the creation of the first generation of *rich* Americans who'll live 150 years.

What I wouldn't give to live 150 years!

Johnny Baker to Sri Billy Lee Mookerjee, May 4, 2056:

Yukio bandaged my blistered palm today and then for a moment let me hold his hand. Despite the pain, I love carving. With Emma's help, it took me three days' hard work with an inch-wide gouge to round the top of the cedar log into the sloping dome that will become the crown of Mamagon Gaia's skull.

Yukio Tanaka to Mariko Tanaka, May 14, 2056:

Dearest Mother,

Happy Mother's Day. I hope you received my red carnation. Johnny asked me what my gift to you symbolizes, and I told him that in the Japanese language of flowers, a red carnation given to one's Mother on Mother's Day is a token of gratitude for her precious love. He then got very sad because, as you know, his Mother committed suicide.

You've often said what a rough time you had raising me in this transient and beautiful world. I know how hard things were for you after father died. I've disappointed you both. Forgive me.

Emma Torchlight

Johnny, completely absorbed in carving Mamagon Gaia, lost interest in my pregnancy. I didn't care. I had an easy first trimester: a little morning and evening sickness, sleepiness, sore nipples, constipation. Nothing I couldn't handle.

Johnny literally made the chips fly. Mamagon Gaia's hooked nose, her pregnant stomach and pendulous breasts emerged from the wood under his hands. He was a born carver. He visualized shapes in three dimensions and loved the feel of wood. Texture was his thing. He textured Mamagon Gaia with sculpted lumps of methyl cellulose paste he carefully added to the carved wood.

I'm proud Johnny was my student and am very sorry that *Mamagon Gaia* is the only wood carving he lived to make.

From John Firth Baker's interview in *The International Review of Manual Art:*

Mamagon Gaia (Plate 5) was my first commission, a big event in the life of a young artist. I gained a lot of self-confidence from pulling it off. I now considered myself a professional.

Johnny Baker to Sri Billy Lee Mookerjee, May 16, 2056:

Yukio and I returning Sat. to NY with your *Mamagon Gaia*.

Late last night, I found myself in my studio there, waiting for Irene to show up for dinner. We were going to order in sushi. She called to say she'd be late. I went to the roof to look at the full moon. I thought to myself, I must be looking into the past; there were no lights on the lunar surface. It was completely dead, like in the old days, and lit only by reflected sunlight.

It was the biggest moon I ever saw and suddenly I realized that it was dangerously near the Earth.

At that moment, the Angel of Death appeared in the night sky, but off in the distance. It flapped towards me on huge bat wings, then glided overhead across the moon. The Angel of Death has a gaping cunt. That woke me up!

I've gotta paint her portrait.

Polly Baker

Emma asked me on the phone to be baby Jeanette's godmother, and I said, "I'd be honored!"

She mentioned that Johnny was hopelessly in love with a straight Japanese boy, the other surviving arsogenic metamorph.

I said, "Birds of a feather," and thought about poor Nadia Kammerovska dead in her grave these eight years.

Nat Glogow

Soon as Johnny and Yukio got back from Alaska, Johnny started painting *The Angel of Death*.

He told me, "Yukio and I are going nowhere."

Unrequited love made Johnny mean. One evening, Yukio forgot to wash some expensive brushes, which got stiff with paint. Johnny, who'd been drinking, blew his top.

"You fail at everything you do! What the fuck good are you around here?" he shouted. "Go back to Japan!"

Yukio said, "I thought we were friends."

"Nat here's my friend, Irene's my friend. I got friends to spare. Be my lover or go back to Japan!"

Johnny Baker to Sri Billy Lee Mookerjee, June 14, 2056:

I'm studying the anatomy of the femayle perineum—clitoris, urethra, vagina, etc.,—for my painting *The Angel of Death*. Ugh!

Yukio and I are now lovers. I've taught him to suck me off. His heart's not in it.

I'm trying to get him to see a shrink. He's obsessed by the relief he felt at hearing of his father's death. A teacher told him the news in the schoolyard on a blustery spring afternoon. Yukio wanted to shout, "Hurrah!" He happened to notice there was an east wind. It put the bee in his bonnet about his father's ghost.

Maybe *I* need a shrink. I constantly relive my last words to Mother: "I never wanna see you again!"

Wakinoya Yoshiharu

At that time, Fritz was giving the Robert Pollack Actual Lectures at Columbia University, which kept us in New York. I saw quite a bit of Yukio. He told me that when he and Johnny made love, he fantasied he was an old-time samurai courting a young male kabuki actor who played wimin's roles.

Sri Billy Lee Mookerjee

The last week in May I installed Johnny's carving of Mamagon Gaia on the wall opposite the front door my church. Johnny's work helped my congregation visualize our Motherworld as creator and destroyer.

The *Mamagon Gaia* became a favorite aid to meditation. One morning, I found a suckling pig with its throat cut, laid out beneath it as an offering. The pig was sprinkled with lavender and thyme.

From Sri Billy Lee Mookerjee's home page, June 2, 2056:

A dead suckling pig was left in my church yesterday as an offering to John Firth Baker's carving of Mamagon Gaia. This pious gesture made by my anonymous congregant doesn't surprise me. Since ancient times dead baby pigs have been offered to images of Mother Earth. Johnny's art has miraculously reactivated long-dormant religious practices in the service of Gaia. His work is destined to have a profound influence on the development of Gaianism.

Sri Billy Lee Mookerjee

The practice of offering dead suckling pigs to Mamagon Gaia in my church caught on. I distributed the pork to the neighborhood noahs who camp out along the Emerson Canal. That led to the annual Emerson Canal barbeque—a feast held in honor of Johnny's image of Mamagon Gaia, which is carried around in a procession.

Nat Glogow

Yukio and Johnny led separate social lives. Yukio hung with a bunch of *pentojin* [penthouse dwellers], rich Japanese kids who lived with their parents in the Nippon Towers overlooking the East River.

Elizabeth Hinosawa

I was one of Yukio's girlfriends. He told me he worked for a famous artist. He was always broke. Yukio's English was nonexistent. We spoke in Japanese with autotranslators.

Yukio seemed much older than he was.

When I said to him, "You seem much older than you are," he was like, "That's because I'm an arsogenic metamorph." I thought that was his religion.

Yukio was what we Japanese-Americans call a "cherry blossom." "Cherry blossoms" are Japanese who are hung up on the glorious Japanese Imperial past, when Japan ruled Asia. Yukio believed the Japanese are a superior race whose emperor is descended from the sun goddess. The last emperor's assassination by Gynarachists drove him wild. Yukio was your typical Japanese chauvinist. He believed Japanese and American men are pussy-whipped and will lose the Gender War. The one thing he could say in favor of Chinese men was their subjection of Chinese wimin. The same for the Arabs.

Yukio sounded off in this vein all the time. But he was a gentle lover, and pleased me no end.

From John Firth Baker's interview in *The International Review of Manual Arts:*

The Angel of Death (Plate 6) is a combination cutout collage and painting done in both gouache and oils. I painted the ultramarine sky in oils. The fingers on the bat wings are badly drawn.

From Sri Billy Lee Mookerjee's home page, June 14, 2056:

John Firth Baker's latest painting is a portrait of *The Angel of Death*. Like his other work, it is a Gaian vision. His Angel of Death has an open womb, which symbolizes the paradox, celebrated by Gaians, that death is the source of life on our Motherworld.

Johnny Baker to Teddy Petrakis, June 16, 2056:

Good news since last we spoke: Billy Lee bought *The Angel of Death* today for $5000. Irene, who stopped by, agrees with his Gaian interpretation of the womb symbol.

She says, "Life can come from death. Look at you! You can't deny that your mother's death gave you new life."

I can't deny it.

Irene's worried about her sick father. She's off to Salt Lake tomorrow to be with him on Father's Day. I'm celebrating here with my father. On Sunday Fritz begins sitting for his portrait.

From the Furies home page, June 18, 2056:

FEMINIZE THE HUMIN RACE!

The explosion which today destroyed the Mormon Temple and caused extensive collateral damage in Salt Lake City's Temple

Square was a BBU-97 FAE (Fuel Air Explosive) bomb detonated by the Furies, the armed resistance movement of the North American Gynarchist League.

We bombed the Mormon Temple because Mormons kidnaped, clitorectomized, and amputated the nipples of Sister Maria Lopez, the former Chairpersin of the North American Gynarchist League.

Wominkind! Rest assured that all your atrocious suffering at the hands of men will likewise be avenged!

Johnny Baker to Teddy Petrakis, June 19, 2056:

No word from Irene. I fear the worst. Her father wanted her to take him to the Father's Day sacrament meeting in the chapel of the Joseph Smith Memorial on Temple Square, where, it's reported, there are over 400 dead.

Johnny Baker to Teddy Petrakis, June 20, 2056:

Clorene got a phone call this morning from Irene's sister, Claudia, in Salt Lake. Just as I feared, Irene's dead. She and her father were killed Sunday morning in the explosion outside the chapel. They were buried this afternoon.

Johnny Baker to Teddy Petrakis, June 21, 2056:

Because I drew the bookplate on which Maria Lopez based the Furies logo, reporters have been after me for a statement about the bombing. I've refused all interviews. To tell the truth, it wasn't easy—I could use the publicity.

I've given up on Gynarchism. The Father's Day bombing shows that wimin can be as cruel as men. Both have a vicious streak. Fritz says it's in the humin genome.

Johnny Baker to Teddy Petrakis, June 25, 2056:

I've stopped work on Fritz's portrait to paint *Life on Mars* in memory of Irene. She believed that huminkind will spread life from world to world. My painting must represent her vision.

Alex came by. He's dedicating a new composition to me, which will have a Sept. premiere at Juilliard.

Johnny Baker to Teddy Petrakis, June 28, 2056:

Immersed in Lunartech-Interares VR tours of the Martian landscape. This afternoon I toured the western equatorial region around Mt. Dilemma, the eerie little two-horned crater about 12 kilometers SSW of Olympus Mons. Listed the amazing variations of red in the stony regolith: crimson, cadmium red (light & medium, deep) naphthol carmine, red, vermilion, etc.

At noon Martian time, wandering down Daedalia Planum, I spotted a scarlet boulder the size of our house in Cather Keep. On one side of a crater, I counted three shades of orange rocks in the bright sunlight—cadmium, hansa yellow-orange, and a rich cadmium red-orange. Never saw so many rocks, pebbles, and boulders in my life.

A sudden crimson sandstorm blew up in a 250-mile-an-hour north wind. The billowing clouds, through which a shrunken yellow sun shone, almost covered the blue-black sky.

But I'm not out to paint another realistic Marscape. I want to portray a scene from the Martian future, when the red planet starts turning green.

Johnny Baker to Teddy Petrakis, June 30, 2056:

Blocked on *Life on Mars*. I haven't the skill to paint the stony Marscape—or a convincing-looking metamorphic plant growing out of it. My conception of the work has collapsed.

Nat Glogow

Johnny panicked when he couldn't solve an artistic problem right away. In order to paint, he upped his dope and booze. But paint he did—six, seven hours a day. I have a memory of his beard streaked with vermilion; some evenings, there was orange in his hair.

Johnny Baker to Teddy Petrakis, July 3, 2056:

Today is Mother's birthday. She would've been 47 years old.

Johnny Baker to Teddy Petrakis, July 9, 2056:

It hit me today that if I can't paint a plant growing on Mars, I can sculpt it. I've decided to sculpt the whole image in relief against a painted sky.

Johnny Baker to Teddy Petrakis, July 12, 2056:

Made a plaster cast of the Martian metamorphic plant out of a ginger root. It looks quite unearthly. My Martian plant makes me think of my dead birth tree. Only this won't die on me—and it'll keep Irene's memory green.

From John Firth Baker's interview in *The International Review of Manual Art:*

Life on Mars (Plate 7) is my first landscape. My ignorance of the roles of perspective led me to combine painting with a sculptured relief to give it the illusion of depth.

From Sri Billy Lee Mookerjee's home page, July 22, 2056:

Today I saw John Firth Baker's latest work, *Life on Mars,* which is destined to become a cherished Gaian icon. It pictures that moment in the near future when metamorphic life from Earth takes root on Mars—when our living Motherworld begins, through us, to reproduce herself by animating another planet.

Alex Thomas jr.

I dedicated my four-part choral invention *True Believer* to Johnny. It's a theme and variation in D-minor—the saddest key—on the spiritual "Sometimes I Feel Like A Motherless Child." You may remember that my composition was inspired by Johnny's grief for Jeanette. Now here he be mourning Irene. I thought he was due for some happiness in his life.

Johnny Baker to Teddy Petrakis, July 24, 2056:

Fritz once wrote, "We scientists will eventually transform our species into a new kind of being; one whose mind will have the same relationship to ours as ours has to life and life to matter. The scientist can now say, with the poet: '*Oh! je serai celui-là qui créera Dieu!*'—'Oh, I am the one who will create God.'"

My portrait of him will be called *Oh, I am the one who will create God.*

Johnny Baker to Teddy Petrakis, July 25, 2056:

Fritz comes in every day from his summer rental in Conn. to watch me work. I listen to him talk.

Today, he said, "In my work, I ask a question, get an answer, and come up with a fresh question. You can't imagine what this means to me as a researcher—what an intellectual passion possesses me. You can't imagine the strange, colorless delight of my intellectual desires.

They're remorseless. Studying evolutionary genetics has made me as remorseless as evolution."

Johnny Baker to Teddy Petrakis, July 26, 2056:

Fritz has a vivid memory of my mother meeting Yukio's mother in an elevator at the Ozaki Institute on the day I was conceived, February 2, 2037. Mother was wearing a blue dress.

Yukio asked, "What was my mother wearing?" and Fritz said, "I don't remember."

Yukio flew into a rage. "My mother's not important enough, is that it?"

Johnny Baker to Teddy Petrakis, July 30, 2056:

This morning at ten, I finished Fritz's portrait, *Oh, I am the one who will create God.* Gave him red eyes.

Fritz said, "I look like Satan masquerading as Christ."

I said, "You've read my mind!"

From John Firth Baker's Interview in *The International Review of Manual Art:*

Oh, I am the one who will create God is my portrait of my father, Frederick Rust Plowman, the genetic engineer, who laced my genome with arsogenes. Like my picture shows, his pride scares me. The work is a composite cutout collage. It's a takeoff on a Byzantine or Russian icon. The scientist who will create God looks to me like Satan posing as the savior of huminkind. (Plate 8)

Plowman—Fritz—bought his portrait for $4500. He, Nat, Yukio, and I had a drink in the studio to celebrate the sale. Fritz stared out the window at the Melville Canal and said that in the last twenty years, the oceans had risen almost three feet, and there was no end in sight. The melting polar ice caps are drowning the world.

Nat went, "God, who's fed up with the humin race, decides to make another flood. He sends the angel Gabriel to the pope with the news, and the pope goes, 'Hallelujah! We'll sing the praises of Christ our Lord in heaven for eternity!'

"Then Gabriel's off to the Grand Mufti of Jerusalem, who goes, 'Allah be praised! We'll spend eternity in Paradise drinking wine served us by beautiful houris.'

"While in Jerusalem, Gabriel slips the bad news to the Chief Rabbi. And the Chief Rabbi says, 'How much time we got?'

" 'Forty-eight hours,' says Gabriel.

"So the Rabbi goes on the Net and says, 'Jews! We got forty-eight hours to learn to live under water!' "

Fritz said, "I could design humin beings to live under water: *Homo aquaticus*. It's not so far-fetched. I could give them gills and webbed hands and feet. Tough, scaly skin. Why, they could visually communicate with each other under water by changing their skin color at will, in individually colored patches all over their bodies, like squid."

I imagined a guy with gills swimming around in the ocean. His scaly face glows with different colors, reds and blues, which communicate his feelings. He feels like me—amazed he's a metamorph.

I portrayed him in a new work as open-mouthed at being himself. My painted collage *Aquamorph* (Plate 9) took me about a month. To tell the truth, it's a disguised self-portrait. I feel I'm always in deep water, way down inside myself.

Johnny Baker to Teddy Petrakis, September 10, 2056:

I gave Fritz my *Aquamorph* as a gift. We're like a real father and son. This morning we shared our thoughts on love. Told him I no longer love Yukio, but still feel tenderly towards him; I pity him. He brings out the mother in me.

Fritz told me that when he was four years old he wanted to marry the boy next door in Little Rock, Arkansas: "Ronald had hazel eyes—like my mother, whom I loathed. But Ronald's hazel eyes turned me on. Go explain love!"

The love of Fritz's life was the world-famous Japanese metamorphic geneticist Yoshida Ozaki, who gave him a parrot that died. Fritz sure misses that parrot. I want to be Fritz's parrot—his lovebird—and perch on his finger.

Johnny Baker to Teddy Petrakis, September 12, 2056:

Last night, alone with Fritz, I got stoned and drunk and said, "Fuck me!"

Fritz said, "No!"

I tried to bite his nose. He threw me on my bed and left. Saw myself for what I am.

Am working on new self-portrait.

Wakinoya Yoshiharu

Fritz gave a final lecture at NYU on the 13th and decided to return immediately to Japan. He wanted Yukio to go with us.

"You're wasting your time here. Make a life for yourself in Japan."

Yukio said, "I won't go back to being a fucking apprentice lacquerer to a fucking portable shrine maker at fucking Torigoe in fucking Tokyo."

Johnny said to Yukio, "You can stay on with me awhile."

Yukio said, "Everybody pities me. God! I hate it!"

Johnny Baker to Teddy Petrakis, September 15, 2056:

Yukio and I made up and talk a blue streak. Today we compared notes on the terror we felt as kids at Nadia Kammerovska's arrest and death. Her fate convinced us that being an arsogenic metamorph was a crime punishable by death. We both stopped drawing for over a year. Both still fear we must pay for our gifts with our lives.

Nat Glogow

Johnny sublet a tiny one-room studio with a northern exposure on the fifth floor of my building for $4800 a month. Yukio kept house. Johnny plunged into work. His new project was another self-portrait.

Sunday nights the two held open house. Billy Lee was always there, along with his crowd of rich Gaians. Alex brought four or five musical arsogenic metamorphs. Because of AANGA, they were scared to come out of the closet. Among them was a future world-famous conductor, who to this day swears she's naturally gifted.

Clorene came too. She introduced me to Pierre Minuit, who'd recorded her poems. I also remember meeting the Manual Arts critic for *The New Yorker,* Philip Lustenader. Yukio got drunk and tried to persuade Lustenader to do a humin-interest story on him—the tragic arsogenic metamorph forced by his father's ghost to renounce his gift. Yukio said, "I'm under a curse." Lustenader looked at him like he was nuts.

Johnny's little studio was the place to be on a Sunday night. Johnny loved being a celebrity—the world's first successful genetically engineered manual artist, the boy who had designed the Fury logo.

Johnny was like, "If Mother could only see me now!"

Yukio went, "She does! The dead see everything!"

From Johnny Baker's interview in *The International Review of Manual Arts:*

My *Self-Portrait with Knife Blades for Teeth* (Plate 10) is the real me.

From Sri Billy Lee Mookerjee's home page, September 22, 2056:

Johnny Baker's *Self-Portrait with Knife Blades for Teeth* will become another Gaian icon. It's a pictorial allegory of his conflicting impulses—her paradoxical inclinations. *Self-Portrait with Knife Blades for Teeth* portrays Baker's divided self. It is a portrait of a soul ripe to resolve its division by gaining Gaian Consciousness.

Nat Glogow

Johnny told me that Billy Lee's Gaian interpretation of *Self-Portrait with Knife Blades for Teeth* was bullshit.

But next Sunday night at his open house, Johnny publicly praised what Billy Lee wrote, saying to him, "I sure hope I gain Gaian Consciousness soon!"

What a smart move! Billy Lee bought the picture on the spot for $7500—Johnny's biggest sale yet!

Yukio Tanaka to Mariko Tanaka, September 23, 2056:

Dearest Mother,

Happy birthday. Please accept my insignificant gift of $500. I'm hard up.

I live here on Johnny's sufferance. It's humbling for me to play second fiddle to him. The gods have not dealt fairly with me. I can't accept my fate. Why won't father's spirit forgive me?

I went to a Buddhist priest in the Bronx and told him I was relieved at my father's death. The priest said, "In another life, you were a parricide."

I have a hangover. My head aches. I miss your soothing hand on my forehead.

Johnny Baker to Alex Thomas jr., September 25, 2056:

I greatly enjoyed the premiere of *True Believer.* Your music speaks to me. I heard the sounds of slavery in it—the clinking of chains in the second part was very powerful. The climax brought tears to my eyes. You say my grief over Mother's death inspired you to use "Sometimes I Feel Like A Motherless Child" as your main theme. Well, your music gave me an idea for a picture!

The party after the performance was imperial. I went home with that hunky tenor in the chorus named Charlie Lee. Did you know that his twin sister, Freya, has a crush on you? Look her up—she's cute.

From John Firth Baker's interview in *The International Review of Manual Art:*

I listened to *True Believer* again and again while walking in the heat along the midtown canals. Alex's anguished music made me think of certain African masks.

Near home I noticed a workbot caulking the crumbling redbrick wall of a building that overlooks the Grand Central Canal. I suddenly itched to get my hands on a caulking gun and draw the picture that the music put in my mind.

I bought a caulking gun that afternoon for $168 and drew *Sometimes I Feel like a Motherless Child* (Plate 11) in three hours. Like my little sketch *Clorene Sleeping* and my portrait of Irene Winter, *Sometimes I Feel like a Motherless Child* is based on African masks. I learned it's easier to draw a work of art than a live model—the artist has already plotted the essential lines.

Alex Thomas jr.

Johnny gave me *Sometimes I Feel like a Motherless Child* as a gift. His work transposes the emotion expressed in my music, composed in an African-American idiom, to a visual medium. It opened for us the possibility of a unique collaboration between composer and manual artist. We were sure we had a great future together.

From *Keepsake Magazine,* October 3, 2056:

In Memoriam.
Baker, Jeanette (July 3, 2009–October 3, 2055)
Wish you were here.
Johnny

Clorene Welles to Johnny Baker, October 4, 2056:

Your sad face about your mother Sunday night; buck up. A rich, long life stretches ahead of you; & remember there's lots & lots of time coming after that. Endless generations, behind and before us.

What are we? So little. But we know—we feel. We're part of it. Even to die is part of it. Dead or alive, we're in the making of it. Come visit me. The roses are blooming on my terrace.

Johnny Baker to Emma Torchlight, October 5, 2056:

How are you?

Emma Torchlight to Johnny Baker, October 5, 2056:

Sleepy. I'm sleepy all the time and pee a lot. Twice today, Jenny kicked me in the bladder.

Nat Glogow

Johnny, Yukio, and I went to visit Clorene Welles on Wednesday afternoon, October 7. It was pouring. We sat among the potted rose bushes under her terrace awning. Clorene reminisced about her days as a dental hygienist for a well-read Philadelphia dentist who encouraged her with her poetry. "He initialed his gold inlays: M.R. for Marvin Rapaport. His name sticks with me after fifty-five years."

Clorene said that if she could do it all over again, she would write her poetry in the African-American vernacular, like Sistah Sally, rather than in a white, "literary" style. She said, "I was ruined as a kid by the poems of Adelaide Crapsey. Her spare wasp voice ravished me; thereafter I wrote white." She and Johnny talked about Irene. Clorene predicted *Life on Mars* would one day become an icon for Martian terraformers—she was right about that!

Clorene then turned to Yukio and Johnny and said that Irene believed that humin metamorphs are the future of our species; that we're destined to enhance our genomes and for better or worse assume responsibility for our own evolution.

Clorene had trouble getting up to go to the bathroom. She said, "If I knew I'd live this long, I would've taken better care of myself."

Afterwards she sat with her bony hands in her lap and watched it rain on her roses.

Clorene Welles to Johnny Baker, October 7, 2056:

Clorene Welles' Obit, Written by Herself

A minor poet died today.
The echo of her voice in verse
will fade away.
But failure fanned
her desire to write poetry,
& the work taught her
to see.
The day before her death

at ninety-three,
she warmed her chilly brain
over a rose she saw on fire
in the rain.[37]

Johnny Baker to Teddy Petrakis, October 11, 2056:

I don't grieve much for Clorene. She got her wish and wrote her death poem.

To tell the truth, I'm glad to be young and alive. It's 4:15 P.M. I just looked out my fifth-story window. A seagull was bobbing in the canal. It drifted up and down on the green water into the violet shadow of the bridge on the corner. Right below me, a bunch of Chinese tourists got off an uptown bus. They were wearing different-colored shirts: white, rose, purple, and yellow. The one in yellow knelt on the quay.

I spend my days looking at oil paintings. Only this morning, I realized that Rubens almost always paints the edge of a gray half-tint shadow next to a flesh tone. Oil painting technique intimidates me. I have so much to learn. Maybe I'll make something worthwhile by the time I'm forty.

Teddy Petrakis to Johnny Baker, October 16, 2056:

Happy birthday, dear boy! Nineteen! Congratulations!!

Johnny Baker to Teddy Petrakis, October 16, 2056:

What's the big deal? At my age Van Dyck was already a Master in Antwerp's Guild of St. Luke. And Picasso, at fifteen, drew as well as Raphael, who painted his *St. Mary Magdalene* at fourteen! To tell the truth, I got second-rate arsogenes.

Johnny Baker to Teddy Petrakis, November 16, 2056:

This evening I made a little oil sketch from memory of the Chinese tourist in a bright yellow shirt kneeling on the white stone quay below my window. The sketch didn't work out, and I wiped it off the canvas,

37. Welles, "Obit," op. cit., p. 213.

but I learned that you need very little yellow paint to make it look very yellow if you lay that color next to a violet or lilac tone.

Yukio called me to bed.

It's time he went back to Japan, but I haven't got the heart to kick him out. Tonight, with tears in his eyes, he told me, "To be packed off from here back to Tokyo would be an unbearable insult!"

Johnny Baker to Teddy Petrakis, November 8, 2056:

Billy Lee brought Ishtar Teratol to my open house tonight. She's accompanied everywhere by a guardbot because of threats to her life from the International Organization of the Naturally Talented.

I sketched her in pencil as the White Queen. She's training for a rematch with Chess Maven next September.

Ishtar still lives with her mother in Beit Tiamat under the Med. The six-hundred-odd Gynarchists there have split into two ideological camps over the Father's Day Bombing. Ishtar is against gynoterrorism. Her mother is for it. The two no longer speak.

Ishtar Teratol

I mislaid Johnny's drawing somewhere when I moved to New York in the fall of sixty-one.

Nat Glogow

Johnny was like a little kid—thrilled to vote for the first time in the presidential elections of forty-eight. Of course, we voted for "Granny" Smith, and we celebrated her landslide victory over Koyle with a dim sum feast at the Forbidden City in Chinatown. Johnny said he had feared Koyle would be elected as a reaction to the Father's Day bombing. He was like, "'Granny' Smith's election restored my faith in America. I love this country.'"

Johnny Baker to Teddy Petrakis, December 1, 2056:

I want to make a brightly painted three-dimensional construction.

But I can't come up with a subject. Feel dead inside. Trying to stimulate my imagination by studying the colors in nature. All around me I see contrasts of red and green, blue and orange, sulphur and lilac.

For three hours this afternoon by the lake in Central Park, I tried painting a little oil of a bare towering bower. Finally, I gave up and went off in the Rambles with a guy in his eighties, who paid me $450. Wrinklies have very big balls.

Yukio and I had a nasty row about my coming home an hour late for the Katsura willow rice garnished with pine weed he'd prepared for our supper.

"You don't appreciate me," yelled Yukio, storming out for the second time in two days.

Johnny Baker to Teddy Petrakis, December 12, 2056:

I'm blocked, scared to work. I'm scared about not living up to my mother's expectations. My mind's a blank.

Emma Torchlight to Johnny Baker, December 15, 2056:

Name: Jeanette Baker Torchlight
Date and time of birth: December 15, 2056, 1:12 P.M.
Weight and length: 7 lbs. 3 oz; 20 inches.
Apgar score: 9

Johnny Baker to Emma Torchlight, December 15, 2056:

Congratulations to us both! Your news made me happy for the first time since Mother died.

Feeling good, I went to bed about midnight. Next thing I know, I'm walking through a graveyard. The graves are all overgrown with ivy. One has a blank tombstone. That grave bursts open and a skeleton's forearm shoots out and, with its index finger, cuts one word into the granite. I won't say what the word is—I'm gonna show you in a painted construction called *A Message for the Living from the Dead*.

I feel alive again!

From John Firth Baker's interview in *The International Review of Manual Arts:*

I re-created my dream in *A Message for the Living from the Dead* with a real skeleton's right forearm arm and hand, which I bought, hinged together, for $650 from an anatomical supply house that supplies specimens to various city teaching hospitals. I wondered, Who was this person whose body parts I'm using in my work?

So I borrowed $550 from Billy Lee and had a DNA analysis done on the bones. Back came a portrait of a thirty-five-year-old alcoholic man, prone to violence, who'd been five-foot-seven, with blond hair and brown eyes and an MMIQ of about 80. Booze had probably killed him. He was straight and allergic to bee stings. He also had the genetic potential to become a good tenor. I named him Andy—after Andy Lynn, the main singer in my favorite group, Hot Ice.

At first, I thought about my Andy a lot. Where was the rest of him? I asked him to forgive me for disturbing his bones. Then I regarded them as elements in my composition, along with the painted cardboard, pieces of wood, plastic ivy, and artificial earth.

A Message for the Living from the Dead (Plate 12) took me a month. The work brings together a text and an image. I need to integrate them. I got this need as a kid from looking at the paintings of Charlotte Salomon. We're both narrative artists.

Emma Torchlight to Johnny Baker, January 18, 2057:

Thanks for showing me *A Message for the Living from the Dead*. To think you dreamed it up! I like your message: "Rejoice!" Come rejoice with me in our daughter, Jenny. Come see us in Anchorage as soon as you can.

From Sri Billy Lee Mookerjee's home page, January 20, 2057:

Yesterday I visited Johnny Baker's studio. Johnny was putting the finishing touches on a painted construction entitled *A Message for the*

Living from the Dead. The message, written on a tombstone by a skeletal hand, is "Rejoice!"

Johnny's construction communicates a Gaian sentiment. As Srimaati Andrews puts it: "Gaianism takes life's transience as a call to embrace earthly joy."

Johnny's unique combination of artistic and spiritual gifts marks him as someone special. We Gaians are proud to claim her as one of our own. Last August, Johnny said to me, "I sure hope I gain Gaian Consciousness soon!"

Hang on, Johnny. It's coming!

Nat Glogow

Johnny parlayed Billy Lee's home page about *A Message from the Living to the Dead* into another $7500 sale. He sold it to a rich Gaian who donated the work to Billy Lee's church. Johnny bought himself a round-trip ticket to Anchorage. He had no warm clothing that fit. I lent him my old coat of many colors and a pair of gloves. He bought himself a pair of blue boots with high heels that showed off his legs. Johnny was vain about his legs.

Emma Torchlight

I've a good memory for dates. Johnny arrived in Anchorage on Wednesday morning, January 24th. I was nursing Jenny when he arrived.

"Here," he went, "lemme me try that," and stripped off his shirt and bra. Johnny had no milk, of course, but Jenny, who'd just drunk her fill, sucked herself to sleep on his right nipple. Thereafter Johnny neither drank nor smoked and, three times a day, was Jenny's living pacifier. By the end of the week, his breasts leaked a little milk into her mouth. I saw tears in his eyes.

Johnny bathed Jenny and diapered her and took her for long walks in her stroller. He pushed her up and down Orchard Street, which is lined with cherry trees. The three of us became a family in a few short, warm winter days.

One evening while putting Jenny to bed, Johnny went, "I've never been so happy!" Next morning, after Jenny fell asleep at his breast, he said, "I had a sad childhood."

"How come?"

"I was only happy when I made Mother happy, and I could make her happy only by making pictures. I resented being loved not for myself but for what I could do. For her, I was a means to an end. I'll always love Jenny for herself alone—whatever she turns out to be. And just think, she'll live a hundred and fifty years! Lucky Jenny!"

At the end of two weeks, on February 6th, Johnny said to me, "I gotta get back to work."

Johnny Baker to Emma Torchlight, February 8, 2057:

What's with Jenny?

Emma Torchlight to Johnny Baker, February 8, 2057:

Whenever I put her down on her back, she turns her head to the right and raises her right forearm. What's with you?

Johnny Baker to Emma Torchlight, February 12, 2057:

I'm making a painted construction called *Mother Earth*. The image came to me Tuesday night while I was rereading my favorite poem, "The Song of the Earth." Mother said it reconciles polarities. That's my theme. To tell the truth, all my work nowadays has themes.

Johnny Baker to Emma Torchlight, February 16, 2057:

Rereading Mother's journal. I talked at six months! Alex and Yukio did, too. Arsogenic metamorphs are born old.

Nat Glogow

I was there when Johnny, Alex, and Yukio found out their mothers had proudly told each of them they spoke their first words at six months. Johnny said "Momma," Alex went "cup," and Yukio, "*hana,*" which is nose in Japanese.

The three looked at me. I could see them thinking, We're far superior to you!

And for the first time, I hated them for being metamorphs.

From John Firth Baker's interview in *The International Review of Manual Arts:*

I made *Mother Earth* (Plate 13) to visually fuse opposites—femayle and male, life and death—into one image.

I cast my own torso and neck in plastifoam and topped it off with a humin skull. Setting a skull on my body in place of my head creeped me out.

Mother Earth is essentially composed of four roundish shapes: a pair of breasts and a skull that are set off by a solar halo. But the construction itself isn't in the round. It can be viewed only from the front, which is a flaw in its conception. *Mother Earth* is incomplete because it's not truly three-dimensional, which is the direction my work is now moving in.

Every month or so, I make something I couldn't make before. It's like being a little kid again.

Doris Peel

I first saw *Mother Earth* at Johnny's open house on Sunday night, February 18, 2057. It was lit up on a bridge table in the corner. A bunch of us gawked at it while Srimaanji quietly recited the poem called "The Song of the Earth." When he was done I gained Gaian Consciousness.

Nat Glogow

Peel's eyes rolled back in her head, and she slowly sank to the floor at Mookerjee's feet with a stupid grin on her face. A few minutes later when she came around, she hailed Johnny as "My giver of Gaian Consciousness."

Johnny, who was stoned, laughed and said, "I give but don't receive."

Peel paid Johnny $8500, his biggest sale yet, for *Mother Earth*, which she then gave to Mookerjee.

Sri Billy Lee Mookerjee

Doris' gaining Gaian Consciousness took me completely by surprise, and I have to admit, I was jealous of Johnny's spiritual gifts.

I placed *Mother Earth* on a high wooden table that faced the congregation in my church in High Bridge Island Park. Starting the very next Sunday, we used it as a visual aid to meditation while we recited Welles' poem in unison. The verse has long been a part of our developing liturgy, which has as its sole aim the gaining of Gaian Consciousness. "The Song of the Earth" is my mantra, the foundation of my spiritual life.

(Recites)

I mother
& devour life.
I father forms
that thrive &
those that fade.
I'm husband
& wife,
windpipe
& knife.
I'm the sheath
that shields
& rusts its blade,
this patch of sunlight,
that patch of shade.

On the first Sunday in March 2057, the combination of poem and Johnny's image worked wonders. Two more people in my congregation, Leah Vogt and Sam Lee, gained Gaian Consciousness during my evening service.

From Sri Billy Lee Moorkerjee's home page, March 5, 2057:

My ex-sheila, the arsogenic metamorph Johnny Baker, has gone on by himself to become the first Gaian artist guru. She has created thirteen works of art, which I call Baker's Dozen. They are visions of his continuing quest to gain Gaian Consciousness and have the power to help others gain Gaian Consciousness for themselves.

From: A Naturally Gifted Manual Artist
To: John Baker, March 7, 2057:

Your 13 heathen visions called Baker's Dozen came to you from hell, which is where you're soon headed.

Signed, a Naturally Gifted Watercolorist

Johnny Baker to Teddy Petrakis, March 6, 2057:

I guess you saw Billy Lee's latest home page. Don't think I've joined the Church of Gaia after quitting yours. I've got my own religion—my work.

Baker's Dozen, as Billy Lee calls it, is the end of a cycle in my development. I'm putting grief behind me. I'm brimming with new ideas. I want to paint from nature as well as my imagination. I want to study colors in the natural world and reproduce them on my palette. Right now, I'm excited by different hues of gray. I recently figured out that gray-green is composed of yellow, black, and a touch—just a touch—of blue.

Yukio leaves me cold. This evening, very stoned, he said, "Why are you the lucky one? You *gaijin* faggot! Remember, your mother committed suicide! Her spirit will avenge itself on you! You'll see! Beware!"

Katherine G. Jackson to John Firth Baker, March 10, 2057:

Dear John Firth Baker:

I am a thirty-three-year-old freelance journalist with a Ph.D. in Art History from Yale. I write about young American manual artists, whose work seems to me to exemplify the mid-twenty-first-century zeitgeist. I want very much to interview you for *The International Review of Manual Art*. It seems to me that as the first arsogenic metamorph and a Gaian she-he, your promising early achievements would not have been possible without the confluence of contemporary science and religion.

I greatly admire Baker's Dozen, which I am now studying. The thirteen widely varied and imaginative works, which include two images of metamorphs, seem to me to constitute a veiled autobiographical narrative. The technique is somewhat reminiscent of Charlotte Salomon in her *Life? or Theater?* Am I right?

I have a particular interest in narrative manual artists. With your cooperation, I'd like to get the story behind Baker's Dozen and any other works you'd care to show me. The only drawing of yours I've seen is the one incorporated in the Furies logo. Though I deplore the political uses to which your drawing was put, I admire your draftspersinship.

I hope you let me interview you. I won't put my words in your mouth. My journalistic ideal is to let my subjects speak for themselves, as you will see by my interview with the sculptor Ann Kahn, which appeared last March in *IRMA*.

If you are interested in being interviewed, please contact me at your earliest possible convenience.

Sincerely,

From John Firth Baker's interview in *The International Review of Manual Art:*

Q: You are an utterly contemporary phenomenon: the first arsogenic metamorph whose brain is also partially the product of a postnatal experiment by the metamorph's own mother. How do you feel towards her?

A: Mother gave me the ability to make images. Making images is my greatest pleasure. I'm grateful to her.

Q: You've been threatened by an anonymous naturally gifted watercolorist. What's your response?

A: Fear.

Katherine G. Jackson

I interviewed Johnny at his studio over a period of three days. He constantly poor-mouthed Yukio. "Yukio can't get his shit together, can you, Yukio?" Johnny said. "Yukio's got a father complex."

At first I was surprised at Johnny's mean streak. Then I remembered his *Self Portrait with Knife Blades for Teeth*.

Johnny Baker to Teddy Petrakis, March 22, 2057:

Today Billy Lee commissioned me ($5000) to do a portrait of Srimaati Andrews. Agreed on condition that I work in her Seattle home. Then told Yukio that I'd be working alone in Seattle for at least a month, and that he ought to take this opportunity to return to his mother in Japan. He went crazy.

"You can't get rid of me so easy!" "You made me a cocksucker!" "I'll drink your blood like wine!"

I calmed him down. He wept.

I said, "Yukio, you've got to get on with your life!"

"I want to draw, but I can't."

"Well, I can't help you!"

He raged again. And again I calmed him down. Finally, he agreed to return to Japan next Sunday, the 25th, the day I go to Seattle.

Johnny Baker to Polly Baker, March 24, 2057:

Dear Aunt Polly,

Yukio's returning to Japan tomorrow. What a relief!

I'm off alone tomorrow morning for Seattle to do a portrait for $5000 plus living expenses!

Late this afternoon, I went to Manhattan Beach to look at the sea. I lingered happily with the setting sun at my back. The crests of the waves rising before me were yellow; those nearer the horizon reflected the light cobalt sky. The shadows of the low clouds rippled over the water, which looked metallic. For an instant, I was the sea gazing at itself.

Dearest Polly. I love you.

Any plans to come East? I miss you. Thought maybe I'd go out to Lincoln for a long weekend towards the end of April. Tell me when's a good time. Let's visit Jenny together! I want to be a good father to her—not like Fritz was to me when I was growing up.

I'm going to be interviewed in the next issue of *The International Review of Manual Art*. Fame—it's wonderful!

Yukio Tanaka to Mariko Tanaka, March 24, 2057 (Delayed):
Dearest Mother,

Farewell! Don't be sad. I found a way to appease my father's spirit. The wind is from the east. Tonight I shall fall among these detestable Americans like a wild cherry blossom. Don't grieve for me.

Nat Glogow

I was there on Johnny and Yukio's last night. Sunday, March 25, 2057. We were smashed on Amae and dope. Yukio's imminent return to Japan was very much in the air; that and Johnny's departure in the morning for Seattle. The booze made Yukio weepy.

"Fuck all," he said. "Everybody dies!"

"Not me," said Johnny. "I'm gonna live forever!"

Yukio said, "Good luck."

I went home about midnight. The cops woke me at six-thirty the next morning. They took me to Johnny's apartment. He was face up on the floor in a huge pool of blood. I gagged at the sight of him.

The New York Times, March 26, 2057:

METAMORPHIC MURDER AND SUICIDE

Arsogenic Metamorphic Manual Artist Slain,
Metamorphic Roommate Kills Self

NEW YORK, March 26 (AP). The world's first successful arsogenic metamorphic artist was stabbed to death here early Friday morning by his roommate, who then mutilated the dead body and killed himself.

John Firth Baker, 19, died of two stab wounds inflicted with a barber scissors to the back of his neck as he slept in the studio he shared with his Japanese roommate, Yukio Tanaka, 19, who was also an arsogenic metamorph. According to police, Mr. Tanaka then used the scissors to gouge out Mr. Baker's eyes.

A short time later, the police said, Mr. Tanaka leaped to his death out of the fifth-story window of the studio that overlooks the Herman Melville Canal.

The authorities were conducting interviews today to determine what led to the killings.

Mr. Baker, Mr. Tanaka and a third arsogenic metamorph, Nadia Kammerovska, were created in an experiment by genetic engineer Dr. Frederick Rust Plowman at the Ozaki Institute of Metamorphic Genetics in 2037. Ms. Kammerovska was killed in Moscow at the age of ten by her father.

"The calamitous destinies of the first three humin beings who were metamorphically endowed with the genetic potential to become manual visual artists will not deter us from our appointed task of creating creative people at will," Professor Plowman said today.

Mr. Baker had recently completed a cycle of thirteen works entitled "Baker's Dozen," which a spokesperson for the Church of Gaia in New York declared today were "visions of his quest for Gaian Consciousness." A she-he and former sheila of Gaian guru Srimaanji Billy Lee Mookerjee, Mr. Baker also recently won notoriety for having made the drawing upon which the Furies' logo used in the Father's Day Bombing was based.

An interview with Mr. Baker conducted by the journalist and art historian Katherine G. Jackson will appear in the next issue of *The International Review of Manual Arts*.

"John Firth Baker was the world's first successful metamorphic manual artist. He was created to create images and he did. I'm convinced his work will last," Dr. Jackson said today.

Katherine G. Jackson and Sri Billy Lee Mookerjee, March 28, 2067:

KGJ: In the ten years since John Firth Baker's murder, his life and work have been largely appropriated by the Church of Gaia, which interprets them entirely according to its own beliefs.

How did that come about?

MOOKERJEE: It came about because Gaians all over the world revere Johnny as an artist-guru, an eminent religious teacher. The American Church of Gaia, which owns most of Johnny's work, is the largest single contributor to Johnny's current show at The Virtual Museum of Modern American Manual Art.

KGJ: The Church of Gaia has turned Johnny into a religious myth. A cult has grown up around him in the United States, Japan, China, India, wherever the Gaian religion has taken root. Why was he mythologized?

MOOKERJEE: Religious teachers are often mythologized by their disciples; their identities sometimes merge after death with various preexisting myths. It's an unconscious process, which is happening with Johnny. Eastern Gaian churches emphasize his androgyny. The New Sino-Japanese Church of Gaia regards her as an avatar of the legendary Lan Ts' Ai' Ho, the Chinese transvestite poet-painter of the Han Dynasty. Our rapidly expanding Indian Church, centered in Varanesi, identifies Johnny with the god Ardharnarisvara, "The Lord Who Is Half Womin," and considers him a reincarnation of the late Shubha Roy, the graphic artist who served the goddess Kali.

Johnny's importance for us American Gaians centers around his last work: Baker's Dozen, images I call "tangible Gaian visions." They are aids to our daily meditation on the Motherworld; they frequently induce Gaian Consciousness.

KGJ: Do you think Johnny's work has artistic value separate from its religious implications?

MOOKERJEE: No.

KGJ: I hope Johnny's upcoming retrospective at The Virtual Museum of Modern American Manual Art will appeal to a larger audience and secure his artistic reputation.

MOOKERJEE: In time, Johnny will be remembered solely as a Gaian guru who illustrated his quest for Gaian Consciousness. Johnny is a religious phenomenon. Scientific and artistic interest in her will fade. In the contest for influence among religion, science, and art, religion always wins, hands down.

From The Virtual Museum of Modern American Manual Art, "Thoughts about John Firth Baker on the Tenth Anniversary of His Death," April 17, 2067

Online Host: Katherine G. Jackson

POLLY BAKER: My thoughts today turn to Jeanette. I now think she was a criminal. Her crime was experimenting on Johnny when he was a baby. She made him into a thing. She crippled Johnny emotionally when she gave him "the lust of the eyes." Thereafter, Johnny had trouble loving somebody other than Jeanette.

EMMA TORCHLIGHT: He loved Jenny.

POLLY BAKER: How true!

THE REV. THEODORE PETRAKIS: I'm pleased to say that Johnny loved me. And, for a time, the dear boy loved Christ. Johnny went from God to Gaia to art. Like all artists, Johnny was an idolater who worshiped images. He also allowed the images he made to be worshiped by others, and that's a mortal sin.

Johnny was a sinner. God have mercy on him! God gave Johnny his gift through a miracle of modern science. But Johnny put it at the service of false gods. And now his work has been appropriated by a neopagan cult that's turned him into a kind of minor deity. My poor Johnny!

NAT GLOGOW: Johnny had a run for his money. By hook or by crook, he was given the ability to convey his emotions with pictorial images. He had the immense gratification of making images that perpetuated his feelings in other people. And he was famous!

Above all, Johnny was committed to learning his craft. He wanted to be a skillful manual artist. He feared he had second-rate arsogenes. But who knows what he would have accomplished, had he lived.

WAKINOYA YOSHIHARU: I wonder the same about Nadia Kammerovska. As you know, her brain showed greater artistic potential than Yukio's or even Johnny's. Nadia's visual cortices and prefrontal lobes were the most developed of the three—probably the result of her mother's loving postnatal care. By all accounts, Anya Kammerovska was a real mamushka—a loving Russian mother.

POLLY BAKER: My question then is, Why did Fritz make a mother–artist-maker out of a depressive like Jeanette?

WAKINOYA YOSHIHARU: If you ask me, it was a heartless thing to do. I'm no psychologist, but I'll bet it's significant that both Ozaki-san and Fritz had deeply neurotic mothers.

I'm not surprised Fritz isn't with us today. Fritz is no longer interested in Johnny. He's totally absorbed in his five-year-old TOE-Heads. Thanks to him, all ten have greatly enlarged parietal lobes—the math center of the brain. He thinks one of them, May Li Chang, is another Einstein.

KATHERINE G. JACKSON: Emma, tell us about Jenny.

EMMA TORCHLIGHT: She's a good kid—open, loving, very self-assured. She knows how to work a roomful of grownups. She's bright, too, and imaginative.

POLLY BAKER: Tell her dream.

EMMA TORCHLIGHT: Dreams interest Jenny, like they interested her Daddy. Three weeks back, she watched a neighbor's dog dreaming. Casey's a grouchy twelve-year-old Welsh terrier with bad breath. Jenny watched her sleeping on her side in Liz Murphy's kitchen. Suddenly Casey's paws twitched, and she barked three times.

"What's she dreaming of, Mommy?" Jenny asked.

I said, "I don't know, dumpling."

Next morning bright and early, Jenny says to me, "I know what Casey dreams, Mommy."

"How, dumpling?"

She was like, "Last night, I dreamed I was Casey on the kitchen floor dreaming she's a puppy again, chasing a butterfly across the lawn."

"What a lovely dream! Your Daddy taught himself how to turn his dreams into art."

Then Jenny said, "I'm sad Daddy's dead."

And I said, "Don't be sad. His work lives. Art is stronger than death."

PLATES

Baker's Dozen

1. THE GROUND BENEATH MY FEET, 2055

Painted paper mâché, textured with architectural modeling material, glass eyes, mounted on canvas, 20" × 16" × 3" (50.80 x 40.64 x 7.62 cm)

Collection of Billy Lee Mookerjee

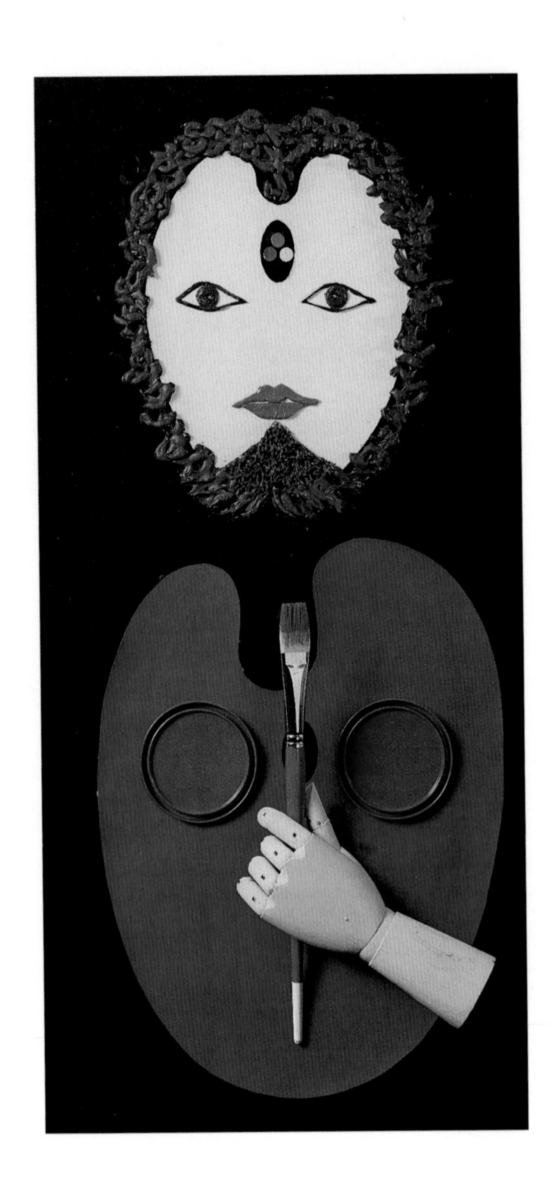

2. SELF-PORTRAIT AS A YOUNG MANUAL ARTIST, 2056

Acrylics, paper cutout, structural paint, brush, paint can lids, painted wooden articulated hand model, on board, 33" × 16" (83.82 x 40.64 cm)

Collection of Doris Peel

3. PORTRAIT OF IRENE WINTER, 2056

Oil paint on plastic foam, paper cutouts, painted paper labels, on paper,

27" × 20" (68.58 x 50.80 cm)

Collection of Gloria L. Cronin

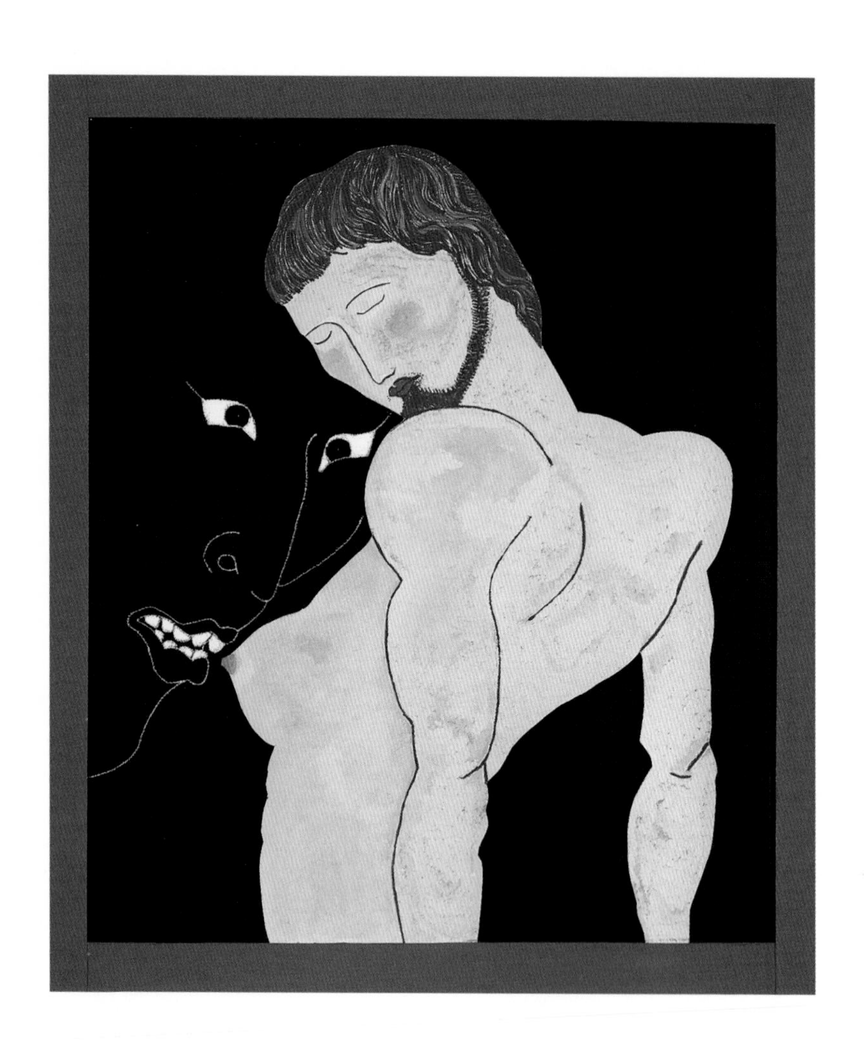

4. THE NIP, 2056

Gouache on paper cutout and scratchboard,

18" × 16" (45.72 x 40.64 cm)

Collection of Polly Baker

5. **MAMAGON GAIA,** 2056
Alkid paints, monkey skull, horsehair, boar's teeth, glass eyes, textured with methylcellulose with water, on red cedar,
35" × 22" × 6" (88.90 x 55.88 x 15.24 cm)
Collection of Billy Lee Mookerjee

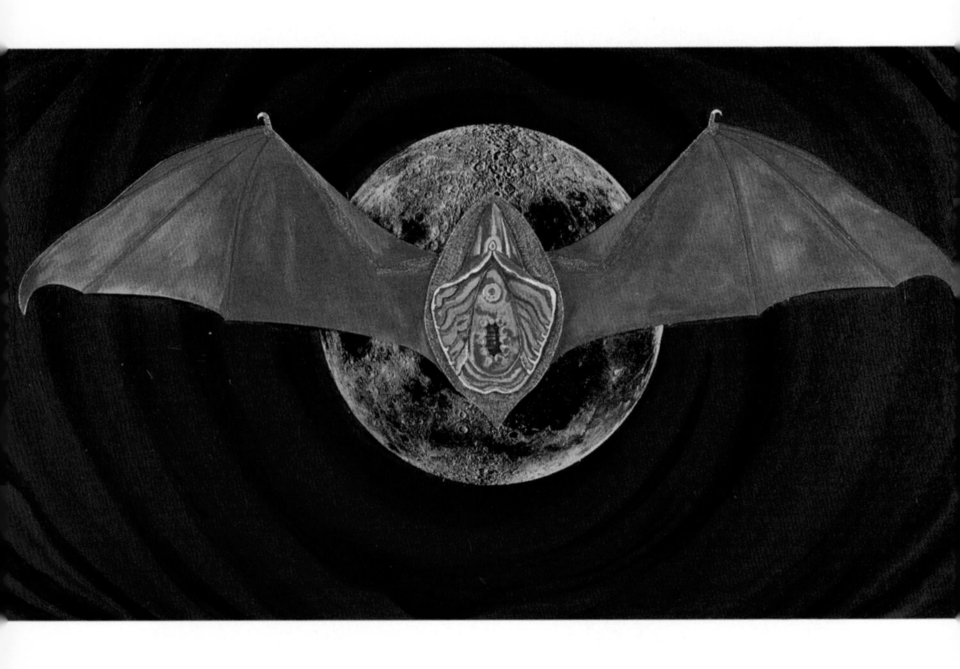

6. THE ANGEL OF DEATH, 2056

Paper cutout, b&w photograph, gouache, oil, mounted on canvas,

25" × 45" (63.50 x 114.30 cm)

Collection of Billy Lee Mookerjee

7. LIFE ON MARS, 2056

Alkid paint on textured plaster mold, methylcellulose mixed with water, on canvas, 24" × 18" × 5" (60.96 x 45.72 x 12.70 cm)

Collection of Billy Lee Mookerjee

8. OH, I AM HE WHO WILL CREATE GOD (portrait of Frederick Rust Plowman), 2056
Alkid paint and gilt on colored paper, scratchboard, 26" × 22" (66.04 x 55.88 cm)
Collection of Frederick Rust Plowman

9. THE AQUAMORPH, 2056

Painted paper cutout, colored paper, methylcellulose mixed with water, painted paper labels, mounted on board, 24" × 19" (60.96 x 48.26 cm)

Collection of Frederick Rust Plowman

10. SELF-PORTRAIT WITH KNIFEBLADES FOR TEETH, 2056
Oil on paper cutouts, X-acto knife blades, gilded latex caulk,
17" × 11" (43.18 x 27.94 cm)
Collection of Billy Lee Mookerjee

11. SOMETIMES I FEEL LIKE A MOTHERLESS CHILD, 2056
Painted latex caulk, mounted on canvas, 20" × 16" (50.80 x 40.64 cm)
Collection of Alex Thomas jr.

12. A MESSAGE FOR THE LIVING FROM THE DEAD, 2057

Human skeleton hand and arm, painted cardboard, painted architectural modeling material, artificial ivy, 18" × 16" × 11" (45.72 x 40.64 x 27.94 cm)

Collection of The American Church of Gaia

13. MOTHER EARTH, 2057

Painted human skull, artificial flowers, painted cast bust of John Firth Baker, gilt on cardboard, 25" × 23" × 5" (63.50 x 58.42 x 12.70 cm)

Collection of Billy Lee Mookerjee